Summer of My Amazing Luck

Summer of my Amazing Luck

a novel by

Miriam Toews

TURNSTONE PRESS

Copyright © 1996 Miriam Toews

Turnstone Press
607 – 100 Arthur Street
Winnipeg, Manitoba
Canada R3B 1H3

Turnstone Press gratefully acknowledges the assistance of
the Canada Council and the Manitoba Arts Council.

Cover art: Rick Sealock

Author photograph: Kathy Countryman

Design: Manuela Dias

This book was printed and bound in Canada
by Friesens for Turnstone Press.

Canadian Cataloguing in Publication Data

Toews, Miriam, 1964–

Summer of my amazing luck

ISBN 0-88801-205-5

I. Title.

PS8589.06352S85 1996   C813'.54   C96-920158-3
PR9199.3.T64S85 1996

dedicated with love and gratitude
to my mother, Elvira Toews

Acknowledgements

Thanks to Cassady, Kaya, Owen, Georgia, Marj, Mom, Dad, Jacque Baskier, Keith Louise Fulton, Heidi Harms, Margaret Ingram, and Carol Loewen.

LISH HAD BEEN A LIFER even before the trouble started with
Serenity Place. She had four daughters, two of them with the
same guy and the other two, twins, with a carefree street performer who had fallen in love with Lish's hands. Perfect for
balls, he'd said, juggling them that is. Now jugglers never make
cracks about balls, Lish informed me, they just don't. Lish knew
a lot about the theatre, about working a room, drawing a
crowd, about blocking and leading, about the superstitions of
theatre people. She had always loved the stage. Or the street, or
wherever it is that people perform. She had met the juggler in
the hospitality suite of the hotel at which all the performers
were staying. Volunteering, for Lish, was a good way to meet
theatre people without violating welfare rules, and it was a nice
break from the kids. This street performer, absent father of the
twins, said he loved Lish and suggested that she join him on the
road. He could teach her to eat fire, juggle knives, walk on stilts.
He showed her a newspaper clipping of himself from *The
Miami Herald* and the headline was "Magic, Music and
Tomfoolery," and then there was a photo of him breaking a
chain with his chest.

Just like Zampano in "La Strada," he'd said. Lish was giddy
with the proposition and the free booze of the hospitality suite,

and so she agreed to join him on the road, on the condition that she could bring her daughters, numbering two at the time. "Not a problem, not a problem," he said, "they'll bring in more cash," and then he made a red handkerchief disappear up Lish's nose. And, of course, reappear. Something he himself had failed to do after impregnating Lish in his hotel room that night, while her long beautiful hands caressed his oily back and the hot summer night got hotter. Lish found him irresistible with his sad eyes and his world-weary bearing and silly jokes that in and of themselves weren't funny at all, but when he said them seemed, at least to Lish, to define comedy. And Lish loved to laugh. What was funniest though to Lish was his utter seriousness about sex.

He didn't say a word or crack a smile throughout, and Lish had to pretend that a snort of laughter she let escape while he focussed in on the homestretch was really an uncontrollable gasp of pleasure. She had hoped he'd think it was her unusual way of expressing herself while in the throes of passion. Snorting. But she wasn't sure. In any case, it didn't matter. The next morning while Lish slept sated and pregnant with not one but two of the busker's babies, he made himself, along with Lish's cotton purse, disappear for good. Lish said he had left a note that said "Catcha on the flip side." Can you believe it? Lish said his juggling was much better than his writing.

For a while Lish wondered if her snorting had made him leave, but really she knew that it hadn't been her. It had been the road, and there was nothing she or anyone else could do about it. Some people were just like that. All the road had to do was look up at them and they were gone. Poof. And so it was with the father of her twins. She wished she had found out what his name was, but hey . . . Lish was the kind of person who enjoyed telling this tale to people. It was romantic, reckless. And if the twins asked about their dad, she could build him up for them, make him a hero, a rogue, a poet, a jester. Once I pointed out to Lish that the twins might like more details, some fleshing out of the story, maybe an address or a present on their birthday, a postcard. Lish said, "Maybe. Maybe not."

I know that Lish still kept a big silver spoon room service had brought up to the hotel room the night she and the busker got together, and the twins, when they were old enough, took turns using it to scoop the natural chunky peanut butter Lish bought at a health food co-op. They'd say, "It's my turn to use Dad's spoon." And Lish would smile and hand it over. Who knew what she was thinking. The older girls had a dad they saw fairly regularly and for a while were willing to let the twins use him as theirs, too. But the twins didn't want him. They were happy enough with their own.

I should tell you right now how I got to where I am: single mother on the dole, public housing, all that. It wasn't a goal of mine, certainly. As a child I never once dreamed, "I will be a poor mother." I had fully intended to be a forest ranger. Now I realize there just isn't enough human contact in that field for me. But then, look where human contact got me. They said I hadn't grieved properly over my mother's death. That was the reason I became promiscuous, they said. They said I snuck out of my bedroom window every night because I needed to forget. I needed to forget, they said, because I couldn't bear the sadness of remembering. That's what they meant by grieving properly: remembering. Remembering everything and reacting to it and releasing it. There was more to it, but I can't remember what it was, ha ha. So I'm not proud of it or anything, but it happened. And it's how I got to where I am. Half-a-Life Housing. Winnipeg, Manitoba, Canada, city with the most hours of sunshine per year (that's another thing they say), centre of the earth.

Somewhere along the line I became pregnant. With Dill, my son who is now nine months old. His full name is Dillinger. I don't know who his father is. Like Lish says, if you eat a whole can of beans, how do you know which one made you fart? I don't think it's the caretaker at my dad's church, because Dill's hands are very big. Those huge hands were the first thing I noticed about Dill. The caretaker, on the other hand, had very small hands. I remember, because after we'd had sex leaning up against the pulpit, he wandered over to the organ and started playing "Midnight Special." I lay on top of the organ, naked as a cherub, and I remember peering down at the caretaker's hands as he played. They were small and cupped and soft like a baby's. So I'm quite sure he's not Dill's father. And, to tell you the truth, there were eight or nine other guys I was with at the time Dill was conceived, and most of them have faded from my memory. If I ever did know their names, I've just about forgotten them. At least I've tried to. And all this because I didn't grieve properly.

The first time I saw Lish, I thought she was insane. In fact, I thought she was a baby snatcher. I had left Dill sitting on the grass in front of Half-a-Life just for a second while I paid the cab. It wasn't really called Half-a-Life, it was called Have-a-Life Housing, like Have a chocolate, or a pretzel, but nobody called it that. Lish told me later that the Public Housing authority people had considered all sorts of names before deciding on Have-a-Life. They tried Seek-a-Life, but it sounded too buddhist or something, and Take-a-Life, but it sounded like a home for murderers. They couldn't call it Get-a-Life, 'cause it sounded rude, or Dial-a-Life, 'cause it was already taken. So they settled for Have-a-Life, which became Half-a-Life, and sometimes Have-a-Light? or Have-a-Laugh or Half-a-Loaf Housing. Anyway, it was the day Dill and I moved in and everything we owned could more or less fit into the trunk and the back seat of the cab. When I turned around I saw Lish picking Dill up and smiling at him and talking to him. I screamed at her to put him down and ran over to where they were. She was wearing a black t-shirt with the sleeves cut off, a purple gauzy skirt, Birkenstocks with socks, and a black beret with a big silver spider brooch stuck on the front of it. She said she was sorry and tried to explain, but I just grabbed Dill and walked away: I'd heard about crazy women who couldn't have babies of their own so they kidnapped somebody else's. Or they'd walk up and down sidewalks with empty strollers, cooing to imaginary babies and buying big packages of diapers for nobody. Back then I was extremely protective of Dill. Kind of paranoid, I guess. He was all I had. Or then again my constant worrying might have been a result of my improper grieving. Who knows. I found out that Lish actually lived in Half-a-Life, too, and had four kids of her own and wasn't interested in having mine.

The next day I was sitting on the floor in my apartment, playing with Dill and taking stock of my material possessions: one single mattress with no wooden frame, one cassette player held together with gaffer tape, one crib, one toaster, one stroller with a wheel that kept falling off, two wooden crates which could be used as table, chair, storage, whatever they were needed for at the moment, various posters, which struck me as childish and out of place in my new home, a few dishes and utensils, one pot, and some toys and clothes, mine and Dill's. I sat on the linoleum floor and decided that I could use area rugs, some plants, and a real table and chairs. And Dill's room could use some bright colours. Maybe paint. The door bell rang. I answered it and guess who? Lish. Wearing the same black hat and spider, the same socks and sandals, and gauzy skirt. She was wearing a t-shirt that had a picture of a giant mosquito and underneath, it read "Blood Lust." She had the twins with her. They looked like they were about four years old.
"Hi."
"Hi."
"Hi."
"Hi."
"Hi."
I was not prepared for this conversation.
"Look, I'm sorry about yesterday. I . . ."
"Don't worry about it. I know what you were thinking. You shouldn't apologize for wanting to protect your kid. Our most

5

noble gestures as mothers are the ones most ridiculed. My name is Lish and these are my daughters, two of them that is, Alba and Letitia."

"My name is Lucy."

"Hi."

"Hi."

"Hi."

"Hi."

Thank god for tactless kids. Lish and I would still be standing at my door grinning at each other if it weren't for the twins marching right in and saying hello to Dill, who was slithering around on the floor, pushing himself backwards toward the sound of our voices in the hall. For the next hour or so the twins passed Dill back and forth and played peekaboo with him, and Lish and I drank coffee and shot the breeze. I was not entirely comfortable with the twins using Dill as a plaything, thinking of his soft spot, but Lish didn't seem worried and I had the feeling they had done this before. Talking with Lish, I kind of got the feeling we, at Half-a-Life, were one big rollicking, happy, impoverished family. I felt ill at ease and remember thinking Lish was probably the freak of the block and she was thinking I was too new to know it and I'd let her in the door. I also had a strange feeling that I had seen her before, years ago on a city bus, wearing cat eye glasses, a *faux* leopard fur coat, ripped tights and a head that was half shaved. I remember thinking, as I walked past her on the bus, that she was weird and probably a punk from the suburbs with really strict parents. Now here she was sitting in my empty kitchen with twin girls and Birkenstocks and a full head of hair. God, she had hair. Thick, black, long hair clinging to her back like an oil slick. I could tell her twins were going to have it too one day, and I hated to think of their bathtub drain.

It was during the course of this conversation in my empty kitchen that I found out that the father of the twins was some kind of performer. He ate fire and made things disappear. I told her I didn't know who Dill's father was and she smiled and said, "Just as well." The problem was knowing, she said, because as soon as you knew, you cared, soon as you cared, you lost. As for Dill, she said, now he could create his own dad in his mind and never be let down. Well, that was Lish. I wouldn't call her a man-hater or anything, she was simply speaking from her own experience. In fact, many weeks later, sometime in June, during the flood, she told me that she would give anything to see the twins' dad again and laugh in bed and wrap her hairy legs around his hot back and that the twins had a right to meet their father in the flesh and spit in his face. She was full of contradictions. And I believed each one. I wondered if she felt more love for this busker guy because he was gone than she would if he actually did show up. But what did it matter? He was gone. Their only encounter had been in a hotel and he didn't even know where she actually lived or that he was the father of two playful girls with thick black hair. And that they were the half-sisters of two older girls, more serious but just as hairy. And that they all lived in a public housing co-op in Winnipeg's inner city. Smack dab in the centre of Winnipeg, which was smack dab in the centre of Canada, which, as a point of interest, was smack dab in the centre of the earth.

Lish and I were single welfare mothers. I was proud to be something finally, to belong to a group of people that had a name and a purpose. It turns out that Lish was considered by most of the people at Half-a-Life to be a freak, but a kind freak and a funny freak as freaks go and, therefore, a good freak. As Joe put it, "Lish is off her nut, but she's not dangerous or anything."

I told you she liked the theatre. Joe had probably never heard of the word "eccentric." Not that she was really. Eccentric. She wasn't self-absorbed enough to be called eccentric. I'd have to say she was just miscast. Again, it all boiled down to money. Lish could have been a performer herself. Not only on the street but in theatres anywhere, had her lust not interfered with her passion. In the world of theatre she would have been considered normal: flamboyant, zany. In Half-a-Life she was just weird. And four kids, are you kidding? And on her own? A life on stage was not practical for Lish.

Well, Lish might not have been practical, but she knew something of life's limitations. Besides, if she couldn't perform for money, she could perform for us at Half-a-Life, and if anybody could use the laugh, it was us. As my mom used to say before she died, "A merry heart doeth good like a medicine." Lish's imitations were the funniest. She imitated her social worker from the dole and bank tellers and her father and just about everybody in a position of authority, however remote. She'd imitate bus drivers and waiters. She didn't do it with spite, not much spite, just dead-on accuracy. Her father, John, for instance: she'd drop her chin to her chest and lower her voice to a booming bass, to say, "Alicia, your mother and I have some concerns about the kids. We think they need a father figure in their lives and uh . . . more . . . uh . . . structure. We feel uh . . . that they are given too many uh . . . freedoms." Lish informed us that words like *freedom, peace, happiness* and *love* all made John nervous, genuinely confused. How he raised a daughter like Lish, I'll never know. But you see, even if her kids or any of ours at Half-a-Life had their dads around, would it make any difference? They'd grow up to be themselves eventually like the rest of us. But that didn't stop us from dreaming of fathers coming home from work with treats and offers to do housework, to take the kids to the park, or read them a story. It didn't stop us from dreaming of falling asleep with a man and waking up with him, going through the motions of an easy, comfortable routine, mom, dad and the kids all playing on the same team. Naturally some of the women in Half-a-Life had spent years with the same guy and it hadn't worked out, causing a nasty separation and the usual poverty for one thing, but still . . . a smoker dying of lung cancer always dreams of one more perfect cigarette. So, during the days we congratulated each other on our independence, busied ourselves with the kids and odd jobs and other people's kids and the headaches and general ups and downs of everyday life on the dole. During the days it was easy to forget about men. There were always distractions.

At night, though, we had more time to scrutinize our bodies, which I might point out, were still fairly young and able to withstand violent contortions and the rough eager enthusiasm men of our age had for sex, or lovemaking, as Lish calls it. I'd never have called it that except that Lish told me it was a good word and I should use it. I would have said *boinking* or *boning*, two words Lish hated.

But every once in a while one of us, I should say *them,* because I was just not interested, did somehow manage to meet a man. Or a woman. After all, there were a couple of lesbians in the block who had managed to get custody of their kids—one, Gail, was given custody because the judge had to decide what was worse, a lesbian or an alcoholic, and because he had had a father who drank and beat him, decided that Gail, as long as she kept her perversions to herself, would be more suitable, god help those kids anyhow. Anyway, these flings and one-night stands helped to take the edge off their desire and remind them of their potential. They'd always laugh about it in the morning and roll their eyes while describing the very personal details of the night before like it had been a Jets game or an encounter at the 7-Eleven. I think I knew more about their boyfriends' genitals than I did about my own. They felt that they had come too far to go back to the silly pretense of romance. We talked as though we were too tough to get duped again by some smooth-talking man. No, I'm not thinking of anyone in particular. But I wish I was. Then I might know who Dill's dad is. All of us, that is, except Lish, who could fall hook, line and sinker for skinny, artistic guys who looked like they had TB, and long hair and goatees. That was her type. Usually they were quiet and not very funny, but I guess she provided the laughs during the usually brief courtships they'd have. I don't know, because Lish didn't talk about her nights of passion as eagerly as the rest of them. She actually respected the privacy of the men she'd had sex with, and besides, it was difficult to talk about those things at Half-a-Life with our kids around all the time.

Inevitably these men Lish fell in love with said they couldn't handle the pressure of being with four children all the time, and she believed them (didn't we all) and had no hard feelings for them, nor they for her. They'd usually remain good friends, and sit around burning incense and drinking tea and talking all night while her children lay sleeping in little heaps around her. Lish didn't believe in cordoned off bedrooms where each child, or maybe two, lay alone, separated from the rest of the family. They did everything else together, why not sleep? She didn't call it the family bed, like some other women in the block, she just let the kids fall asleep where they felt like and let the experts go to hell. She'd point out the absurdity of situations by saying in a nasal kind of ditzy voice, "Okay, now you go into this tiny dark room and sleep and You, you get this walled-off area here to sleep in and I'll go *way* over here and sleep in this little room. Good night dears, have no fears." If Lish wanted to fall asleep with her arms around two of her daughters and the other two near by, she would. Of course, on the occasions when she had one of her tubercular lovers over, she'd lead him to the kitchen or the bathroom or some room without children sleeping in it and there remove her spider hat and her gauzy skirt and let all her hair, and his, cushion them from the cold, cheap tile of public housing.

Lish didn't have a problem picking up men. Usually they were guys who hung out at the local natural food collective or worked in the artists' co-op next door to it. I think these guys found Lish's long black hair irresistible and Lish herself a lot easier to handle than women with careers and ambitions and problems with sex and an inability to nurture. These are the types of things unemployed guys sometimes say about employed women. The type of women these guys thought wanted to take over the world. But Lish didn't care. It felt good to be with a man and touch his hair and it made her feel powerful. The thing is none of these guys, not one single one of them, made her feel the way her busker did, the father of her twins, the love of her life, the one that got away. She longed to see him again, I knew this, even though she laughed it off and joked about a spoon being a pathetic reminder of the man you love.

It's hard to talk about this kind of stuff, because the independence that we strutted around throughout the days is what people knew us as. All that longing and female desire and pent-up lust and yearning to have a man as not only a lover but a friend and father to our kids, too. Well, that wasn't what the public got or how they thought of us. Out in the city, in the welfare office, at the grocery store, at the school, we carried ourselves like gangsters, warriors, we were just fine, didn't need anybody, we had a job to do and we'd do it without anybody's help if we had to. We were Single Mothers. Only Lish was brave enough to give herself up to the possibility of love, to follow the whims and wants of her four daughters during the day, and to enjoy herself during the night, and throughout all those days and nights to flirt with the wild possibility of the twins' father finding his way to Half-a-Life and into Lish's happy dream.

A lot of the women in Half-a-Life thought Lish was fooling herself. She didn't even know the guy's real name, and he didn't know where she lived, as they had met and parted in a hotel, never knowing he'd sired not one but two adorable girls, and besides, just because he was connected with theatre, had gorgeous hair, made her laugh and caused a stir in the sack, didn't mean he wouldn't turn out to be like the rest of them. We all thought Lish had just been another easy lay for him on the road. Probably he had a wife and kids somewhere else, and he had completely forgotten about the crazy chick with the spider on her hat from the centre of the universe. I felt guilty about not sharing Lish's optimism. And not believing, like Lish, that maybe someday she'd see him again, made me feel like one of those old, cheated people who don't believe in anything.

Lish was the one who showed me the ropes at Half-a-Life. First of all she explained to me the problem with the women in Serenity Place. Well, it wasn't a problem with all of them, just one in particular. But you know how that works. Serenity Place was the name of the public housing block directly across the street from Half-a-Life. It was a low-slung building with fake street lanterns outside it and actual flowers out front. It looked better than Half-a-Life. Half-a-Life and Serenity Place. Sounds like Heaven and Hell. But actually it was all the same: cheap housing, tons of women and kids. Where there's smoke, there's fire, where there's cheap housing, there's women and kids. Anyway, this one woman in Serenity Place was giving Sarah, who lives in Half-a-Life, a lot of problems. Sarah had a son, and they lived on the second floor of Half-a-Life. She was also the caretaker along with Sing Dylan, whose real name was Bhupinder Singh Dhillon, but was called Sing Dylan because he liked to play sad folk songs on his guitar late at night in his little suite next to the furnace room in the basement of Half-a-Life. We all knew they weren't having sex because Sikhs don't have sex before they're married, but we didn't know anything else because Sarah was mute, or rather, she had chosen to stop talking after the traumatic circumstances of her pregnancy.

Either her brother or her father had raped her and then denied the whole thing. According to Lish, Sarah had tried to talk to people, to get them to believe her, but nobody cared to hear the unsavoury details and dismissed her as crazy. Sarah then just said, fuck it, from this day on I will never say another word. She didn't, either, but she did write furiously on little stick-it note pads, to her son, to us, to herself, to Sing Dylan, who didn't read English, but somehow related to Sarah. Little messages, like "Right now I'm thinking about something so hilarious if I said it you wouldn't stop laughing for a week." Or, to her son who was nine, "Good thing you're such a blabber-mouth sweetie, blab on." Strange messages, but never information, you know, hard information about herself, what happened to her, what she saw happen to other people. All her messages were cheerful and odd and not conversation starters at all, just detached snippets from the reel going round inside her head. When Emmanuel was five and starting school, Sarah fell in love with his teacher, a gentle, handsome man with startling blue eyes. As they say. She also made friends with the mother of one of Emmanuel's classmates.

Her name was Sindy (Lish told me to spell it with an S) and she happened to live in Serenity Place with her kids. Everybody in Half-a-Life felt very protective of Sarah and so when Sindy made her move they all saw red. Sarah wrote a special note to

Sindy and it said something like, "I'm finding myself interested in Mr. Myron." Well, that was it, if this pathetic dumpy mute could entertain thoughts of boinking Myron, then, thought Sindy, so could she. So Sindy schemed and connived and eventually got ol' Myron over to her place under the pretense of discussing her own son's lack of social skills in the classroom, and Myron, not being professional enough to resist her advances, took Sindy right there on her velour sectional and then did it again the next night and the next. She didn't mention any of this to Sarah, but when she saw Myron giving Sarah the once-over in the coat room as she bent to tie Emmanuel's boots, she used her trump card. That night she told Myron that Sarah's kid was a freak, an unnatural product of an unnatural coupling. *Pssst . . .* Sarah's own father was the kid's father. And, if that didn't take the cake, Sarah was hunting for a father for the kid, intending to pass him off as someone else's.

Mr. Myron was appalled at Sindy's vicious telling of this tale, but also put off by the notion of having anything to do with Sarah or her kid. Emmanuel was transferred to a different classroom, one for slow learners, or whatever they're called now, and Sarah was told, essentially, that Emmanuel must be told of his origins or he'd be angry later on and possibly run the risk of a lifetime in jail, maybe even take his rage out on his mother or himself. Anyway, he'd be a burden to society on some level. Appointments were set up, Emmanuel was told the terrible secret, and his mother was evaluated by a clinical psychologist who said she was suffering from post-traumatic stress disorder and should try to begin talking in order to begin healing. If she didn't, Child and Family Services would have to be notified and Emmanuel might have to be placed in a normal home where people spoke to one another and didn't scribble on stick-it pads all day.

Because she'd do anything not to lose Emmanuel, Sarah began to talk in a scratchy voice that was raw from not being used. Emmanuel, once bubbly and carefree, stopped talking and laughing and refused to go to school, so that the school principal was forced to call Child and Family Services and they sent out a social worker to investigate. Sarah had been trying to help Emmanuel and had been making progress. The two of them, over something funny on TV, would turn to each other and smile now, and Emmanuel could be heard through the walls of his bedroom experimenting with swear words, like *fuck* and *shit* and *bloody hell,* which Sing Dylan used a lot. But when the social worker visited Sarah and Emmanuel and tried to get some sort of promise that Emmanuel would be sent to school, Sarah began to cry and Emmanuel ran to his room and slammed the door. This was enough for the social worker to recommend a foster home for Emmanuel on the basis of his and her lack of cooperation regarding school attendance. So two days later Emmanuel was packed into the back of the social worker's car, staring straight ahead at nothing, and Sarah collapsed in the arms of Sing Dylan.

Sindy and Mr. Myron ended up living together, and all of Serenity Place heard the story, at least Sindy's version of it, and all of them agreed that poor Emmanuel was much better off in a foster home and hadn't Sarah handled the situation badly. After that Sarah helped Sing Dylan clean Half-a-Life, and prepared herself and her apartment for Emmanuel's ninety-minute visits every other Sunday afternoon as if preparing to meet the love of her life, which she was.

After hearing this story I understood the feelings the Lifers had for Serenity Place and its tenants. Most of us shunned the women who lived there, even the new ones moving in, innocent women who knew nothing of its terrible reputation. And the women in Serenity Place hated us Lifers as well. Our children and theirs did not play together. I guess it was stupid. Elaine, the Irish girl, said we were just like Northern Ireland without the bombs.

Lish also introduced Dill and me to a trio of women who practised witchcraft and treated each other's various infections and rashes with rare herbs and potions and went to bed and woke with the sun. Lish herself was part of a group that met on every full moon out back behind the parking lot in the grassy area, making circles and doing mysterious things, and she packed her share of tiger balm on the heaving chests of her children and treated ear infections with half an onion strapped to the ear with one of her Indian scarves.

Once, just before the rains, when the atmosphere was preparing for the upheaval and the ground was bracing itself, the vibrations of these forces tunnelled themselves right into Dill's inner ear, according to Terrapin, the enormous dark beauty of the trio. I noticed that whenever she spoke her voice went up at the end of the sentence as though it were a question, which it usually wasn't. Like, "I can't believe the amount of junk my kids got on Hallowe'en?" I had to sneak Dill's antibiotics past her in the elevator. I was sure she'd disapprove. Maybe even invoke the name of Serenity Place, stating that was something one of them would do for infection.

I appreciated their natural wisdom. I had never witnessed anything like it in my life. Almost an entire floor of hippies, but I couldn't repress my cravings for hot dogs and Kraft Dinner and Tylenol and coffee for killer hangovers. I hid my 7-Eleven bags in Dill's diaper bag. I was not able to keep plants alive and incense made me choke. Lish said it was all bogus anyway, and if the trio sometimes went overboard it was only because they had nothing else to do. As their kids got older, she said, they'd probably give it up for something else. They didn't seem any calmer than the rest of us anyway. Still, Lish continued her full moon ritual and munched on organic fruit all day long and didn't lose her sense of humour. Though she seemed bitter some days and pitied herself stuck in a dive like Half-a-Life while the men who had once whispered proclamations of undying love in her ear now travelled the world with no cares, and at times she was tempted to chuck the silver spoon.

When Terrapin asked Lish if she had eaten the twins' placentas, Lish gagged on her fruit leather and said in her mock enthusiastic voice, sort of high and puckered, "Oh yeah, it was incredible and when they turn six I plan to sacrifice them both to the goddess. Won't you come? I think it'll be a potluck." I laughed at that and Terrapin said, "Oh Lish, you're never serious." Which wasn't exactly true, but the trio brought enough

New Age brooding into our lives and Lish and I enjoyed tormenting them with our demented humour. Well, I should say Lish's, because I was more an enthusiastic fan than an actual accomplice, a role I didn't mind and Lish seemed to need.

During the days Lish and I would sit and talk and drink chamomile tea or cider, sometimes cheap champagne for the hell of it, getting up only to sort out problems between the children or to rummage around in boxes looking for artifacts to support the stories we told to each other of our lives. And loves, in Lish's case.

Her four-year-old twins were born on a full moon under the sign of Pisces which, according to Lish, made them very emotional and eager to please. They adored Dill, dressing him up in ridiculous costumes and bathing him and letting him crawl all over them while they giggled and screamed. Their paintings covered all of the walls, which Lish had painted dark colours of burnt red and midnight blue. Alba took diving lessons at the Pan Am pool and Letitia was saving up for a video camera so she could make movies about bugs and show them to children. Both girls cried easily if Lish raised her voice, and whenever she did, which wasn't often, she'd scoop them both up and beg their forgiveness. Then she would berate herself for being inconsistent. Alba and Letitia were identical twins, and during their nightly performances of dance and spontaneous poetry they were enchanting. Lish lit candles and operated the tapes, and the older girls prepared treats which were passed around before and after the performances. They also gave stage directions to the twins and operated the curtain which was made from a wool blanket given to Lish by a macrobiotic shoemaker and always made her break out in itchy hives. It was a royal bank blue with a big yellow star in the middle.

The older girls, Maya and Hope, I didn't know as well because they were in school all day and had many friends in the block with whom they were always hatching plans that would terrify and infuriate Sing Dylan. "Bloody Hell," he'd say in a clipped way, "Bloody Hell." They were nine and ten. Lish hadn't wanted them to go to school. She didn't trust schools and

16

knew that she could do a much better job of teaching her kids herself. This she would do by filling the apartment with books, art supplies, fresh vegetables and soul-stirring music, by visits from local artisans and writers, by naps after lunch, by evening walks and bike rides. At night the girls could release all the energy of the day and dream and rest next to Lish and the twins.

But Maya and Hope were just like their mother. They needed an audience and loved to talk and laugh with other girls their age. And the boys at school held a special appeal their own household lacked. Nothing Lish could say could keep them from going to school, and as each year passed their love for its comforting routine grew. Every morning Lish shook her head and looked desolate as Maya and Hope scrambled around the apartment gathering their books and lunches, not even trying to conceal their excitement. And every morning Lish would mutter as she covered them with kisses and hair, "Don't take any shit, my sweet petunias. Remember you can quit any time and return to the land of the living." And off they'd run, laughing and screeching.

I tried to console poor Lish. Maybe Alba and Letitia would stick around and let Lish teach them at home, but the way they followed Maya and Hope with their eyes down the street and beyond the giant BFI containers until they were out of sight, it wasn't likely.

Lish reminded me of my own mother. When I was young she'd pull me out of school, actually out of my bed, and announce that we were taking the train to Vancouver to visit her sister. Or that we must hurry to the airport to catch a plane to Grenada or wherever. I only realized later that these spontaneous trips always followed confrontations with my dad, where he sat in furious helpless rage and my mother tried to get him to talk to her. My mother was indifferent to school and never forced me to go or questioned my grades or really showed any interest in it whatsoever. The only course she insisted I take was typing. She said it would serve me well. If I got into trouble at school, which I did frequently, I'd regale her with the whole story and she'd laugh in collusion, slapping her thigh in appreciation of my rebellious spirit. My dad, a geology professor, would sit silently and occasionally twitch his mouth as he sipped his black coffee from a tiny cup. My mother drank from a big ceramic mug, at least fifteen cups a day.

Throughout my life I have tried to make my dad laugh or shout, to get a rise out of him, as my mom said. Once, on one of his up days when I was about twelve, he invited me into his classroom and asked me what colour he had just painted the supply counter. I thought hard for a moment and then said, "Rose." That made him so excited he actually jumped up off the floor, all two hundred and fifty pounds of him, which is one eighth of a ton, and whooped like Dill does when he's in his Jolly Jumper. He grabbed my hand and shook it and then pulled a fiver out of his wallet and pressed it into my other hand. I guess he hadn't wanted me to say plain ordinary pink. Maybe he was concerned about his masculinity or maybe as a child he had had an argument about the colour with an adult who had laughed at him and walked away, and now, finally, was his chance to be vindicated. But then again, what did I know from pink? Since that episode I have given him books with rose covers, sport shirts with rose buttons, and offered to paint his picnic table rose, wink wink, but he either doesn't remember or doesn't want to be reminded of that day he got excited and shook my hand. Sometimes I get this image in my head of thousands of fathers rubbing small peepholes on frosty windows and standing in snow and looking into warm houses, watching their families inside. Well, in our cases, mine and Lish's, there weren't any fathers looking in, more like us, at least her, looking out wondering where in the hell *they* could be. Or who they could be. Or where that one, that dark-eyed, sinewy, rogue magician, had disappeared to.

Hope and Maya's dad was a long-haired musician who wore round glasses and worked in a book store part time. He'd frequently stop in and visit his daughters, and occasionally take them over to his mom's place where they'd play Clue and eat

Fudgeos, a rare treat. He and Lish had no hard feelings toward one another except that Lish wished he'd live in a building instead of his VW van, the location of Maya and Hope's conception, so that Maya and Hope could stay with him when they needed a change from Half-a-Life.

Not all the women in Half-a-Life had friendly relationships with their exes. No sirree. When I heard their stories I was glad I didn't know who Dill's dad was. I was amazed that love could turn so rotten. Lish's second cousin, Naomi, for instance, was involved in an endless battle with the father of her second child. The father of her first choked on his own vomit and died one snowy evening when Naomi was out working. He had been a really nice guy, but a notorious drunk. When Naomi returned home, she found Tina, the child, sitting on top of Rob's cold body watching TV and drinking apple juice from the box. In shock, Naomi married the first man to come along, a firefighter with a soothing voice and a sympathetic ear and a genuine interest in Tina. Not until it was too late did Naomi discover his interest in Tina was sexual and his hatred for Naomi boundless. He turned out to be one of those creeps who prey on single mothers as a means of getting to their kids. Lish warned me never to get involved with a man who was immediately crazy about Dill. She said it takes a normal man a bit of time to warm to somebody else's kid, that is, if it ever happens at all. All this after Naomi had fallen in love with him and given birth to their son, a child he found irritating and time-consuming. Believe it or not, it was months before Naomi could act upon her discovery. One night while the guy slept, Naomi silently stuffed her kids into their snowsuits, packed a bag of diapers and crackers and toys and slipped away. She carried both children and the bag and walked, bare-headed and without gloves, for a mile before stopping to rest in a snow bank. There she considered falling asleep with the children, peacefully slipping away into another place and joining Rob, a man she had always taken for granted, not knowing any others.

But just then Tina woke up and complained of hunger and the boy opened his eyes and grinned at the snow around them

and Naomi decided to get focussed, as Lish put it. They had a
snack of crackers in the snow and then Naomi told Tina she
would have to walk and carry the toys. She threw the rest of the
bag's contents in the snow, heaved the boy over her shoulder,
and together the family trekked across town from their comfortable suburb where split-level homes with Christmas lights
lit the night sky, to the shabby front door of Half-a-Life and up
four floors to Lish's open arms. Hell, said Lish, she had let
enough men live with her expense-free, why not Naomi? They
lived with Lish and her two daughters (this was before the twins
arrived) for three weeks until housing authorities found out and
forbade that many people in a two-bedroom apartment and
commissioned Sing Dylan to spray for roaches in number
thirty-four and help Naomi move in. Lish had pulled a few
strings to get them their own spot in Half-a-Life. One of her
skinny tubercular lovers was the son of the chairman of the
board of Manitoba Housing.

Naomi lived next door to Terrapin, and the two of them
were constantly arguing. Naomi found Terrapin's organic cru-
sade stupid and phony and Terrapin found Naomi crude and
dirty. Both were right about the other, I thought. Terrapin was a
royal pain in the ass with her earnest preaching about better living and Naomi had, since walking across town with her kids
and no tuque, given up on surface things for awhile. She said
what she felt like saying about anything, including Terrapin.
One afternoon I heard Terrapin reminding Naomi that she
shouldn't leave her leftover Hamburger Helper garbage in the
hallway because it made her nauseous, and Naomi, in a voice
similar to Lish's, said, "If you'd rather be a cow than eat one, get
fucked." One time Terrapin had asked Naomi if she was a natural blonde and Naomi had said, "Are you a natural asshole?"
Naomi, after that rush of adrenaline she had used to rescue her
children and herself from the firefighter, had needed some time
to lie around and re-charge, plan her next move. Her mind was
working overtime trying to keep herself sane, and her heart was
heavy with guilt and shock and the unbearable sorrow she felt
thinking of her daughter. So Lish helped her get Tina to school

and looked after the boy, Keith, quite a lot. This whole time Naomi was trying to get sole custody of the boy and figure out how to get the firefighter to court on assault charges. Tina wouldn't talk about it and there was no physical proof that it happened. Naomi was close to having a nervous breakdown and eventually Lish told Terrapin to quit harping about her tinctures and homebirths and leave Naomi the hell alone.

A couple of the other women in Half-a-Life I got to know were more like me, not possessing any well-defined goals or on the run from nightmarish pasts. We were just there because we were poor and had kids. Most of us were unlucky when it came to men. Lish said poor self-esteem made us incapable of maintaining relationships, but I firmly believed that it took a lot of self-esteem to get out of them.

Teresa lived next door to me. I thought she was beautiful, and it took a while before I gave up trying to be like her. Her grammar wasn't great and her nails were chewed down to almost nothing, but her skin was incredibly smooth and thin and her lips were always very red, naturally. She gave me a lot of food tips for Dill and would, from time to time, give me a Safeway bag of her son's old clothing for Dill. As I removed these articles I sniffed them, trying to smell Teresa. Don't get the wrong idea, but everything about Half-a-Life was so new to me and I wanted to become familiar with everything about it. I was, after all, trying to fit in and maybe even find a family for Dill and me. Teresa had an eight-year-old daughter and a five-year-old son. The father of the eight-year-old lived in New York City and worked as a book editor. I wondered if Teresa's lack of grammar skills had ever bothered him, but I'm smart enough to know that ruby red lips can take the sting off dangling participles and I admired Teresa's nonchalant power. Anyway, the editor was long gone, wouldn't be back for many a day, and Teresa had "taken up," as my mom would have said, with another.

This guy, turns out, ended up impregnating Teresa's neighbour and Teresa almost simultaneously. I guess he felt more in tune with the neighbour or maybe more afraid of Teresa, but he let the neighbour in on his predicament, and not Teresa. Then, for one whole year, he bounced back and forth between the two apartments like a madman, never, not even for a second, piquing Teresa's curiosity with his impulsive exits and nightly fatigue. Not even when he grabbed his coat and scarf and left behind his shoes on his way, supposedly to pick up a litre of milk in the middle of November, did Teresa suspect. Anyway, after one whole year of this, when his sons were three months old and he had, miraculously, managed to attend the births of each, born within twelve hours of each other, and both with confused expressions, he spilled the beans. Lish told me all about it. She had been at Teresa's watching *Y & R* when it happened. He couldn't handle the stress any longer and he kneeled at Teresa's feet and wept and asked for forgiveness and understanding. Teresa ate one entire carrot in silence, except for the crunching, while the baby sucked at her breast and then snapped, "Cry me a river lover boy, get the hell out of here and don't never come back." When this guy moaned and begged to be able to see his son, Teresa said with all the melodrama she could muster, "The kid ain't yours, you two-timing prick, he's mine." Since then Teresa and her neighbour, Marjorie, have become great friends. Marjorie gave him the boot, too, hearing that he had gone all soft for Teresa in the end, when she had been the one who had maintained the secret and kept him even knowing she was one of two of his true loves.

And I thought this was very wise of her. Usually the woman keeps the man and shits on the other woman when all the problems originated with the man's stupidity. Now the two of them organize Scrabble tournaments for the block and their sons, both five and both with that kind of confused, peeved expression, are *unseparable,* as Teresa says. Teresa is taking French *immersions,* she calls it that, which I don't think is wise. Why not master one language first, but I don't know her well enough to tell her, and besides, with her beautiful skin and red red lips, who the hell cares?

There was another woman in the block. She was pregnant and almost due to have the baby. She waddled up and down the halls for exercise and had eaten so many carrots for Vitamin A that her face and hands were orange. Whenever anyone asked how she was she'd say, "Never better." Every time. So it seemed like she was just getting better and better all the time. Or maybe she meant her face. It was getting more and more orange all the time, so maybe that was a goal of hers. I had no idea how that sort of thing would end. She didn't know who the father was either, but she, at least, had narrowed it down to two men. One was a big six-foot-five fireman. (It seems firemen pop up in the women's lives all the time. Lish told me the first time this one went out to a fire he fell off the back of the truck. So now he takes cabs to fires and he's joined a men's group because of the unfair teasing he gets just because he isn't "man enough" to hold onto the back of a fire truck.) The other was a five-foot six-inch stripper with a great, but small, body, according to Teresa. She obviously doesn't have a type. Both men know they could be the child's father, so both of them are vying for it. They buy bigger and bigger gifts and are offering more and more amounts of child support, to beat out the other one. They are bringing her food and giving her tickets to the theatre and stopping their smoking and rug-doctoring her carpets and freezing food for after the baby arrives and decking out the baby's room with toys and new paint and expensive cribs and change tables. Maybe that's what she means when she says, "Never better." I realize it is very unusual for two men to be clamouring to be the Father, and peacefully at that. When one's there the other waits outside in the hall or in his car until the first is gone before he does his bidding. She says she'll get a blood test eventually (the men, naturally, have agreed to split the four-hundred-dollar cost of that), but in the meantime she's never been better.

Just before the rain started a woman and her kids moved into a suite across from Lish's. Apparently they came from the Northwest Territories. Lish said they couldn't handle the cold winters there, which I later realized was a joke of hers. You see, Winnipeg is one of the two coldest points in the world, the other being somewhere in Outer Mongolia. Her name was Angela, and we'd chat about superficial things. She told me she thought Dill had an old soul because of his rather stoic expression. Lish told me that Angela's oldest daughter and her youngest daughter had the same father, but the middle girl had a different one. The father of the oldest and the youngest was an Irish rock musician she had picked up in a bar. He had returned a second time to play in the same bar and had just about the same amount of time to kill before hitting the road. The oldest and the youngest looked exactly alike, round-faced, red-haired, pale. The middle child was small and dark and furtive and always wore sweaters that were much too big for her. She was always shooting her arms straight up into the air, to allow her tiny hands to free themselves from the sleeves. She looked like a scruffy midget cheerleader, but she seemed happy enough being the oddball around both her chubby red-haired sisters. Her father was a well-known writer from the Northwest Territories and at the time of her conception was also being hailed as family man of the north, an honour some women's group got together to bestow upon some unsuspecting local father. They didn't know about Angela, of course, and neither did the writer's wife and teenage sons. Lish figures he gave her some money to go away and Half-a-Life is where she ended up. I asked Lish if Angela could blackmail him and get more money out of him, maybe take a cruise with the kids, and Lish replied that writers don't have any money but do have lots of imagination to dream up excuses and lies about their lives and that a blackmail job didn't stand a snowball's chance in hell. When Robert De Niro or Mick Jagger are dumped with paternity suits by desperate women, does anybody care? Nope, Angela would have to take her knocks like the rest of us and write her own stories about unhappy love.

Like I said, with Angela's arrival in early June came the rain. The clouds broke like a million amniotic sacs and didn't stop dumping rain on us until one month later. Lish and Angela got along quite well. They'd sit around and talk while their girls played together. Angela taught Lish how to bake bread. Neither one of them faked a big interest in the other's kids, and if they wanted to yell from time to time, they did. I wasn't crazy about Angela and in a way I was jealous of the attention Lish gave to her. I told myself it was because they both had daughters of the same age. Anyway, Angela and I were the newcomers and Lish, as *de facto* mother hen of the block, had decided to take us both under her wing.

Once on a Friday evening when all the fathers lined up their cars and half-tons outside the block, Deadbeat Dad's Row we called it, Lish thought she had seen the dark head of the fire-eater in one of the cars. She said to me, "Watch my kids," and took off out the door of her apartment like her hair was on fire. I had never seen Lish move that fast. Her long black hair shot out behind her and her bracelets jangled as she sprinted. A few minutes later she came back and looked at us all as if we were vaguely familiar and sat down at her kitchen table. She played with her hair for a few seconds and then burst out laughing. We all laughed then, relieved.

That evening I bathed Dill in the big tub for the first time and wondered if I had ruined his life by not knowing who his father was. And is, I guess. Somewhere out there in the suburbs, probably, some guy is living with his parents, fixing his car, studying for exams, drinking at socials with guys, trying to pick up girls, Dill's father. Doesn't even know it. He'll probably marry someone pretty and competent and have a family and be proud of them, put up pictures in his office and tumble around with them before bed, never knowing that on the other side of town some girl he boinked when he was too pissed to remember is living on the dole and raising his son. If only Dill's dad were dead, that would be so much easier. I have imagined the scene in my mind. And I've imagined Dill as a seven-year-old or maybe even younger saying, "By the way Mom, who's my dad?"

And what would I say? "Well, Dill, I really don't know." Or would I launch into some inane parable to try and derail his thinking? What would other kids say? Hey Dill, I hear your old lady's a slut. Doesn't even know who your old man is. This was my thinking late at night. During the day Lish and some of the others and I would laugh at the bleak humour of our situations. We'd roll our eyes at the thought of trying to parent with some fumbling man and pity women who had to. This was another way in which we separated ourselves from the women in Serenity Place who, we told each other, resented being single mothers and would marry the first man who asked them. Lish would say, "If I had a dollar for every time a man asked me to marry him, I'd be a wealthy woman." And then she'd pause, and say, "But I've got four kids already, I can't handle another one." We'd usually join in with the last part of that sentence and then snort through our noses with our mouths shut, like we were some kind of a chorus line. But really it was just an act for me. I'd say it, but I'd cross my fingers under the table, or my toes in my shoe—so I wouldn't jinx my entire life. I always thought I would have a husband. If I had a dollar for every time I imagined who he might be, I'd be a wealthy woman. Well, I'd be able to buy some furniture anyway.

The first week of rain was bearable. The mosquitoes hadn't arrived and the rain had provided us all at Half-a-Life with a few interesting challenges. None of us had cars or money for cabs. Even the bus was an extravagance. One bus fare can get you a box of Kraft Dinner or a litre of milk. So with kids and babies and strollers and bags of groceries, and tricycles the little ones would start out on and then abandon, wanting instead to be carried, and the rain coming down on top of everything else, we at Half-a-Life were accustomed to getting wet. Not only that, but the road in front of Half-a-Life had sunk and dipped, so crossing it meant wading through one foot of water. Lish had called the city works department about it, but they had said if they started with our road they'd have to fix everyone's. We didn't see the problem with this. Anyway, we couldn't stay in all day. At least I couldn't. Lish could because her apartment was a real home and being in it so much of the time didn't make her crazy like it did me. In fact I had known her to spend entire days curled up in her big brown chair. She'd get up to prepare food for the kids or find a lost toy, but that was about it. She wasn't despondent or anything, just content. People would come and go and she would hold court from her brown chair. My apartment was kind of empty and white. Or eggshell really. Stuff sat around in boxes. Terrapin said maybe I was depressed and couldn't motivate myself to unpack. But I was after all only eighteen years old and had never set up a home of my own before. She offered me something called echinacea she had purchased from Vita Health, promising it would pick me up. I told her I didn't need picking up, I needed a break from Dill to think and organize and maybe go out and pick up some things from the Goodwill. Maybe even from my dad's house. Her head tilted to one side and moved up and down like a big oil drill and she made herself look empathetic. She could have offered to babysit Dill so I could set up my place properly. But no. Terrapin smiled wanly, tilting her oil drill head, and then hugged me. I was horrified. And then immediately relieved that she hadn't offered to babysit Dill because the thought of her holding Dill against her scratchy Guatemalan vest and anointing him with god knows what kind of oils and tinctures gave me the creeps.

Anyway, the less stuff I had cluttering up my apartment, the easier it was for Sing Dylan to spray for roaches. Lish would have babysat gladly, but I was nervous about her girls lugging Dill around and maybe dropping him. Besides, when I went out Lish and the twins usually came along. If I didn't want them to I'd have to sneak out the back door past Sing Dylan's apartment and traipse across the gravel parking lot. Dill's umbrella stroller was falling apart as it was and the gravel made it worse. With the puddles and the muck, crossing it was almost impossible. So I usually just went out the front door and took my chances.

Every day it rained. The day I had to go to the welfare office for my regular lecture, it was raining like mad. Sing Dylan skittered about outside trying to keep the rain from going into the window wells and flooding his basement apartment. He wore a big Super-Valu plastic bag over his head so his turban wouldn't get soaked. Sarah tried to help but, for the most part, just stood there in the rain, letting her hair get plastered to her head and her pants get stuck to her legs. She kept trying to put back one snaky strand of hair from her face to where it belonged. Sing Dylan was laughing. He seemed to think it was a big joke. Anyway I had to go. My appointment was for 2:15. That really didn't mean a thing because when you got to the office everyone just threw their name and case number into a pail and then sat down for about two or three hours. The names were picked at random as far as I could tell.

The very first time I had been to the dole, I had waited with Dill for about two-and-a-half hours. Right next to the dole headquarters was the Sals. I had jokingly suggested to my worker when I finally got in to see her that there should be some kind of intercom system installed between the dole building and the Sals and that way we could all sit in the Sals drinking coffee and eating cheese nips until we were called in to confess our sins of poverty and joblessness. She looked at me as if I had just told her she had an enormous butt.

Before I turned eighteen, my dad had to support me or I would have been made a ward of Child and Family Services and they'd in theory have to take care of Dill's and my needs. My dad preferred to give me money than to have me go public, so to speak, because the idea of me as a ward of Children's Aid horrified him. But I know he was somewhat consoled by the fact that I was only a single mother and not a drug addict or a prostitute. I don't think it occurred to him that a person could be all three. So from the day Dill was born until the day I turned eighteen, which was one month before I moved into Half-a-Life, my father gave me four hundred and fifty bucks a month.

28

I didn't see him, I just received his cheques in the mail. At that time I was living in a different dive, but it was a dive for all kinds of people, not only women and kids. When I turned eighteen he gave me a book for my birthday. It was a thick historical romance epic novel with a picture of a man and woman on the front, the wind blowing their hair back and the man towering over the woman who had her head tilted backwards and her mouth open and eyes closed, like an eighteenth century Cosmo cover girl, and the man looked as if he was strangling her. On the inside cover he had written, "Best wishes on your eighteenth birthday Lucy; from your dad." I kept the book just for that.

When I was a kid I scratched my name into the wet concrete that was put in down the street. That was long before they had guards to watch over it as it dried. As a matter of fact, Teresa had that job once for awhile. She got it through welfare: they figured it was something she was qualified to do. Anyway, I scratched my name, Lucy Van Alstyne, into the sidewalk that my dad walked up and down four times a day for thirty years. To the university, back for lunch, back to the U and home again. At first I was nervous, wondering what he'd say. Then I forgot about it. He didn't mention it once, not once. He still walks that way and back and there and back, and I wonder what he thinks when he sees my childish scrawl in the cement. Does he wonder what happened to that kid? Is he ashamed? Does he smile to himself? Guess I'll never know.

Anyway, I was on my way to my second dole appointment. I had to wake Dill up in the middle of his nap to make it on time. He was not happy about that. I was supposed to bring proof of all sorts of things, photocopies of this and that, and my appointment slip. I stuffed all of it into a plastic Safeway bag. (In Half-a-Life just about everyone carries their stuff in plastic grocery bags: you can put half-eaten chocolate bars and wet diapers and washcloths in them.) I got Dill into his little pink rain jacket, passed on to me from Lish, and carried him and the stroller and the bag down the stairs to the front entrance. It was pouring. You can't miss a welfare appointment. If you do you will not get any money and your future's at stake. If you can call a future on welfare at stake. And you have to wait until they have another opening. Some of the workers will insist on knowing the reason why you can't make it, and ask for written proof to back it up and make sure it was a damn good reason. When Sarah's sister died, she had to bring a photocopy of the death certificate to the dole because the funeral fell on the same day as her appointment. After a few months on City welfare single mothers get bumped over to Provincial welfare, which means that they think you're a lifer and good for nothing else. Then you get visits only about twice a year and your cheque in the mail every month. It's like a graduation. In fact Lish was telling me about Provincial parties some of the women in Half-a-Life had. They'd celebrate, usually with tequila, because once you were in the hole (called that because they just about forget about you), life was much easier. For some reason everyone in this block drinks tequila whenever they're on a tear. I hate it myself and I worry about it seeping into my breast milk and getting Dill drunk. But I was still on City.

To get to the dole office, I had to walk for about twenty minutes. Half-a-Life wasn't too far away. Both were in the Core, the centre of the city. Dill's umbrella stroller was falling apart. One of the wheels kept coming off and every ten yards or so I'd have to stop and kick it back on. Or I'd have to tip the stroller a bit so it was only riding on three wheels, but that got tiring fast. The rain was pissing down on us. Dill was crying and then made himself puke by sticking the string of his hood too far down his throat. Cars whizzed past two feet away and splashed us all the way to the front doors of the dole. A guy on a mountain bike wearing some Gor-Tex jacket and cut-offs over long johns rode on the sidewalk beside me for a while with a big ecstatic grin on his face as though he had just spent a year in the Sahara.

"Isn't it great?" he puffed.

"What?" I said, removing the string from Dill's mouth.

"The rain, it's amazing. It's like a great equalizer, you know?"

It's funny how some people just start talking to you when they see you have a kid.

"Oh yeah, for sure."

I hated Gortex Guy.

"Well, take her easy," he said as he wheeled away, probably on his way to some philosophy or film studies course. Even with the plastic Safeway bag, all my proofs and papers and Dill's extra diapers were soaking wet. Dill had kicked off one of his yellow boots and I hadn't noticed. It took me about fifteen minutes just to get in through the bloody doors of the dole office. There were about five guys standing around in the lobby all staring at me and nobody did anything to help. At one point I had pushed the front of the stroller in and the door came swinging back shoving one of the curvy handles of the stroller into my stomach. Eventually I got Dill and the stroller and myself into the building. Water was dripping off the end of my nose. The rain had made the vomit on Dill's jacket runny and it was sliding down the shiny plastic onto his lap. He was very intrigued with it and moved one chubby index finger around in circles through the puke.

I asked the secretary, "Can I leave my stroller in the lobby?"

"No, you can't."

"Where can I put it?"

"I don't know."

"Ah."

"Most people don't bring 'em."

"Well, I did."

"I'm just saying most people don't."

Getting past the receptionist into the holding tank/waiting area was never pleasant. I shook the water out of the stroller in front of her. I didn't care because she was only the secretary. She wasn't the one giving me the money.

Some guy with a black eye and fresh blood on his cheek said he could watch the stroller for me. Like I was born yesterday. To get into the bigger waiting area I had to follow one of three lines painted on the floor. Yellow, Red, or Blue. Which line you followed all depended on how long you had been on the dole. Following a colour is easier than following signs, for people who can't read. The receptionist glanced at my wet appointment slip.

"Red line."

"Thank you ever so much."

I started off down the red line. The wheel on Dill's stroller fell off. I stuffed it into my Safeway bag full of sidewalk muck and sand. I reminded myself, the main thing to remember when you walk into the waiting room is not to look at anybody. That's only an invitation for boring conversations and hard-luck stories that can go on for two or three hours. The thing to do is just find a seat and sit and look tough. And also remember that these people aren't necessarily as pathetic as they look. Or they're far more pathetic than they look. Either way, don't talk to anybody. I sat down holding Dill on my lap and shaking things in front of his face like keys and the stroller wheel. And I thought of Gortex Guy beaming with delight in his cultural anthropology class at the wonder of it all. The old guy next to me appeared to be having some kind of asthma attack, he kept smacking his shiny lips together after every gasp and hack. A woman said "Hi baby" to Dill. She offered him a nickel.

I was trying hard to look tough. I didn't stare at anybody or offer the old man assistance or coo at Dill or smile sympathetically at the crazy woman or take her dirty nickel. I sat and looked at the walls and ceiling and waited for my name to be called. Then I saw Terrapin. Oh great. She saw me and dragged her two little sullen girls over to me and Dill.

"Lucy! Why didn't you tell me you were coming here? We could have walked together. Isn't the rain beautiful? This is your first time isn't it?" Blah, blah, blah. She was wearing a t-shirt that read, "Extinct is Forever."

I had wanted to give the impression that I had been on the dole all my life, that I had seen the world from every angle, that I didn't need anybody, that I had been to hell and back and survived.

"Hi."

"Hey Lucy, would you like to share our snack? I brought some veggies and raisins, and Sunshine (her other daughter's name was Rain) brought a board game she made by herself out of odds and ends. We may as well enjoy ourselves while we wait."

My cover was shot to hell. The other hard-cores had no respect for me. They were staring at Terrapin and me and I felt trapped. I don't know why I wanted the respect of long-term dole recipients. Wherever I went I tried to fit in and the dole was no different. There was something terrible about being at the dole for the second time. I didn't want them to pity me and I didn't want to pity them. I just wanted to be anonymous. But I think they felt about me the same way I felt about Gortex Guy.

A couple of women from Serenity Place came in, and Terrapin whispered in my ear that one of them was making over five thousand bucks a month as a prostitute as well as collecting the dole. I wondered if it would work for me. The women from Serenity Place sat way off in a corner next to a group of Indians who hadn't said one word to each other the whole time.

I'm not sure, but I think someone who worked at the dole must have told my case worker to see me as soon as possible, because Dill kept crawling off into the blue and yellow line rooms, where we were not supposed to go, and I'd chase him, he'd laugh, I'd sigh, and the dole workers would clear their throats or look away. With the puke now on his pants and one boot missing he looked horrible, and I think seeing him depressed the dole staff. Anyway, they got me in and out of there pretty quickly. My worker asked me if I knew yet who Dill's father was. As if since the last visit an angel had appeared in my kitchen and said "psst, it was Tiffany's brother, whatsisname." Was I supposed to line up all the guys I'd had sex with over that period and check out their features and insist that they all go for blood tests and report back to me so I could then get the sheriff after them to give me child support and get off the dole? Actually it might have been a good thing I didn't know.

A lot of women in Half-a-Life did know who the fathers were, and as soon as their dole workers knew they knew, they were expected to get money from them, which would be docked from the mothers' welfare cheques. If the guy didn't pay,

too bad, you were still out the money. You could put them on
maintenance enforcement if they were still in the province.
Sometimes this worked. But sometimes, if the guy was an asshole, he could blackmail the woman and get her welfare can-
celled. Like if a woman babysat or sewed stuff or did any little
amount of work in her apartment for pay, it was supposed to be
reported to the dole, so they could dock that amount from the
cheque. Also, if you left your kids sleeping while you went
downstairs to do the laundry or ran over to a friend's for an egg,
the guy could sue for custody, claiming you were an unfit mother. Some mothers simply didn't want to anger their children's
fathers. They would rather tell the dole they were receiving a
hundred bucks or fifty bucks a month from the father even
when they weren't and lose it from their cheque than risk the
dole and the courts getting involved and going after the man.
Most of them are far more afraid of these men than they are of
poverty. For those with a lot of pride, it's rough. When your
case worker sits there punching information into a computer,
and says, "Father's name and address," you can say, "I don't
know," which for me is true and hard to admit, but even when
it's not true, a lot of women say it to save themselves the grief of
trying to extract cash from fathers long gone.

It's not hard to ask for money for new winter snowsuits, or
a crib, even though it's kind of degrading, but there's something
about saying you don't know who the father of your child is
when you do. And when that child was conceived you really
loved the guy and he loved you, maybe, and the child was perfect, and you almost believed that you'd be together, a family,
forever. That you had actually made a decision to have a relationship with a certain man and to become pregnant and give
birth and become a mother and be responsible. Then to just
toss that out the window and say you don't know—for some of
these women, that was the hardest thing. They hung on to their
memories of perfect love, of perfect union, these were the
beginnings of their children. Yeah, they were alone now, the guy
had split. But their intentions had been grand and they'd be
damned if anybody was going to take that away. These are the

women who say *Yes* of course they know who the father is, and *No* they have no idea where he is and no way of finding out. That really surprises the workers. Their hands are tied. They have to issue the full amount on the cheque and they can't go after the guy for maintenance. They hate it.

Anyway, I wasn't one of those. I had to answer the question. I sighed and said, "No, I still don't know who the father is. I should tell you right now, I probably never will."

"Well, if it happens again," the dole officer said, "we might not be so helpful."

That pissed me off. Helpful? This was his job. It was policy. It was all politically motivated. People like him needed people like me. I had read this in an editorial in the newspaper, and besides, I could have a dozen children and not know the father of any one of them and they'd still have to give me money. I knew that. "Oh," I said.

"Yes, oh. If you find yourself in a similar position in the future, I'd advise you to a) utilize some type of proven contraceptive device, or b) obtain the identity of the male, be that through direct communication, that is, by asking him his name, or if need be, that is, if he is not forthcoming and refuses to co-operate, by taking down his license plate number, providing he owns a vehicle, and from thereon in his identity can be traced by the police, that is, if the need arises."

I concentrated on breathing. I noticed the sign on his door. It said F. Podborczintski. His eyes were small and blue and his nose was large and red. He had managed to comb a few strips of hair over his shiny scalp. His shirt tugged around his armpits and was the colour of dust. He looked sad and tired. I wondered if he was married and had kids of his own. I wondered if he always talked this way about sex.

"Okay," I said.

Type, type, type. He put more information into my file and then he gave me a slip which meant I should follow the red line out of there and then switch onto the green line towards the tellers who would dole out my money. There were about seven of them and they sat behind bulletproof windows that had little slits at the bottom close to the counter where we slipped them our papers and they slipped us our cash. We didn't have to say anything to each other. Before I left his office, Mr. Podborczintski tweaked Dill's cheek and this made him cry. Podborczintski looked so uncomfortable. It would have been nice if Dill had smiled at him. I had to stand in a teller's line for about fifteen minutes, while Dill tried to lift my shirt and get his mouth on my breast. After that tweak, he needed some soothing. Lish had told me that feeding your child is nothing to be ashamed of and if people didn't like it they shouldn't look, so I stood there while Dill slurped away to his heart's content. I knew the receptionist was staring, and sure enough, after a few minutes, she clomped over to me and said she was sorry, but breast-feeding wasn't allowed in the building. There had been complaints. I felt like ripping off my shirt and shaking my milky tits in her face. Just then Terrapin came around the corner and waved. I motioned to her to come over and then asked her to chase Dill around because if he couldn't eat, he sure wasn't going to stand there in the line-up with me and I didn't want to lose my spot. I had heard a woman behind me say, "That's disgusting," after the wet *thwop* sound that happened every time I took my nipple out of Dill's mouth before he was ready to let go. It was still raining outside.

On the way home, the stroller was working remarkably well, so I decided to take a chance and go to the mall to pay my phone bill. One more day and I was going to be disconnected. As soon as Dill and I hit the mall, the stroller started acting up. Every ten yards, kick kick. Dill had fallen asleep by then and I was trying to ram the thing back on gently so he wouldn't wake up. I deposited my dole cheque into the instant teller and then expected to get cash back. But because I had no funds in my account to cover it I was told there would be a two-day hold. *Have a nice day* the instant teller told me and then the window slid shut over the screen. I looked in my pocket and counted two dollars and twenty-seven cents. CRASH! I had put my heavy leather jacket on the stroller handles and the weight of it pulled the stroller over backwards onto the floor. Dill woke up screaming and staring up at the ceiling. I picked up the stroller and Dill from the floor and took off for the phone place to tell them that they'd just have to wait. I'd explain and pay in full as soon as I got my money. Every ten yards the wheel came off and I'd kick it back on, but then it started coming off every five yards. I was kicking it harder and harder. Dill was really screaming now. People were staring. I thought I saw Gortex Guy going into the Gap store. My head was starting to pound and my jaw was clenched like a psychopath's.

Suddenly I stopped.

"I CAN'T FUCKING STAND THIS FUCKING FUCKING PIECE OF FUCKING SHIT NO FUCKING MORE!" I screamed. I thought to myself that I sounded like Teresa. I scooped Dill from the stroller and then starting kicking the stroller for all I was worth. I kicked it and kicked it. I kicked it at least fifty yards down the mall. Everybody was staring at me. Dill was crying. Then I picked it up and carried it over to the fountain in the centre and heaved it right in. Over the heads of a few old people that were sitting around it killing time.

I remembered my mother getting pissed off at an umbrella that wouldn't close. She was standing in the doorway, she had just come back from the neighbours', and she couldn't get the umbrella to close nor could she get it through the door into the house. The wind was howling. The rain was coming down so hard it hurt. I was sitting on a chair at the kitchen table watching her fight with the umbrella. Then the door shut. I looked out the window and there was the umbrella tumbling through the sky lifting higher and higher. It was beautiful. My mom had thrown it away, let it go. I was impressed. I clapped. My mom put a pot of coffee on and sat down with the crossword puzzle.

I shifted Dill over to my other hip, stuffed the Safeway bag and our jackets under my arm and marched all the way to the other end of the mall and into the Sears store. Dill had stopped crying and I felt quite good. I walked over to the baby appliance section and put Dill into the first floor model stroller I saw, heaped my jacket and the bag on top of him, and walked right out of the store. I walked out of the mall into the rain and I didn't have to stop until I got to the front doors of good ol' Half-a-Life.

Dill loved his new stolen stroller. He'd sit in it for hours and Alba and Letitia would push him up and down the hall. I stayed away from the mall for a while.

One morning I looked out my living room window and on the fence surrounding the small parking lot (parking lots for public housing are always small because they know few of us have cars and they think they discourage overnight visitors that way) was painted in big red letters FUCK THE RICH THAN EAT THEM. When I saw that I thought Teresa must have done it because of the spelling of "then," but I realized it might have been a kid, or kids. Besides, Teresa hadn't seemed miserable at all, especially since she had been studying French two evenings a week. Sing Dylan was in the parking lot trying to scrub the painted letters off, but he wasn't having much success. This time Sarah was laughing. She was standing in the rain again wearing one of Emmanuel's t-shirts and her jeans were rolled up. She was barefoot. I had never seen her laugh before. Sing Dylan was shouting at her for something and this made her laugh even harder. At first I was worried that she had finally gone insane over Emmanuel. But eventually she stopped laughing and handed Sing Dylan his pail and acted normal again.

She had cut her hair and she looked like a little boy. She looked good. Seeing Sarah and Sing Dylan out there laughing and shouting in the rain made me feel terrible. I wanted to run out there and be crazy too. I actually envied Sarah for a second, not having her kid with her. I was an old woman. I never had any fun anymore. I should have been hanging out in cars with guys my age, drinking beer and staying up all night, sleeping in. At least I could go out into the rain and laugh for awhile. But that would have been ridiculous, walking out there and then just laughing. Sarah and Sing Dylan would have thought I was insane and I would have felt like Gortex Guy. They were content, just the two of them, and my life seemed like one big mistake from start to finish. I thought of my mom and wondered if it hurt her to see me this way, that is, if she could. My mom was always telling me, "Good Luck Lucy, Good Luck." I'd leave for school, she'd say Good Luck, I'd take out the garbage, she'd say Good Luck, I'd go to bed, she'd say Good Luck. I'd tell her I wanted scrambled eggs and bacon for breakfast, she'd say Good Luck. Ha Ha. But she didn't just say Good Luck just like that. She said it like it was two sentences, both with exclamation marks after them. GOOD! LUCK! and move her chin down with each word, like someone saying FUCK! YOU! but of course not at all the same as that, just with the same vigour. Was I lucky? Had it worked? Is this the kind of life my mom would think was lucky?

I remembered some crazy woman in a laundromat on Broadway telling me her mother was very disappointed in all of her children, but mostly in her, because she once had had potential as a TV journalist and now had become like all the rest of her siblings: her older sister ran away from her kids and joined the army, her younger sister was dead, well not technically, but she may as well have been because she let men walk all over her and never batted an eye, and her brother was, well he seemed to be okay, but his wife kept trying to kill herself, so he must not have been that hot. This woman in the laundromat said that she could live with her own disappointment, but she just couldn't handle her mother's.

She said she was going to start telling her mom big lies about all her career successes and start sending fake positive upbeat letters from her siblings who, from what I could tell, lived in Northern Ontario, and then she was going to replace her mom's liver medicine with vitamins so she'd die fast and terribly thrilled with the way her family had worked out. She said that if I mentioned it to anyone she'd find out where I lived and slit my throat from ear to ear, it wouldn't bother her. I could see her actually carrying out her plan with the liver medicine and the letters and everything, but I had a really hard time imagining her as a TV journalist.

My apartment seemed too big for Dill and me: we had an extra room and some of the other women used theirs for craft things, easels, sewing machines, drum kits. But I didn't have a hobby. I hated crafts. Angela was forever making piñatas for the kids in the block. Terrapin and her organic friends, Gypsy and Deb, made jewellery and wove friendship bracelets and tried to sell the stuff on the street and through a women's co-op. There was a woman in the block who was sculpting sex toys out of clay: rocking chairs with big multi-coloured phalluses sticking out of the seats. She had a teenage son, and his girlfriend lived there, too. The woman was very shy. I don't even know her name but I think her son and his girlfriend forced her to be their slave.

My apartment, like most, had a long hall as its central feature. On one end was the bathroom, on the other the kitchen. In between were the bedrooms and living room, which were more or less the same size. The rooms had big windows that opened out. Off the living room was a door to the outside balcony. Lish had woven a fishnet around the bars of hers and put a plastic wading pool out there that was continuously filling up with rainwater. The kids loved it. The couple below weren't thrilled about the water splashing over the sides down onto their balcony, but their kids played in it too, so they couldn't really complain.

Joe and Pillar had been at Half-a-Life almost as long as Lish had. Theirs had been one of those perfect storybook marriages. Until about one week after the wedding. That's when their first kid was born. Apparently they both fell so in love with the kid that neither one wanted to leave the house and work. Joe had always been kind of unemployable and Pillar had once been a computer programmer. But after Duncan, they hung around at home, had more kids, fell in love with them, went on the dole when their money ran out, and eventually joined the ranks of the *nouveau* poor. Give a big warm welcome to Joe and Pillar!

Like I said, they lived right under Lish, and whenever she had one of her skinny boyfriends over and her moaning and groaning got too loud, Joe would stand in his apartment, in his kitchen, right under her kitchen, where she always *did it* with her boyfriends, and imitate her moaning. Then Pillar would call him a jerk and they'd fight and all along Lish didn't even hear it or care because she was too wrapped up in her own fun.

I didn't have enough stuff to fill my apartment. I marvelled at Lish's apartment. It was full of junk mostly, secondhand furniture that she painted or the kids had painted, art from a lot of her boyfriends, kids' art, plants, old books, records (she didn't have a stereo to play them on), jars of organic food stuff, boxes of leather bits and material the kids could use to make things with, lamps with big fringy shades and two or three old-fashioned typewriters, photographs of her kids and her family, her great-grandparents, her friends. She almost always had music playing in the background and incense burning and big vats of soup or vegetables boiling on the stove. Mint and dill were her favourite smells, and she put huge amounts of garlic into everything she cooked. She had transformed her standard issue public housing suite into a marvellous home. I loved going over there. In comparison, my apartment was cold and depressing.

Over the summer it got better. Lish took me to all the secondhand furniture shops and gave me some blue and yellow cloth to hang over my windows. I bought an old Persian carpet from an estate sale and my dad gave me the bedside lamp from Mom's side of the bed. Rodger, Hope and Maya's dad, let us use his van to pick up the stuff. When I picked up the lamp my dad wasn't home, but he had left a note telling me where the lamp was, as if I had forgotten where my mom had slept. We picked old wooden chairs out of back lanes and sanded them down and painted them green and mustard, fuchsia and black, I draped a lacy tablecloth over my old couch and bought a few plants from Safeway. Lish suggested I take the cupboard doors off my kitchen cupboards. That way the dishes and food would be visible and make the room look more lived in and colourful. I wasn't so sure boxes of Kraft Dinner and Melmac plates were so hot to look at, but off came the cupboard doors anyway. Angela gave me a big clay pot and I hid my crappy food behind it. Lish told me I needed a cast iron frying pan and wooden mixing spoons. These I got from my dad's place, too. Again he wasn't home when I picked them up. I guess there's a lot to do when you're a geology professor. My mom had never used these things because they were lodged too far back in the cupboard and she didn't really care whether she was cooking on iron or Teflon.

My dad never cooked for himself. He ate all his meals at The Waffle Shop or at the Pizza Hut. When I was a kid he'd take me to The Waffle Shop. We would walk there holding hands. Well, it was more like me flying behind him like a kite because he was a huge man and covered the ground with enormous quick strides. My dad had this weird talent. He could pick out four-leafed clovers in the grass. One four-leafed clover surrounded by thousands of regular three-leafed ones and grass and stuff and he'd see it. Every once in a while that would happen on our way to The Waffle Shop and he'd stop and home in on the thing and then point it out to me, but that was it. He never picked them and I never asked him how he did it and he never told me. It was very strange. I remember telling my grade two class that my dad could do this weird thing with four-leaf clovers and they were not impressed. A boy got up and said his dad could crow like a rooster and they were impressed. Then I told them, *well*, my dad was the only baby ever in the world to be born wearing a little grey suit. I had overheard my mother tell this to one of her friends on the phone. They were not impressed and my teacher asked me to please sit down.

I don't think my dad could even feel my hand in his big one. I think often he forgot I was with him until we actually got to The Waffle Shop. That's when I landed back on the ground beside him, huffing and puffing. Every time we were at The Waffle Shop he'd say the same thing to the waitress: "An egg salad sandwich for my bombshell blonde." My dad was human when he was outside of our house. He talked a bit and smiled. He tousled my hair. Inside the house he was dead, terrifying. He sat in his chair and silently shook his head at me when I made a lot of noise or ran around too much. On weekends when he wasn't working, he stayed in bed all day. We'd forget about him.

There was a woman in the block who was really truly crazy. She took seventeen pills a day to try and keep herself "between the ditches" as she said. She hadn't always been nuts. At one point she had been studying for her Master's degree in English Literature. She was married to an engineer and they had a son. When her son turned five, things started to unravel for her. She lost it. Her husband left and took the kid with him. He couldn't handle her madness. Somehow she got to Half-a-Life, probably because her son was allowed to spend one week of every year with her. I don't know. I never asked her because I didn't want to upset her. She scared me. Once she dropped in on Lish and me, at Lish's place, and started talking to us like we were old friends. Before that she had never spoken to us. The kids used her as their ultimate insult. "You love Betty." "No, you." She was pleasant around them, always saying, "Hi, how're you doing?" But all that medication made her twitch and shudder a lot. It scared the kids just like it did me. She showed us a picture of a guy she had been writing to and was hoping to visit. She got his name from a prison pen pal catalogue at the library. He was in jail in Baltimore for murdering a woman. That's all he had told her. She told us she was going to hitchhike out there and they were going to get married. She was worried about telling him she was nuts. Lish pointed out to her that he had a few quirks himself. This made her laugh. Once, she broiled frozen bagels for us in Lish's oven. She took them out gingerly and said "ouch" because they were hot. I noticed that the oven hadn't even been on. But she smeared cream cheese over them anyway and handed them out to us. Frozen bagels with cream cheese. Then she went running upstairs and brought down the dress she was going to wear to get married in. It was really stunning. It was beige silk, simple and very elegant. I thought she had good taste for a nutcase. She asked us about ten times if we

43

thought she had a soft laugh because Andre, the murderer she planned to marry, told her over the phone that she did and he liked it.

Lish told her that she didn't think it was a good idea to plan to marry this con without visiting him first. "The guy's a murderer for Christ's sake," Lish said. Betty said, "Yeah, but it could just have been a backhand that happened to kill this woman." "Or he might have chopped her into little bits," Lish said. "The two are very different." "If he chopped her into little bits," Betty had said, "I'd reconsider." But basically, she thought he was a very sweet guy. He was completing a university degree in psychology. She also pointed out that he was black, male, poor and eighteen when he killed this woman, and might be taking the rap for someone. People like him are thrown into prison in the States all the time, Betty claimed. Anyway, she was excited about hitchhiking out to Baltimore to see him and was preparing herself for the trip.

"I want to get really long fingernails so I look like one of those Jewish broads who've never worked a day in their lives," she told us. I looked at Lish. She had longish nails. I thought she might say something to set Betty straight, but she just laughed. A couple of days later Betty told us that Andre had called her and said he wanted to be honest with her. He had killed his grandmother, doused her with gasoline and lit her on fire. But he had been young and she had always nagged him. Betty decided she didn't care whom he had killed or how. She wanted to wear that silk dress more than anything and be Andre's wife. Though she had wondered out loud whether or not they would actually be married if they didn't have sex. Apparently that prison didn't have a conjugal trailer or room or whatever.

After that first visit we'd had, I'd say Hi to Betty when I saw her in the hallway. She'd purse her lips at me and wouldn't say a thing. Once I saw her with big black stitches on her chin and she told me she had fallen off her bike. Lish told me that Betty had shown her the photograph of Andre and had told Lish it was her brother Dean. Toward the end of the summer she moved out and none of us saw her again.

The woman who moved into her apartment was very friendly. Her name was Tanya. She had two children, a boy and a girl. They had different fathers. On the weekend her son went to his dad's place in the country. His dad had a girlfriend who had a daughter. His dad and the girlfriend had a son together. So Tanya's son had a half-sister and a mother with whom he lived during the week, but on the weekend he had a step-sister and a half-brother and a step-mom. The girl went to her dad's place in the suburbs on the weekend. Her dad had a girlfriend who had a son. Her dad and the girlfriend had a daughter together. So Tanya's daughter had a half-brother and a mother with whom she lived during the week, but on the weekend she had a step-brother and a half-sister and a step-mom.

Tanya had the weekends to herself. On the weekends she brewed beer in huge vats and bootlegged it to people in the block. Once, somebody from Serenity Place called the cops on Tanya. One of the cops turned out to be the full brother of Tanya's daughter's weekend step-mom. Tanya and this woman got along all right. The cop knew that his sister wouldn't invite him over for Sunday dinners anymore if he arrested Tanya and, like most cops, he was lonely. So he gave Tanya a warning, tongue in cheek, enjoyed a mug of home brew with his partner, and left. You see, it pays to be well-connected and Tanya certainly was. She made a fine beer with a higher than usual alcohol content. She let us buy it on credit and half the time she'd forget about it. She really enjoyed brewing beer. When her kids came home she put all the tubes and funnels and bags of sugar away and she and Sing Dylan and Sarah carried the bubbling vats of beer downstairs to Sing Dylan's apartment. Sing Dylan didn't drink it, of course, but he didn't mind storing it for her. I don't think her kids ever knew their mother was the Beer Queen of Half-a-Life.

There was one other woman in Half-a-Life I sort of got to know. Her name was Mercy. Lish told me that her real name was Mercedes. Her mother had given her that name when she was still in the womb because it was the last thing she saw of Mercy's father after she told him she was pregnant: a big black

Mercedes pulling out of the driveway of her parents' home. He was the son of a banker or a judge. Mercy's mom raised her alone on the top floor of her parents' elegant home in River Heights. Lish said Mercy and her mom were invited downstairs to join the grandparents for dinner every Thursday night. Other than Thursday nights they never saw each other. When Mercy turned eighteen she turned wild. She set fires around town until she was caught. She did every type of drug available. She screwed anything that moved, male or female. Eventually her grandparents turfed her. Heartbroken, her mother committed suicide on a Friday afternoon and they didn't find her body until the next Thursday evening when she didn't show up for dinner. Or so the story goes around Half-a-Life.

Anyway, Mercy belonged to our group only because we loved to gossip about her. Actually she would have been very funny if she hadn't been so uptight about everything. After a while her uptightness became the joke. She confused me. She had one daughter. The father of this girl was a Trinidadian Rastafarian. But he lived with a different white woman and they had a whole whack of children together. From time to time he'd stay overnight with Mercy. Seems his wife knew about Mercy, and Mercy certainly knew about his wife and that was the situation. I knew he had hit her a couple of times. I found it interesting how a person like Mercy could be attracted to a violent married man. She and her daughter went to bed every night at 7:30. She saved money on everything she bought. She always rode her bike everywhere with her daughter bobbing around behind her in a kid's bicycle seat. Her apartment was spotless. They seemed to bathe incessantly. When her daughter had been a baby, she had changed her diaper every time she urinated, even the smallest amount, to prevent diaper rash. She rarely got a sitter. She only read books by female feminist authors, mostly black ones, and she didn't own a TV. She was in control of everything—everything except her peculiar and violent love life. This guy walked all over her, showing up drunk late at night, banging on her door, agreeing to take the girl out to the park, then not showing up, asking her to marry him and the next day telling her she was a whore and hitting her. She put up with his shit. I guess he was the only unpredictable thing she could handle. She probably didn't want to end up alone like her mom had, so she didn't complain. She compensated for his randomness with her own precision.

One Saturday morning she asked Dill and me over for tea. Her daughter was surprisingly free and charming. Every time Dill dragged some book or toy out of place Mercy quickly put it back. When he spilled his juice, she spent about fifteen minutes wiping it off the floor, not complaining about it, just very focussed on it. Mercy showed me photographs of her trips to Trinidad. She travelled there with her daughter every year. She saved money on food and clothes and stuff so she could do this. She said she wanted her daughter to know where she was from. But these pictures were very odd. A lot of black people crowded into the photo, smiling and barefoot, holding chickens, wearing ripped t-shirts, dancing. Then there in the middle of the shot was Mercy. She was always wearing bright white knee socks and long khaki shorts. She had on hiking boots and long-sleeved men's white shirts. She wore a big-brimmed straw hat, tied around her little head with a yellow ribbon. Her face was obliterated almost entirely by huge black sunglasses. Her expression was always grim. Her daughter was usually off in the background dancing with her cousins. When she had finished showing me these pictures she carefully put them back into their plastic-backed envelope and then into another one and then another. Then she put them into a file folder entitled Trip Photos and put that file up high on a shelf in a cardboard box made especially for folders.

Each time she went to Trinidad she brought the family of her daughter's father gifts. For the children she brought thick-soled leather hi-top runners and puzzles and books. For the women she brought perfume and tampons and for the men she brought white dress shirts like the ones she wore. Mercy told me that in Trinidad she and her daughter slept in a dirty one-room shack with about six other people. There was no running water and no electricity. Almost everyone went barefoot. They joyously welcomed Mercy and her daughter, their granddaughter and cousin, into their home and hated to see them go.

She was also the only one of us who worked—outside of the home, that is. Once I asked Terrapin if she worked. She said, "Yes, I work very hard raising Sunshine and Rain. If you mean do I work outside the home for wages, no, I do not. It's more important for me to be at home with my children." I was going to ask her why her kids always looked so grim, but instead I said, "Oh. Cool." I had decided not to talk to Terrapin about anything concerning me or Dill, anything that was meaningful, anything about life or kids, nothing but *Hello, nice day* for her. God, she bugged me. One time Lish and I were moving a dresser from Lish's apartment to mine and Terrapin happened to show up on the stairs. She was wearing a shirt that read "Have a Special Delivery." She asked us how we were managing. Lish said, "Oh terrible, this is so heavy I'm going to have a miscarriage and I'm not even pregnant." I laughed and Terrapin said, "That might not be funny for all of us?"

Lish sighed, "Yeah, that's very true, Paraffin. What, am I supposed to be like court jester here or what?"

Actually, that is exactly what we expected Lish to be. She was funny. She was meant to be funny. Even if she wasn't making you laugh outright, she was uplifting, good for the soul. She had an attitude towards life that I wish I had. She did her own thing and she never noticed when people stared at her stupid spider hat or her long square-toed shoes. She loved to hang out with her kids, but if they wanted to do foolish things like attend school or join girl scouts, that was okay with her. She let them do their own thing because she knew how much she needed to be able to do hers. She had successfully separated her identity from her kids' identities and so she could really enjoy them. She wasn't afraid to be alone, as I suspected a lot of us at Half-a-Life were.

One morning, it was raining as usual, I cleaned up Dill's breakfast mess, and took him over to Lish's place. I couldn't call to tell her I was coming because her phone had been disconnected. But she knew just about everybody in the block and could use one of theirs anytime, provided they hadn't been disconnected, too. I brought my own coffee because Lish had stopped buying it. "Too expensive for something that makes me all jittery," she'd said. I knocked but nobody answered. So I walked right in to the living room. Hope and Maya were in school. Alba and Letitia were in there playing and singing the alphabet song as best they could. "A B C D E F G H I J K alimony please." I was about to say "Hi" to them when I heard moaning from the other room. At first I thought it was Lish and whoever having sex in her bedroom.

"Good morning Lucy Goosie and Dilly Willy," said Letitia in her most agreeable teacher's voice. They were playing school. Then I heard it again. It wasn't sex at all, Lish was crying. She must have been muffling it in her pillow or in all her hair, because it sounded far away. Nothing sounds far away in a Half-a-Life apartment. I didn't know what to do. Lish crying. It was too weird. She never cried.

Alba said, "Lish is crying because she has a tummy ache. And she can't come to school right now."

"But she'll come in the afternoon."

"Yeah."

I figured I'd just slip out and come back later, but by then Dill had been made a pupil and was being taught the alphabet. Alimony please. He'd scream if I tried to take him home now and then Lish would come into the room and be embarrassed. So I stood there smiling at the kids, wondering what the hell I should do. I flipped through a wicker basket full of letters she had saved. Love letters? I was tempted to read some but I was afraid the twins would tell her I'd been snooping through her stuff while she wept in the other room. I looked around at her photographs. Her parents looked normal. John was even smiling. Her mom had a happy expression and was holding John's hand. A picture of her brother from the '70s when he had an Afro. Someone had stuck two straws into his hair to look like antennae. A picture of Lish and Hope and her dad. Lish was enormously pregnant, with Maya, I guess, and wearing a bikini. They were on the beach. A picture beside it showed Rodger digging a hole in the sand and Lish standing beside him laughing. Hope was playing in the background. Then another picture beside that one. Lish was lying on her stomach with her huge belly nestled comfortably in the hole Rodger had dug for it and reading a book. Maya was sitting on her back and Rodger was drinking a beer. You couldn't even tell Lish was pregnant.

Pregnant, that was it. Maybe Lish was pregnant and that's why she was crying. No, Lish loved being pregnant. She'd be celebrating if she was. Not with tequila though. She kept crying. I stood there. I tiptoed over to the kitchen table, thinking I'd just sit there quietly and wait for Lish to be through.

That's where I saw the program. It was a festival program from years ago. 1989. It was open to the page with the buskers' descriptions and one of them was circled, about a hundred times, as if someone had spent a whole day with a pen going round and round it. The picture was small and blurry and black and white. It was a close-up of a dark-haired guy eating fire. It was the busker, the twins' dad. She was crying her eyes out over this guy. The twins were four years old. How long had she been crying in her hair over him? Four years, my god. I would have had to have started crying at fourteen and not stopped to have been crying for four years. Lish was so funny. Why was she crying after all this time? Obviously she was really hooked on this guy. I was envious. She had a real reason to get worked up. To throw herself down on her bed and sob, bawl her eyes out thinking of lost love, of happier times. I thought then that would be easier than looking forward to them like I was. At least she knew what life was like, at least what it could be like. She could see it. I was still trying to picture it. Alimony please . . . Dill wasn't catching on quickly to Alba and Letitia's teachings. I stared at the picture of the performer. I read his blurb. Fire-eater, magician, not afraid to risk his life for your cheap thrills . . . Lish kept on with her muffled crying. I guess she thought she was keeping it a secret from the kids. That bastard, I thought. Why did this always happen? I had built Half-a-Life and the women in it into a kind of shrine I worshipped. I had to, it was all I had. I really wanted it to be a good thing. I

50

wanted the women in it to laugh all the time. I wanted them to be tough. I wanted them to roll their eyes at trouble and crack a joke. I enjoyed the stupid arguments but I didn't want them to become complicated. In my mind these women had escaped from horrible lives and had come to seek solace in Half-a-Life. And Lish? I needed her to laugh at her life, not cry. Then my life would be funny, too. And Dill would be a lucky boy.

I looked at the wicker basket full of letters. Each one had been opened very carefully, and they were stacked neatly, according to size, smallest to largest. I ran my finger around the rim of the basket. Lish was still crying and the kids were having a good time. I looked out the window and it was then that I had my brilliant idea. I felt like I was Pierre Elliot Trudeau and I had just gone for a walk in the snow. I looked up, big wet snowflakes like chunks of cake falling on my face, and there it was, the answer: QUIT POLITICS. Or it could have been, probably, QUITEZ LES POLITIC. I'd have to ask Teresa. Anyway, in my case, of course, it wasn't QUIT POLITICS or anything, it was WRITE LETTERS. And I wasn't really walking in the snow, I was staring out the window at the rain—but still. It came to me.

And I would sign them, "Love, Gotcha."

When I was a kid my cousin Delia and I played a trick on her brother. He had told his mom that there was a girl he liked. Delia and I overheard him talking about her. He said her name was Sandy and she had hair like Farrah Fawcett and was really cute. He had doubled her on his bike all the way to the Mac Store. "I hope she likes me," he'd told his mom. Delia and I made a plan. We wrote her brother a letter from Sandy. She must have been three or four years older than us so we wrote the letter in big swooping letters instead of printing it in our own square hand. We dabbed my aunt's perfume on it. *Dear David, I like you a lot. Please meet me at the Mohawk after school if you like me too. And if you don't already have a girlfriend. Love Sandy.* Then we dropped this letter in the mailbox and waited. We were bursting to find out what happened. We couldn't even look at each other without laughing our heads off. We were so brilliant. After school we ran home and threw ourselves on the couch, pretending to watch TV like any other day. We waited and waited and waited. Finally the front door opened. Slowly David walked into the house. He dropped his jacket and his books on the floor in front of the door and started walking down the hall to his bedroom. He had on his stiff new Lee jeans. When he saw us in the living room, he said in a really nice soft voice, "Hi." He kept on walking slowly toward his bedroom. I was worried and I could tell Delia was, too. We were frozen, staring at the TV. "What if he shoots himself?" I whispered to Delia. "As if. He doesn't even have a gun," she whispered back. I wanted to cry. We had always played jokes on David and he'd get mad and tell my aunt and she'd tell us to leave him alone. But this was different. We'd broken his heart. What if he became a homosexual or a serial killer of women because of us? The next day his mom found out what happened and she took both of us into her sewing room. She told us we had done a very cruel thing and had made David very sad. We would have to apologize and promise never to do anything like it again. I had hoped David would beat us up like he usually did when we bugged him, but instead he just sat there. After we apologized he said, "Kay." Then we said we were sorry. We told him we had been assholes. Neither one of us had ever said that word out loud before. We hoped this would really convince him we were sorry. He just said "OK" again. After that we stopped bugging him and he never beat us up again. I think we were all sad about that for a long time. Anyway, now he's married to a nurse and almost bald and helps disturbed teenagers by canoeing with them and teaching them to camp. I don't know what became of Sandy.

But that whole thing with my cousin Delia had been a bad joke. I was much older now, and serious about keeping Lish happy. I think even Pierre Trudeau would have approved.

Even Terrapin had stopped marvelling at the rain. The mid-western United States was starting to flood. Rivers were running over farmers' fields and into their homes. Entire towns were being threatened by swollen rivers. Major highways and bridges were being wiped out. It was only a matter of time before the Red and the Assiniboine, Winnipeg's rivers, would feel the pressure and begin to rise. With the rain came the mosquitoes. Every puddle, large or small, became fertile breeding grounds for those damn bugs. Our children were covered in bites. Some were too young to spray with repellent because the chemicals in the spray seeped through the skin into their blood. Others had mothers who didn't believe in it. They tried to ward off the mosquitoes with home remedies, Avon's Skin so Soft and Citronella, but nothing worked. Soon some kids, especially the ones that were too young to slap mosquitoes off, had started a second layer of bites. Dill had three mosquito bites one on top of the other above his right eye. One morning he woke up and his eye was swollen shut.

We couldn't even open our windows, because the buggers managed to get through the miniscule holes in the screens, those that had them. At night you could hear the collective scratching of all of Half-a-Life's bite victims. We scratched until we bled. It was common for the kids to walk around with the dark bodies of mosquitoes squished onto their skin. They couldn't be bothered to flick them off anymore after they had slapped them. If the mosquito was slapped with a belly full of fresh blood, skin and clothing were stained. The walls in our apartments had ugly smears of dead mosquitoes. Large chunks of our days were devoted to tracking mosquitoes, creeping from room to room, standing on chairs and furniture, cornering them, and adding to their death toll. We were told by the experts on the six o'clock news to wear white long sleeves and pants. But it didn't matter what we wore. They still got through. Even the animals were suffering. Farmers couldn't sell their meat for as much as they were used to. Big pork hams had ugly bites all over the skin and nobody wanted to buy them.

Terrapin advised us all to take an organic pill containing kelp and hyssop and tree bark. She said it would make our broken skin heal faster. People didn't want to go out for any reason, not even for beer. Tanya bought herself a beat-up old van and put one of Sing Dylan's old fridges inside. A friend of hers gave her a cell phone and she was in business. She was bootlegging her homemade beer at twenty-five bucks for a twelve, fifteen for a six. She didn't even have to work the normal bootleg hours of two to five in the morning. People were willing to pay any time as long as they didn't have to leave their houses.

On top of the rain and the mosquitoes there was the heat. With our windows shut to keep the bugs out and the heat and the humidity building up inside, it felt like we were living in Viet Nam or someplace. We were all getting nasty yeast infections and Terrapin's yogurt remedy wasn't working for any of us. Lish said to her one day after many yogurt applications, "Hey Hairpin, got any peach? Sean's allergic to avocado." Terrapin advised Lish that if she wanted to cure the yeast infection she should stay away from men for awhile. Lish laughed.

Lish's hair became thick and wavy. She complained daily about it being out of control. I thought it was beautiful. She had cut off the bottom of her gauzy skirts to make them into minis. She tied the bottom of her black t-shirts up under her breasts. A white roll of flab hung over her waistband and occasionally she would grab it and insist that we look at it, saying, "Isn't it disgusting?" It wasn't really, and I don't think she actually cared. Her legs were long and thin and her calves were seriously hairy. They were hairier than any man's I had seen. She ditched the Birkenstocks and traipsed around in her big bare feet. Only on the very hottest days did she take off her hat with the spider on it. Without it she looked younger and paler. Her older daughters wore Lish's t-shirts as dresses. Most of the time the young twins didn't wear anything at all. Some days they jumped in and out of a baking soda bath that Lish had prepared for them to take the edge off their itchy bites.

Every day Mercy went to work on her bike with her daughter sitting on the seat behind her. She'd drop her off at the daycare on the way. Both of them wore regulation fibreglass bike helmets and cheese cloth underneath covering their faces and necks. They looked like bee farmers. God, it was hot. And muggy. *Muggy* was a favorite word of my mom's. Every evening I'd give Dill a bath, but before I did, I had to stretch him out on the bed and peel away the dirt and lint that had stuck deep in the rolls of his fat. His neck had a thin ring of dirt all the way around it. I made cleaning him a game and he laughed his loud big-mouthed laugh the whole time. He chuckled and drooled. Even laughing made us sweat. Even Sing Dylan who came from India said it was "Bloody hot."

It was June. Terrapin was organizing a solstice party. I had no idea what that was and I was too embarrassed to ask her or even Lish, who groaned when Terrapin told her she was having one. I asked Terrapin when she was having it and she just kind of cocked her head at me like a dog and said, "What do you mean *When?*" She was wearing a t-shirt that read "Food" on the back, and on the front it had a picture of a ukulele or something and read "Winnipeg Folk Festival."

Her kids had made some playdough out of salt and flour and carrot juice for colour and wanted to give it to Dill to play with. I guess it was the kind he could eat when he was finished playing with it. From Terrapin's tone when she said *when*, I assumed I was supposed to take my cues from her aura or her vibe or maybe check my *I Ching* to get the answer. What was I thinking being so direct about something so vague and wispy as the solstice? I was determined not to appear ignorant around Hairpin. Besides, I had already given the impression that I knew what the solstice was and I had a pretty good idea that if I knew what it was I was supposed to know when it was. Kind of like a Grey Cup party.

Thank goodness the library was only a couple of blocks away from Half-a-Life. The mosquitoes were bad, so I had to run as fast as I could, pushing Dill in the stroller. At least the sidewalk was smooth the whole way so I wouldn't run the risk of smashing into shifting concrete and watching Dill get flung out of his stroller. He loved the speed anyway, and the mosquitoes would have to work too hard to get us. They were getting slower and bigger from all the blood they were drinking. They looked more like prehistoric miniature flying dinosaurs now, but they were sluggish and sated. Drinking blood for them had become more sport than survival. Now that they had the city to themselves they were living it up, sitting around in outdoor cafés ordering Bloody Marys and slapping each other on the back. Dill and I managed to get to the library with two bites apiece. Not bad. A greater difficulty faced me: getting to the front doors, gasping for air, removing Dill from his stroller, plopping him on the grass, folding the stroller up, making sure Dill didn't crawl into the wet dirt of the flower bed beside the grass, and then carrying him and the stroller inside. This process resulted in another half a dozen bites for each of us. Each time I performed this operation I counted the seconds it took to complete: one thousand, two thousand, three thousand.

I had, in the past, removed Dill from his stroller, folded it up, and got in the library with both of them in eight seconds. In a rodeo this is the amount of time you have to tear out of the chute on your horse, rope the little calf, yank it off its feet, leap down from your horse, flip the calf onto its back, and tie its feet together. Then you jump up and back from the calf with your arms in the air. If your cowboy hat is still on your head you can take it off and wave it around and then wipe your brow with your sleeve. I guess after that someone comes around and unties the calf and drags it back to its mother.

So anyway, I could do this in eight seconds, too, not every time, but often enough. If someone I knew came over to talk to me, someone from Half-a-Life or the dole or wherever, I had to forfeit. It would be disconcerting for them if I was moving around like greased lightning muttering *thousands* or *mississippis* under my breath and then hurtling myself and Dill and the stroller into the library and slamming the door in their face, peering out at them with a victorious expression on my face and my arms in the air. But with the mosquitoes and the rain I wasn't meeting many people outside.

The library was one of my favourite places. The building was old and had a lot of dark wood in it. The book stacks were on the main floor. The library had dim yellow lighting and no windows. The floors creaked and the books were sort of greasy. All winter long the rads hissed and banged. A whole shelf of rare books the library had somehow managed to score had been soaked when one of the rads exploded overnight. The librarians took turns blowing hot air on them with a hair dryer. Downstairs was a room for story time and crafts. Lish and some of the others brought their kids to story time every week. It was free and close and a good break. The parents had to stay in the library but they could go upstairs and talk quietly or read, uninterrupted, for one whole hour. The woman in charge of story time was kind and energetic. Her face had a permanent grin on it and she didn't mind spilled glue and paint as long as the kids were enjoying themselves. Often she'd be a minute or two late. Then she'd come running into the room grinning and panting. "I'm sorry, I'm sorry. Here I am. I misplaced my glasses, so if I can't read the words we'll have to make them up ha ha ha." The kids would cheer and clap and gaze up at her from their spots on the ratty carpet. When she read, the kids listened. There was also a chess club downstairs. Clusters of old men smoking and playing chess and speaking in different languages.

The only problem with this library was the old librarian upstairs. She seemed to work irregularly, so I never knew when she'd be there. For some reason she hated me. Or at least I thought she did. It might have been because I let Dill crawl around on the floor while I looked for books. Sometimes he'd pull out a bunch of books from the lower shelves and she'd clear her throat and try to catch my eye. After a while I stopped looking at her after she had cleared her throat. I'd just go over to where Dill was and clean up the books like it was no big deal. Silently I encouraged him to keep doing it. Sometimes I met other moms from Half-a-Life and we'd talk and laugh and our kids would run around making too much noise. Usually there wasn't anybody else in the library so I didn't see what the big deal was. We'd take out piles of books for our kids, even Dill.

Anyway, this librarian, Mrs. Hobbs, was always on my case. I'd check out books and she'd look at me over the tops of her half-glasses. She'd pull up my file on the computer and then get close to it and squint at it for at least half a minute with her chin resting in her hand. She'd drum her skinny fingers against her slack cheek while she stared at the computer. She'd sigh and look at me again with a very stern expression.

Anyway, I'd found a book that had something in it on the solstice and I wanted to take it out. "You owe twelve dollars and fifty-nine cents in overdue fines," said Mrs. Hobbs.

"Really?"

"Do you wish to pay for that with a cheque or cash?"

"Uh, could I work it off?" I smiled.

"Cheque or cash?"

In the meantime I had put Dill on the floor and he was heading over to the table with the rare wet books.

"You can't take any books out until you pay your fine," said Mrs. Hobbs.

Just then Emily the smiling story time woman came over to the desk.

"No, no, Sadie, don't you remember? The fine has to be brought down to ten dollars. As long as it's only ten dollars she can take out the books."

"Oh. Okay," I said, "I'll pay two dollars and fifty-nine cents now and then I can take out the books."

With Emily the Good at my side I felt more confident.

"Hey," I added, laughing, "I could go on bringing my fine down to ten dollars forever. I don't ever have to pay the ten dollars. When I die my estate would have to take care of it."

Emily laughed. Just then there was a huge crash. Dill had managed to pull a few of the thick hardcovers off the drying table and was standing there chuckling. Then he knocked the hair dryer off the table and a piece of plastic broke off it and flew up in the air. Now Emily was really laughing. Sadie stood frozen to the spot, her half-glasses suspended like icicles on the bridge of her nose. She must have thought they were slipping down because she started flaring her nostrils, I guess in an attempt to widen her nose and create a broader base for her glasses to rest on. The flaring must have upset the delicate equilibrium and the glasses fell. For a second they caught on her lower lip and then clunked onto her chest. They clacked against a peacock brooch she was wearing and then they were still.

I didn't really need a book on the solstice. I could just have asked Lish. Or I could have looked up the meaning of solstice and then left without checking out the book from the library. Or I could have paid the full amount of twelve dollars and fifty-nine cents. Well, actually I couldn't have, not then, but I could have been nicer to Mrs. Hobbs. And in the future I was. We had established an unspoken truce. She smiled at me. I smiled back. I brought my fine down to ten bucks every time and she checked out my books. Dill pulled books off the shelves. I put them back. Mrs. Hobbs did not clear her throat as much.

If I had made a movie about me and Mrs. Hobbs, it would have had a lot of dream sequences of me blindfolded and sitting on a cement floor in the basement of the library. And Mrs. Hobbs would be lighting a cigarette for me and putting it in my mouth. You know that hostage phenomenon where you grow fond of your captor? That's what would happen.

"I hate asking you to pay your fines, Lucy," she'd say. "But until you do, I can't release you."

"I know, Mrs. Hobbs, I know. You're just doing your job," I'd say. "You're as much of a prisoner as I am. Here, have a drag of my cigarette."

"Thank you, Lucy. I'm glad we've had these seven hundred and thirty-one days to get to know each other."

"Me too, Mrs. Hobbs, me too."

Credits roll, orchestra starts up. I told Lish about my movie idea and she said, "God Lucy, give her a break, she's a fucking librarian! What do you know about her life anyway?"

And I said, "Me? You're the one who's always freaking out whenever someone tells you what to do! I was simply trying to illustrate the nature of our relationship!"

"I would not pay to see that movie, Lucy," she said.

Lish and I went on like that for a while. It was our first stupid fight.

Day after day of rain and bugs kept us virtually imprisoned within the walls of Half-a-Life. Lish wasn't cracking as many jokes. Terrapin had lost some of her glow. Sarah was looking sad again and not doing as much talking anymore. Emmanuel's visits had been cut back to once a month. Sing Dylan was still trying to scrub the graffiti from the wall. Naomi was fighting more than ever with the fireman for sole custody of their son. She hit him once when he came over and he charged her with assault. She was worried about the charge affecting her custody case. Every day was more or less the same: trying to get by, keep the kids amused, and not lose our minds. We could hole up inside our apartments or we could wander around the halls, talk in the laundry room or in someone's kitchen. It was difficult for those of us with hobbies and jobs to concentrate on them because of the heat and the constant interruptions from restless kids and restless moms looking for someone to talk with. Joe and Pillar were fighting an awful lot even though neither one of them was working. Lish told me that Pillar had told her that one of the reasons why she had married Joe was because he had reminded her of her old best friend, back when she was a kid in a town called Sarto. Especially his profile and the way he smells. Pillar told Lish that when Joe is drunk and sleeping she tilts his head just so he looks more like her old friend, Peggy, and then she lies there looking at him looking like her and smelling him smelling like her and remembering her childhood. And Pillar thinks Sing Dylan is weird for not drinking. Life is strange. But life in Half-a-Life is even stranger.

During that June I looked forward to the time of the day Mercy and her daughter came home just for something to watch outside other than the rain. Watching Mercy and her girl get off the bike, dragging it over to the lockers and then getting into Half-a-Life was like watching a choreographed performance: every move was precise and it never changed. Getting the mail was another high point of the day, even though most of our mail consisted of library fines or disconnection notices or advertising for places and things none of us could afford. Samples of shampoo were nice.

One afternoon Lish trekked downstairs with Alba and Letitia to get the mail. The twins were singing. "It's raining. It's boring. The old man is scoring." Lish looked tired. Her skin was breaking out around her chin and her black hair was greasy. It was bread day for her. Every Tuesday she had to pick up the bread at Prairie Song and deliver it to the co-op. In return she got member prices on the stuff at the co-op. But it meant putting the twins in the wagon, walking four blocks to the Wheat's End Bakery, loading the bread in and around the girls in the wagon, and in a big hockey bag that she draped over her shoulder, and then walking another four blocks to the co-op to deliver the bread. It also meant either getting soaked or eaten alive when the mosquitoes were bad. I don't know why she didn't ask one of her boyfriends to help her. One of them must have had a car they could lend or give her a ride in. But she said, "Men are a nighttime indoors thing." Going outside with them during the day with kids and bread and problems to solve would ruin it for her. Nope. She'd rather do it on her own. Teresa and I were standing around the mailboxes in the lobby talking about Marjorie. Teresa had a gut feeling Marjorie had started seeing that guy again, the father of her son and of Teresa's, and not telling Teresa, who didn't want to care, and who didn't want to appear suspicious, either.

It was really none of her business anyway. Out of her control. I agreed. She didn't love this guy anymore and certainly didn't want him hanging around her place. But I knew Teresa was wondering if maybe Marjorie was getting more cash for her son than she was getting for hers. If Marjorie was sleeping with this guy again, it would stand to reason she was also reaping fringe benefits like take-out food, new clothes, occasional movies, a new toy for her son. Their son. At least while the bloom was still on the rose. If he was spending money on

Marjorie, he was, in Teresa's mind, spending more money on Marjorie's son too, even in a roundabout way. That would make his son with Marjorie better off than his son with Teresa simply because he was having sex with Marjorie instead of Teresa. That is, if his actual presence could be considered an advantage to Marjorie's boy. Both boys knew he was their father but neither one had really known him and so couldn't really miss him. It was complicated. Teresa was trying to put a price on time and affection. If in her opinion, Marjorie's son reaped some extra benefit, then Teresa's son should too. Just because Marjorie and this guy were having sex didn't mean that Teresa's son should have less money than Marjorie's son, did it? That was what we were talking about. Or rather what Teresa was talking about. While she was talking I was running up and down the stairs. Dill went up. I brought him down. He went up. I brought him down. It was a good form of exercise, and when I was up, it gave Teresa time to formulate her next thought on the whole mess with her ex and Marjorie.

"What are you guys talking about?" asked Lish, coming down the stairs.

"Men and sex and money," answered Teresa, her red lips pursed.

"Jesus Christ, is that all we ever talk about? Bitch bitch bitch let's change the subject." She rammed her key into her mailbox and flung it open.

"To what?" Teresa slapped a mosquito that had landed on her arm and her own blood smeared her skin. Alba and Letitia picked Dill up and started fighting over him. "Men and Sex and Money. Men and Sex and Money," they chanted while they tugged at Dill from opposite sides. I noticed we were all barefoot.

That's when Lish grabbed my arm hard. "Oh my god. Oh my god. I can't believe this. Oh my god. This is too weird." That was the day she got her first letter from the busker. He had stolen her wallet from the hotel room, he had written, and had carried her address around with him since. In my opinion she could do better than a petty thief. I know, I know, I was kind of one in a way, Dill's stroller, other things, but still I had a personal bias against *unnecessary* theft.

My mother was killed in a botched robbery attempt. My dad and I told her over and over again she was crazy to pick up hitchhikers. Didn't she read the papers? But she'd say, "Why would anyone want to kill a little old lady like me?" So it was her policy to pick up any hitchhiker with a bag or a suitcase. If they had a bag they were serious. Sometimes she scared the hitchhikers: why would a single lone female be so eager to pick them up? Didn't she read the newspapers? She'd slow down and stop beside them, a big grin on her face. They'd back away and wave her off and shake their heads. She'd laugh. Suit yourself. Sorry for you if you're afraid of a little old lady. And she'd spin out in her big old Ford with her window wide open, her elbow sticking out and her hand tapping on the roof of the car, always in a hurry to get where she was going. I guess she liked the company and the potential risk of picking up strangers. When you think about it, we had both been affected for life by picking up strangers. She had lost her life and I got Dill.

The day she was killed she was on her way to a farm just outside the city. She was a family therapist. Her office used to be my playroom. There was a lot of talking and yelling and crying going on in that room. It bothered my dad that my mom had all these unstable people streaming in and out of our house, so whenever he was at home and she had clients he would mow the lawn—or shovel the driveway in the winter. He'd mow the lawn right outside the window to the playroom/office, bumping up against the house and going over the same patch of grass many times. Our lawn had never looked trimmer. Actually it was bald in patches. I think this was his way of telling my mom's clients to get a life, get busy like him and leave his wife alone. Or he'd start crashing around in the kitchen, washing dishes and slamming cupboards. The only time he washed the dishes was when my mom was trying to work. My friends said, "Oh wow, your dad washes dishes. That's nice." But I knew it wasn't. My mom did her best to ignore him. When it got to be too much she'd wake me in the middle of the night and off we'd go on the train to my cousins in Vancouver for a week or two. If that was impossible she'd run to the piano and play songs like "Moon River" and "Alfie" and "Five Foot Two" as loud as she could over and over until my dad left the house. Then she'd walk away from the piano, beaming, red in the face, swish over to the counter and make herself a pot of coffee. Once she spit into every pot and dish and cup he had washed and then threw them out the back door into the yard for all to see. My dad stood by saying, "What are you doing? What are you doing?"

The day she was killed she was driving off to some little town to counsel abused farm women. I think she was trying to tell them, "Get the hell off that farm. Take your kids and leave. Move to the city and go on welfare if need be. Start a new life. Just get away." Like Naomi. But she had to get the women to come to that conclusion themselves by repeating a lot of what they said. My mom said she acted as a kind of mirror. That was her job, as far as I could tell.

So on her way she had picked up a hitchhiker, a drifter with a bag. Only the bag had knives and guns in it. Right beside a billboard advertising fresh honey on the number 75 highway, he asked her to stop and get out of the car. She said, fine, she would, but not without her briefcase, which contained all sorts of confidential files and tapes of women and my mom talking. The guy was nervous and said No. So she said something like, "Look, you can have the car, you can have my money, just give me my bag." Then she reached over into the back seat to get it and he freaked.

He didn't shoot her, he just smashed her over the head with his gun. This is how he told the story after he was caught a couple of days later. She wasn't dead then. He dragged her out to the ditch, threw her briefcase on top of her and took off. A while later she died in the ditch. My mom had always done what she had wanted to do, more or less. She'd done it quickly, too. Even at home, cleaning up or whatever, she'd almost run to get it over with. Swish, swish across the linoleum, in her red down-filled slippers. Sometimes she'd have power naps. She could hold a spoon in her hand, she said, and fall asleep. At the moment it dropped she would have had enough rest to feel completely refreshed. Then *boom*, she'd be up. Swish, swish. She could make herself a tuna salad sandwich in three minutes and a pot of coffee in one. "If that was lunch, I've had it," she'd say and then coerce me into playing a quick game of Dutch Blitz before she had to go back to work. She always lost because her fingers were shorter and fatter than mine and she'd have to take sips of her coffee.

At her funeral I was thinking that would be a good thing to put on her tombstone: "If that was lunch, I've had it." But things like that had already been worked out and it would never have happened. I couldn't imagine my dad and me standing there weeping in front of a tombstone with those words written on it. At her funeral my dad, all two hundred and fifty pounds of him, leaned against me in the front row and cried. I wondered, what was he going to do without her? What was I going to do with him? I looked down at his hand holding mine. A very strange hand. He was shaking against my shoulder. He shook and he shook and then he let out a moan that terrified me. There were so many people in the church. Loudspeakers were set up outside in the parking lot so those who couldn't get in could hear what was going on. Lots of half-tons with women in them crying and kids running around the parking lot laughing while the minister's voice boomed out at them. "Let us celebrate, let us celebrate," he kept saying. "Let us celebrate the life." A kid outside must have been playing with a car horn and it got stuck. The horn blasted through the open windows of the church and the minister had to cut his speech short. Everybody else was looking around wondering what to do. My dad didn't care about the speech or the horn. He sat there. He didn't look up. He leaned against me and cried.

Of course, I didn't have to read the letter Lish received to know what it was all about: the busker missed her and wanted to see

her again. Lish was acting like a little kid. Her face shone and
she bounced around her apartment. She still killed mosquitoes
but she called them *dear* and *honey* before she squished the life
out of them. She took her girls and me and Dill out for curry in
a cab. She paid for it all with her laundry quarters. Forty-eight
dollars and seventy-five cents' worth. Hope and Maya were concerned. They needed clean clothes for school.

"Darlings, there are more important things in life than
clean clothes."

"Curry?" replied Maya.

"Oh, Maya, lighten up, have some fun. I'll wash your precious school clothes by hand if I have to."

"Well, you will."

We did have fun. Lish was being extravagant all because of
this stupid letter. I offered to pay for my and Dill's share, but
she refused. Lish and I drank red wine and I listened to her
retell the story of the blissful week she and the busker spent
together almost five years ago. The kids started to run around
the restaurant. Dill was crawling up to other people's tables and
pulling himself up and grinning at them. A few found him
amusing.

Alba and Letitia were performing a drama for some others.
From what I remember the plot revolved around two women
getting drunk. The dialogue was very repetitive. The girls
teetered around the restaurant, pretending that their apple juice
was beer. They tried to get Dill to join them, but he was busy
playing peekaboo with a young couple at another table. Maya
read her book and Hope listened to our conversation and drew
on her napkin. Some people stared at Lish. She was wearing her
black hat with the spider on it and a gauzy skirt with ripped
tights underneath. She had taken off her sandals and was resting
her big bare feet on one of the twins' empty chairs. A couple of
times she burped. Once she imitated the waiter's expression and
both of us laughed too loud. I noticed a few words being
exchanged between the waiter and a guy who looked like the
manager. The manager came over to us and very politely said
that some of the other patrons might be bothered by the

children and the noise they were making. Whoops. This guy didn't know Lish. First, she recrossed her feet on the chair and then she pushed back her black hat a bit and stared up at him. She had another sip of wine and asked, "This is a public restaurant, isn't it?"

"Well yes, of course—"

"My kids are people, right, at least for the most part?" She smiled at me. I didn't smile back. I was getting embarrassed.

"Yes, but I—"

"Right. If they're people, then they're part of the public. This isn't an adults' restaurant. This is a public restaurant. Like a public washroom or a public library?"

"All I'm saying—"

"All you're saying is that your establishment discriminates against the young. You'd rather put them on a spit and sprinkle them with curry, wouldn't you?"

Oh god, I thought and put my hand over my eyes.

"No I really wouldn't —"

"It's a joke, Chuckles." She crossed her eyes and stuck out her tongue. Now everyone was staring at us. Alba and Letitia were still getting drunk and Dill had wandered away and was sitting on some woman's lap. Maya sighed and kept reading and Letitia made faces at the manager. Lish was getting worked up.

"Lish," I whispered, "don't worry about it. He's right, you know, the kids should sit down."

But Lish just kept on going. "You know, you people remind me of those other people who put up signs in their store windows that say 'No Strollers.' Basically they're saying *No women and children*. Especially no poor women who have to cart their kids and everything else around in strollers. I'd like to see a sign in a window that said 'No Suits' or 'No Toupées' or 'No Body Odour' for a change, you know? Eh, Luce?" she said, "wouldn't you?"

I smiled at the manager, and shrugged my shoulders. "Don't worry," I said to him, "she's not violent." And then I muttered into my glass, "I think she's having an allergic reaction to the wine, or something, I don't know . . ."

The manager nodded. "I'm sorry, but you'll have to leave," he said.

"You know what really makes me mad, Luce?" Lish said.

"C'mon Lish, let's go," I said and smiled at the manager, who was staring at Lish incredulously.

"It's okay," I whispered to him, "we're going."

"The people that make curbs at a ninety-degree angle so you have to break your back to lift the stroller over them or wreck your stroller or wake up your kid getting up them. There are no smooth curbs anywhere in this WHOLE GODDAMN CITY."

Lish was standing up now. Her black hair was all over the place, a strand of it was caught in her mouth, and her hat was crooked. The spider was almost covering her right eye. She was gathering up the leftover food in napkins and ramming it into her plastic Safeway bag. I got Dill away from the couple. He screamed. He was having a good time. The twins came over to where we were and said, "We're so drunk. Ooh oooh, let's drink more beer." Maya and Hope were giggling with each other now. A middle-aged man next to us was smiling at Lish with what looked like admiration. His wife glared at him and when he noticed her scowling at him he went back to his goat dish. I tried to get Dill into his pink rain jacket, but I gave up and stuffed it into my Safeway bag and tried to hold him the way he was.

"Call us a cab, we are leaving!" Lish barked at nobody in particular. Part of her was just play-acting, having a tantrum. Like I said, Lish could have been an actress. It's too bad she had to create her own scenes. Had the cops shown up and the manager broken into song or something, she would have been thrilled. As it was, everyone just thought she was crazy. The manager muttered something logical about wanting to be paid for the food. Lish heard him and said, "Oh sure, you want to get paid for ruining our evening. Well, fine." She took out a little bread bag from her Safeway bag. She had a big grin on her face. Her hat was back in place. She dumped all the quarters, forty-eight dollars and seventy-five cents' worth, onto the red carpet. The next morning, when she was sober, she told me it had been an accident, but I didn't believe her. It was actually quite a beautiful thing to see. All that silver mixed with the red. Dill convulsed with excitement and I almost dropped him. A bunch of the quarters rolled under the table of the old couple with the goat dishes.

"Shall we, ladies . . . and gentleman?"

With that, Lish polished off the rest of the wine from her glass and mine. She grabbed the wine bottle, and, holding it over her head like a beacon of hope, led us out of the restaurant and into the dark street. I guess nobody had called us a cab, but it was probably a good thing. Lish threw up twice on the way home. She dumped the leftover curry in a puddle and accidentally dropped the wine bottle, too. It smashed on the sidewalk and an old guy looked out of his window and shook his fist. Lish tried to moon him, but it was too much work. She wasn't much of a drinker.

We walked the whole way in the rain singing dumb songs like "It's a Long Way to Tipperary" and "Show Me the Way To Go Home." I taught Lish a couple of the songs my mom sang to me as lullabies when I was a little kid. "I'm Gonna Wash That Man Right Out Of My Hair" was one. She used to sing that song with quite a lot of conviction. "Take Me Out To The Ball Game" was another one. When she came to the line *I don't care if I never come back* my mom's voice would get loud and brazen and her top lip would roll up to her nose. Before she got to the *one two three strikes you're out* part, she'd shift me around on her lap so she could do her umpire routine. At "You're out" she'd say it like a real umpire, *You're* really fast and high and *out* low and dragged out. Then, if I was in the right position on her lap, she'd slice her arm across and out in front of her with her index finger pointing to the closet door. There was just enough space between the bed and the closet for her to do this, but still, every time she did her umpire act, I worried that she'd thwack her hand on the closet door. Afterwards, she'd lie down with me and close her eyes, her chest heaving from all that singing. I'd watch my skinny arm going up and down on her chest until I fell asleep.

Walking home from the curry place Dill fell asleep in my arms and the twins walked backwards all the way to Half-a-Life. When we got there Sing Dylan was at the wall, scrubbing the graffiti in the dark. He stopped and looked closely at all of us. He said, "Good evening. How are you?" I was about to say *fine* when Lish lurched over to him and said, "The answer to that, my good friend Sing Dylan, is blowin' in the wind." And then, of course, she started to sing. Sing Dylan shook his head and went back to his scrubbing. I could see how the busker would have missed Lish.

The next morning the sun was shining. At about 6:30 Lish pounded on my door, yelling at me to get up and come outside, the sun was shining, the sun was shining. The twins had their pails and shovels, and the older kids had their beat-up old bicycles. Lish had planned a walk to the park on the corner of Broadway and Young. She said, "Even the mosquitoes are too stunned by the sunshine to bite." She was wearing a hot pink dress. Her black hair shone. She stood right in the middle of a sunray that had pierced through the window into my kitchen. Little bits of dust flew up around her. She was eating a bagel with cream cheese. She told me I had a crusty line of red wine on my lower lip. By the time I had thrown on a pair of cut-offs and a t-shirt and changed Dill's diaper and gotten him dressed and given him some cereal, the sun was starting to disappear.

We hurried outside and caught the tail end of the sunshine. It had shone for twenty-four minutes. The rest of the time we played in the rain. A couple of guys at the park were sleeping in the grass next to the sandbox. They were covered with a big orange shag carpet. They woke up when the kids started hollering and they said, "Good morning." We played in the thunder and the lightning. Maya told me that the chances of us getting hit by lightning were slimmer than the chances of us being killed by terrorists. Lish and I lay on the wet ground. We tried to ignore the mosquitoes. Once you start slapping, that's it, you'll never quit, and you have to admit defeat and go inside. So we lay there quietly and agreed with each other that life was grand and we were made for just this sort of activity: lying on the grass, talking, looking after the kids. For Lish it was especially grand. She was the one who got the letter. We had to admit, however, that it would have been grander still without the rain and the mosquitoes. Eventually we had to leave the park because Maya and Hope had to go to school.

When we got back to Half-a-Life, Sing Dylan was outside trying to get the water to run somewhere other than into his apartment. He had given up trying to get the graffiti off the wall for the time being. When he was done digging and draining and piling and drilling, Sing Dylan asked us if we could help Sarah drag out his soaked carpet. It must have weighed two thousand pounds. Each of us, even the twins, grabbed a handful of wet carpet and pushed and pulled it up the stairs and out the back door. By this time we were surrounded by swarms of mosquitoes.

I thought about my friends from high school. What would they be doing now? When Dill was born, they were all really enthusiastic. They brought me and Dill presents and they asked to hold him and offered to babysit. They loved to hear me talk about his birth. "Didn't it *hurt*?" Then one by one they stopped calling. Once in a while I'd meet one of them somewhere and they were always really friendly, promising to call to get together. But that never happened. I had heard that Sheila had moved to Toronto to study law. She was living out there with a lawyer in a place called Forest Hill next to a castle. I thought of Lish. I thought of the two of them together. Sheila had been really poor as a kid; her dad had tried to kill her mom and was eventually committed to some kind of looney bin. Her mom sometimes put make-up on one eye and forgot to do the other one.

Lish, on the other hand, had grown up in a wealthy home. Her dad had invested in the future, made sure they were all secure. Her mom stayed at home and sewed them Hallowe'en costumes and cooked their favourite meals. In the evenings they played board games together. They had a summer home in

France and a French *au pair* to help their mom look after them there and teach them the right kind of French. Her dad flew in for a few days at a time. Now Lish lived in Half-a-Life, trying to raise four kids on welfare. So much for security. As my mom would have said, "Tricky life, this."

We got the wet rug out onto the grass. Sing Dylan gave each of the kids a loonie for their help, even Dill, who had made Sarah trip on the last step. Dill tried to put the loonie in his mouth and Letitia grabbed it away from him and gave it to me. She had a very solemn expression on her face. Sing Dylan patted the kids on their heads and then he slapped Sarah's cheek. She smiled and said thanks. A big glob of blood stained her cheek and Sing Dylan flicked the remains of the mosquito off his hand. Somehow his safari suit managed to stay white even with all that blood and rain and dirt.

That afternoon Lish came over to my place with the twins. Dill was having his afternoon nap, so the twins played quietly and Lish and I watched *Y & R*: our lives were nice and dull compared to those in the soap. Some people watched them to escape from their normal lives. We watched them to appreciate ours. I had heard of a soap opera in Brazil where the audience was allowed to vote on what would happen next: should Officer João Carlos go to the chair for killing those street kids or should he be promoted? Should Branca tell her chubby husband that he repulses her or should she just go ahead and have an affair with the handsome doctor? "Well, that's an easy one," Lish said. If it had been up to me I would have brought all the couples together. They would stop trying to kill each other and fool around behind each others' backs and steal the kids. They would be funny, I told Lish and instead of all that skulking around they would shout out their problems and cry and laugh freely and love one another and leave the kids alone. "Oh, pa-leeze Lucy," said Lish. "People don't want to see that. They want blood and revenge and sorrow. That's what makes them feel better."

Good grief, I thought, if that was the case my mom may as well have said FUCK! YOU! to me every time I went out instead of GOOD! LUCK! But what about the letter? Hadn't the letter from the busker made Lish happy? She had been full of energy since she got it: laughing and singing and buzzing around her apartment organizing things, throwing stuff out, putting up different pictures and posters, washing her cupboards. She had taken a book out of the library called *Clutter's Last Stand*, determined that it would help her to get rid of her junk. Her *unnecessary* junk. If any one of us in Half-a-Life got rid of all our junk our apartments would be bare. Was she expecting him to appear at her door? The letter said simply, "I'm thinking of you. I miss you. I haven't met anyone else that could make me laugh like you. Do you still have your spider hat? Oh Right. I'm sorry about taking your wallet, I was going through a bit of a hard time when I met you. I'm sorry. But hey, how would I have had your address if I hadn't stolen your wallet? I'm on the road now, a different city or town almost every day so there's no point in writing me. I'm going to try to make it to Winnipeg sometime this summer. I hear it's very wet. Right now I'm in Cleveland. Take care of yourself Lish, say Hi to your daughters from me." It was signed, "The guy in rm. 204."

Lish had read it to me. She assumed that he assumed that she knew his name. He had never actually told her his real name. All she knew him as was "Gotcha," his show name. I guess if people were always calling you that, you would want to run away. And that's all that he was called in that old program she'd found. I thought about the letter and it made sense that Lish was ambivalent about it. Excited, yes, to have heard from him, the love of her life and the father of the twins. But on the other hand, it hadn't been too specific. Would he visit or wouldn't he? And if he had been thinking about her all these months—years—why didn't he sound more passionate in his letter? Maybe she would think he wrote letters like this to all his one-night stands. Maybe she would think he was just drunk and lonely and feeling bad about stealing her wallet. And so what if he was the twins' father? They didn't know him. How could they miss him? They were happy enough the way they were. I would have to be a lot more convincing for her to think he really cared.

Anyway, Lish seemed to think this letter was a sign—a sign that he would, when he could, show up at Half-a-Life. In her heart she was thinking they could put the past behind them, start anew, make love desperately at first and then in a more knowing, confident way. The twins could hate him at first for leaving and then come to love him as a father should be loved. They could all tour in the summertime and maybe even become an entire performing family. They'd be good at it. And even if something bad happened, at least the twins would know that he had made the effort. And that was the most important thing, wasn't it: that he had tried to find them? But so far Lish hadn't told the twins or anybody except me about the letter. In Half-a-Life it had happened often enough that one of the women would get her hopes up over some guy and then have them dashed soon afterwards. There was no point in even talking about it until it was real, until the guy had maybe moved a few clothes in or offered to take care of the kids for a while. Besides, the others in Half-a-Life thought Lish was fooling herself thinking life was more simple than it really was. I didn't think that she thought that life itself was simple at all: it was just her take on it that she had smoothed over and over, whittled and refined, until it became simple. Do what makes you happy because there is no sure thing. Just because you can pick out four-leafed clovers doesn't mean you'll get lucky.

Another reason why the women in Half-a-Life didn't publicize every encounter with a man was because it could lead to trouble with welfare. Most of us were friends or had at least a grudging tolerance for each other. Even Naomi and Terrapin were seen laughing over something in the hallway. Public housing isn't called public housing for nothing. If you've got some dirt on your neighbour, chances are she's got some on you. So, in an unspoken form of a truce, we stick together. Most of the time. Our problem was more Serenity Place. And theirs was us. We were two opposing teams in the game of welfare.

The game revolves around men. A man's penis might as well have a price tag on it. There are a thousand strange rules regarding women on welfare and their men. And they have only to do with men. The Mensa minds down at Social Assistance headquarters haven't twigged to the fact that some mothers have decided to make love to other women and sometimes have live-in relationships with them. Often one of the women will work outside the home and the other stay at home with the children. In instances like this welfare officials only consider the working woman to be a roommate, not a lover, so a portion of the stay-at-home mother's welfare rent supplement would be docked, because technically the roommate would be paying half the rent. And that would be the only financial penalty. The "roommate" could be making seventy-five thousand dollars a year and welfare wouldn't care, believing, presumably, that two women would not have sex, especially because one of them, the mother, had already demonstrated her gender preferences. So living with another woman presents no problems. But *men*, they were trouble.

At least having sex with them was trouble. Life became very messy. More messy than usual, that is, under those circumstances. Actually, it was okay to have quick sex during certain hours. But if a man stays overnight you're off the dole. Welfare equates men with financial support. This always made us laugh. Lish said they obviously didn't know the same men we knew. I guess they figured we'd had our chances at love and screwed up and now we could just think about that for awhile, at least while we were dependent on the generosity of the state and its tax payers. So, naturally, we were breaking the law all the time. Us and the women in Serenity Place. Men were crawling in and out of our beds, eating bits of our food that had been paid for by the dole, showering with water that was paid for by the dole, and, of course, pleasuring themselves with us, women who were kept by the dole. That cost. The woman anyway. We were prostitutes for the state.

Okay, I'm repeating everything Lish told me. I actually had never thought of myself as a prostitute for the state. Anyway, no man had been in my bed since I had been on the dole. Never, actually, since I had never had sex in a bed. I lived with my father until I became pregnant. I had a pink frilly room with a single bed and a matching dresser. I had sex in fields, in cars, in stairwells, in basement cellars, in dark cemeteries, in the dark-room of my high school, in half-built houses, in between build-ings, up against buildings, and in abandoned buildings. Groping, painful, wordless sex. The cigarettes afterwards were about as fulfilling. I was a kid. Anyway, the point is you have to be careful when you're on the dole. The women at Serenity Place tried to catch us with men during daylight hours and we tried to catch them. If the same guy visited more than two or three times, rumours started to fly. Elaborate traps were set. Usually we didn't even carry our plans out. It was just some-thing to talk about and to solidify our own alliance. We could inform on someone in Serenity Place, but never on our own. The only reason why we even cared to rat on somebody in Serenity Place was because of the whole Sarah/Emmanuel inci-dent. But still, Lish was playing it safe by not telling anyone, except me, about the letter and the possibility of the busker coming for a visit. Maybe even to stay. This was a good thing. I hoped she wouldn't tell the twins. At least not for some time.

On TV we saw that thousands of families in the States were being evacuated from flooded towns and cities and farms. Water pipes had been turned off. Sandbagging was the activity of the day. After work, after school, everybody bagged. School gymnasiums and machinery warehouses were filling up with homeless families and even their pets. We read stories of stub-born old women who refused to leave their homes, moving up from the main floor to the second floor, to the attic, and then onto the roofs of their homes. From there they were rescued by helicopters and taken to refugee centres or next of kin. Lish told me about some guy in Iowa who had lost five cans of beer in the flood. He was devastated. The sixth can of the six pack had been the last beer his brother had drunk before he collapsed of a heart attack and died. The remaining five cans had been placed on the mantle in homage to the dead brother. Nobody was allowed to touch them. They were washed right off the mantle, out the front door, and then sank to the bottom of the swirling brown cesspool outside. *Maclean's* magazine showed a picture of this guy on his knees crying for his beer cans and his brother. More highways were wiped out and closed. Bridges crumbled and livestock drowned. The U.S. was registering more deaths from electrocution than ever before. Rock bands were getting together to plan a benefit for the flood victims. Bill Clinton surveyed the area in hipwaders, and placed one sandbag on a pile outside Des Moines for the photographers. In case there was some doubt in people's minds, he officially declared the mess a disaster area.

In Winnipeg, the flooding had damaged much of the antiquated sewer system. Filthy ground water was pouring in through the cracks, the weeping tiles, and the windows in people's basements. Toilets were backing up all over the city. When people plugged their toilets with bricks and boards and rocks, the shit came up through their sinks. Pieces of human waste, tampons and used condoms were bumping up against rec room pool tables and entertainment units. Washers and dryers, freezers and bathroom cabinets were floating around in three or four feet of water. The hospitals were dealing with more heart attack and stroke victims than ever. Usually old men. While they were being admitted, their wives were on the phone making arrangements with insurance companies, sons and daughters, grandsons and granddaughters, trying to take care of the details.

A makeshift disaster relief agency had been set up by the provincial government to assist those without flood insurance. The lineup to the office stretched for blocks, fights broke out, crafty entrepreneurs walked up and down the lineups selling mosquito spray, umbrellas and fold-up lawn chairs for exorbitant prices. Those people who were renting homes and woke up to raw sewage threw up their hands, packed their bags and moved. Those who owned homes, though, stayed and fought the flood and panicked. The resale value of flooded homes plummeted. It's impossible to remove the foul stench of raw sewage without spending thousands of dollars on cleaning, repair and renovation. The stink gets behind the walls into the insulation: it seeps under the carpet, under the tiles and into the floor boards. The mould and mildew from the water keeps growing and permeates the house and gets into the lungs of small children and frail adults. Flood victims moved in with extended family or with neighbours: eight kids to a bedroom, four adults on the living room floor. The heat, the bugs, the despair, the loss, the constant smell of wet dog. Cops were busy around the clock with domestic assaults; abandoned flooded homes were being broken into by gangs of kids, sometimes neighbours. Grown men cried and cursed the skies, shook their fists at the clouds and screamed for the rain to stop. Mothers told their kids to think of it as a great adventure and cried in corners. University psychologists were called in to assess the children. Panels of experts informed us that we were under a lot of stress and our tempers would be short, but that disasters like this would bring us together. International disaster analysts told us that we in Canada and the U.S. were living under a false sense of security. We had no reason to be shocked at the magnitude of the flood. What made us think that we could shut out the forces of nature with our well-built houses, expensive building materials and sophisticated engineering? People living in underdeveloped countries handled disasters better than we did because they prepared for them mentally. They expected them.

Sing Dylan said this was a load of crap: it doesn't matter how often shit falls on your head, it still smells bad. Sing Dylan had been hit by the flood three times. After the second time he didn't even bother getting his carpet cleaned and putting it back in. He made sure all of his stuff was in plastic pails or high up on boards or in closets. Every time he went out he unplugged everything. Sarah helped him keep back the rain water as best she could. He couldn't apply to the disaster relief agency for money to cover his losses or to cover cleaning costs and repairs because he was an illegal immigrant and he worried they'd find him out. The public housing agency in charge of Half-a-Life knew he was here illegally and so they knew he wouldn't complain to anyone if they didn't immediately clean up his apartment and replace the damaged stuff. About all Sing Dylan could do was curse the skies like everyone else. In the meantime Sarah let him store some stuff, pictures of his family in India, letters, and rare books he had brought over to Canada, in Emmanuel's empty bedroom. Sing Dylan would say, "Only until the boy returns home. Thank you. Thank you kindly." Sing Dylan always said that. Thank you. Thank you kindly. Never just Thank you or Thanks or just Thank you kindly but always Thank you. Thank you kindly.

Sing Dylan came from The Punjab, Lish said. I had never heard of The Punjab. It was the place in India where a lot of Sikhs come from, Lish said. She told me the Sikhs want their own country. They're not thrilled with the Indian government and they want to change the name of The Punjab to Khalistan. So naturally there was some fighting going on and Lish figured maybe Sing Dylan was involved in it. Lish thought that maybe Sing Dylan came to Canada because his life was in danger. But we didn't want to ask. I thought Khalistan sounded a lot more sophisticated than The Punjab. So anyway, it made sense that Sing Dylan always said to Sarah, "Only until the boy returns home." Sing Dylan was the kind of guy who could really believe that one day Emmanuel would come home. He had to. Just like he believed that one day he could go back to his home, his Khalistan. Emmanuel and Sing Dylan were two homeless guys.

Lish told me about Sing Dylan first coming to Half-a-Life. She told me that every morning when he first arrived he put a pot of coffee on his stove. He would have one cup and keep the rest for company. But company never came. Everyone in Half-a-Life was freaked by having a wild Sikh freedom fighter as their caretaker. At 11:30 every morning Sing Dylan turned off the element under the coffee and poured the coffee down the drain in his kitchen sink. Lish found out about it because one morning she went down to Sing Dylan's place for a mop and he invited her in. He said, "I'm sorry, my coffee is gone." He explained to Lish his morning ritual. Lish just said, "Oh yeah? Well, thanks anyway," and took the mop and left. Then she started to ask people in the block if they had ever gone down to Sing Dylan's for a cup of coffee and everybody said no, no, no, no way, are you kidding, why, what, no, no. No. On and on until she had asked everyone in the block.

Eventually Sarah went down. Mute Sarah. They had a cup of coffee together. Both sitting there, quietly, Sing Dylan wanting his Khalistan and Sarah wanting her Emmanuel. Lish said not a lot of people visited Sarah either, not because she was that weird really, but because she didn't talk. And so conversations, well, you know. Lish said that if Sing Dylan took off his turban and if Sarah talked, life would be different for them.

Lately Sarah had been talking a bit more. Her droopy eyes were opening up a bit and she was even playing music in her apartment. Lish told me that Family Services was considering extending Sarah's visiting rights with Emmanuel. The boy had told his social worker that he didn't care who his father or his grandfather was and whether or not they were the same person. He missed his mom. At the same time, Sarah told her social worker that she promised to talk normally and to send Emmanuel to school. She told her social worker that she was over the trauma that had paralyzed her and she really wanted to get on with her life together with Emmanuel. These visits with the social worker exhausted her. We coached her on what to say, not that we really knew. We told her to stay calm and focussed and always agreeable no matter what the social worker said. We told her to tell the social worker that she did not consider welfare a career option and that she would like to get into a helping profession because from her experience they were all doing such a good job. She understood what had happened, why it had happened and her role in it, and that the future was not bright or easy but that she would do her best to create a positive home environment for Emmanuel. We told her to tell her social worker, when she was leaving, that she appreciated everything she was doing for Emmanuel and for herself, to smile graciously and to say "Bye bye for now," instead of "Kay" when the social worker said, "We'll see you in two months' time."

The last time Sarah had a meeting with her social worker, she walked home in the rain. A few of us watched out the window as she got off the bus in front of Half-a-Life. She had a Safeway bag with a few groceries in it. She walked through a puddle in the parking lot instead of around it. Lish said that was a good sign; I said it was a bad sign.

It turned out to be a good sign, though, because that evening Sarah and Sing Dylan were back at the wall trying to wash the FUCK THE RICH THAN EAT THEM graffiti, and Sarah sprayed Sing Dylan with the hose. They looked like a beer commercial, spraying each other: a non-drinking sikh and a welfare mom whose child has been apprehended. It could be called Real Beer. Still—they were having fun. Scrubbing the paint off the wall was very difficult and time-consuming, but Sing Dylan's plan was to wash off the first letter of each word at least so the message would be more obscure, less obscene. So far he had UCK HE ICH HAN EAT THEM. Lish and I agreed this was much classier than before. Lish said she was going to write "Confucius" under it, but she didn't want to piss off Sing Dylan.

That evening I sneaked Dill's dirty disposable diapers past Terrapin's place. I knew she was disappointed that I was still using them instead of cloth ones or tree moss or whatever it was her kids peed on. She told me wildlife had been found with bits of disposable diapers lodged in their throats. I said, "Oh my goodness, they must have misread the instructions on the package. Ha Ha." Anyway, I was sneaking the diapers down, in the dark, to the BFI container. There was Sing Dylan at the wall, alone and still scrubbing.

"Hi, Sing Dylan."

"Hello, Lucy."

"Still scrubbing, eh?"

"Here today. Here tomorrow," he said. He was smiling. Sing Dylan hardly spoke any English, but I thought that was a pretty good joke.

"Well. Good! Luck! . . . with the wall, I mean."

"Thank you. Thank you kindly."

You would not believe the amount of noodles we consumed in Half-a-Life. Noodles were the national dish of Half-a-Life. We all had different ways of preparing them, but still the humble noodle was the starting point of most of our meals. Lish prepared rotini noodles, sometimes herbal ones, with a lot of garlic which she shaved with a razor, and extra virgin olive oil. Sometimes she added mushrooms or a green or red pepper for a dash of colour and zippy taste. I poured tomato sauce on mine and grated Parmesan cheese. Teresa heaped butter and ketchup onto hers. But our kids ate the noodles plain, sometimes with a bit of butter or cheese, but never any sauce—and god forbid garlic or peppers. Simplicity was the key with noodles. Don't overboil them or they're mushy and lifeless. Don't add too many spices or too many vegetables or the noodles get upstaged and their taste is lost and they just end up as filling, fattening dead weight in the pit of your stomach. Savour the taste and the texture of the noodles. Especially the homemade Italian ones that we got for cheap from Mario's because Tanya gave him a cut rate on her beer and because Teresa had slept with one of his younger brothers and found out that his grocery was really just a front for the local Mafia. A laundromat really. Roberto had hit Teresa for some reason and she said, "If you ever do that again I will blow this illegal laundering joint right out of the water and you'll be picking olives back in Sicily so fast you won't know what hit *you*!" Roberto told Mario and Mario told him to tell Teresa that she and all the whores in Half-a-Life could have special rates on pasta as long as they kept their mouths shut.

Mario gave Roberto two black eyes for telling Teresa about the front and told him never to hit Teresa again. But he didn't have a chance to because shortly afterward Mario set him up in Toronto with a cappuccino bar and a nice Italian girl who'd keep her mouth shut.

Men played cards in the back of the grocery and watched soccer. Sometimes one of their wives, one of the old ones, dressed in black and kind of beakish and hairy, would haul her husband home for supper or bed. The others would laugh and ridicule him and then later get hauled home by their wives. We ate a lot of Mario's noodles. And oatmeal. Porridge is very cheap, very easy, very filling, and very healthy. What more do you want? Well sure, there's taste. But Mario's noodles have that. Hardly any of us, except Naomi and Angela and Tanya, prepared a lot of meat. Kids hardly ever eat it, and it seems odd tucking into a big pork chop all by yourself, kind of depraved.

Anyway, one day Lish and I and Teresa were sitting around in Lish's kitchen eating noodles in different-coloured plastic bowls and reading the paper. Teresa had got the three for the price of one deal from the box on the corner so we all had our own copy. I wished Teresa hadn't shown up because her kid was rough with Dill and it made me uptight. Also, I had really wanted to talk about the busker with Lish. It was exciting, titillating to talk about him. He was perfect because he wasn't around. Lish wasn't shy about telling me the details of how they had sex, and what he told her, all that stuff. But she wouldn't say anything with Teresa around. Lish knew better than to tell Teresa anything even if Roberto hadn't. Teresa read and talked at the same time. She told us she was taking some kind of flagging course at the community college. She had quit French Immersion because her French teacher had come on to her, she said, and besides the grammar didn't make any sense. I thought that must have been the real reason. She thought if she could get this flagging course under her belt she'd have a chance in the movie industry. Apparently flagging is an essential part of any shoot. The flagger must stand around waving a flag which indicates to the truck drivers and dolly operators and whatever where they are to go.

Lish snorted. "You have to go to school to learn how to wave a flag, Teresa?"

"Yeah, it's a one-year course. It's not as easy as you think."

"My god, you're going to study flagging for a whole year? What's there to study? The psychology of flagging? Ha Ha. The Origins of Flagging, or how about Flagging: Art or Science? The Post-Modern Implications of Flagging . . . Ha Ha Ha . . ."

"Excuse me," said Teresa, "are you finished?"

"The Great Flaggers of Our Time: A Retrospective," said Lish. "Women In Flagging . . . HA HA HA!"

"Ha Ha Fucking Ha," said Teresa, "just you wait. I'm gonna extinguish myself."

"*What?*" said Lish, "what did you say? HA HA HA. Are you on fire, Teresa? Oh god. HA HA HA. Go stand in the rain! *Dis*, Teresa, the word is *distinguish. D-I-S-T-*"

Teresa was pissed off. I gave her a look that was supposed to be sympathetic, but I don't think she noticed. She had stood up to Lish before and she could do it again.

"Yeah well, Lish," she said, "what the hell are you doing? Watching tomato plants grow on your window sill, hovering over your kids, laughing at everyone. At least I'm doing *something*."

"Oh relax, Teresa, I'm just kidding around. Some of my best friends are flaggers. Why, just the other night Kevin started flagging only five minutes into the greatest fu—"

"Fucking bitch!!!" Teresa slammed down her coffee cup, spilling a bit.

"What, what, what's your fucking problem?" Lish was mad now too. "I was joking. Jesus, can't you—"

"No, no, not you," said Teresa. "Her. What a fucking cunt. Sorry. Look, Bunnie Hutchison has decided to take away our fucking child tax credit money."

"*What?!*" Lish grabbed Teresa's newspaper.

Teresa was shaking her head. "I can't fucking believe it." I didn't know who Bunnie Hutchison was or what the child tax credit money was, but by Lish and Teresa's reactions I knew it was serious.

"More coffee?" I asked.

"*What?!*" Both Teresa and Lish stared at me as if I had just handed them a plate of snot.

"Don't you know anything? God, Lucy, this is major. It affects you too, you know, you're not in Kansas anymore, Dorothy . . . fuck . . ."

I just shut up then. Who the hell did they think they were? How was I supposed to know about political things just because

I was a mother on welfare? I didn't know that Bunnie Hutch (as she was called by the Lifers because she had them trapped) was the minister in charge of welfare mothers and I didn't know that the child tax credit was fifteen hundred dollars. Fifteen hundred dollars was a lot of money when your annual income is only nine thousand six hundred. Well, that was mine because I only had one kid. Lish had four so she got eleven hundred dollars a month instead of eight hundred. Everybody with kids got the child tax credit money. Now, Bunnie Hutchison wanted to take it away. That is, away from mothers on welfare. Everybody else would still get it.

The word got around fast and the women in Half-a-Life were mad. Lish and Angela and Teresa decided to get a petition going and bring it down to Bunnie's office. Terrapin said she'd chain herself to the big buffalo in the foyer of the legislative building.

"It's a bison, Nellie McClung," said Lish. "And please don't. You'd be ignored all day and then when it was time for everybody to go home, some dopey caretaker would come and cut the chain and tell you to go home, they're closing."

"Can't you call me by my name, Lish, just once?"

"I would if I knew it. What is your real name, anyway? Your mother can't have named you after a turtle. What's your real name? Karen? Barb? Look, I don't even care. Go chain yourself to the buffalo if you like. Chain your kids to it, too. Nothing's gonna change. Why don't we just get drunk tonight and kvetch amongst ourselves until morning. Oh fuck, now it's pouring again."

I had never thought of Terrapin as having a mother. She was trying so hard to be everybody else's. Trying very hard, and not succeeding. We were all trying very hard to be good mothers. But were we succeeding? If we weren't good mothers, then what were we? Losers. What if all our kids hated us for not letting them have fathers, for being poor and for living in a dump like

Half-a-Life? What would we do when we couldn't have babies anymore, when they had all left us? Then what? What could we do to make our kids proud of us? To make *us* proud of us? Chain ourselves to buffaloes? Become flaggers? Maybe I shouldn't have had a baby. Dill was doomed and it was my fault. I wanted my life to be funny, and I wanted Dill to be a lucky boy, as lucky as his namesake, John Dillinger. Some people believe he's still alive. I do. His girlfriend only pretended to be setting him up. But the guy who was shot by J. Edgar Hoover's men outside the theatre in Chicago was somebody else. Dillinger had a notoriously long dick, twelve inches, and the guy who was shot coming out of the theatre had a dick that was only nine inches. Even so it was pickled and now sits in a jar on some shelf at the Smithsonian Institute. I think the lady in red, Dillinger's girlfriend, collected the cash from the FBI for helping them get their guy, and together she and Dillinger disappeared, never to be heard from again. John Dillinger never killed anybody; he just said, "Lie down and nobody gets hurt." He was a lucky man.

I never got to see my mother's dead body on account of its being all beat up. I never actually saw her go into the ground. It could all have been an elaborate plot on her part to get away from my dad. All those trips to Vancouver had been part of the experiment. But who would she have convinced to take the fall for her? Maybe a suicidal client who wanted to die anyway, or maybe she conned some cop into identifying some dead drifter as her. The guy at the morgue could have put one of my mom's sweaters onto the stiff, shown an edge of it to my dad, who would have been too distraught to look at the face. He would have positively identified her, the briefcase, the car, all that, and asked for a closed casket funeral. After ten or twenty years my mom could have created a whole new life for herself, maybe somewhere in South America. Maybe Southern California. She liked warm climates. Someday she might come marching through the doors of Half-a-Life with tickets for me and Dill and we'll go back with her to her sunny *hacienda*. Oh god, she'd love Dill. She loved babies, loved to hold them and smell their heads and she always called them precious, precious things. Lish could meet her. They'd really get along. Lish could use the cheering up, too. We all could, really.

The first letter from the busker had worked. It had cheered Lish up. If Lish's life had been a Brazilian soap opera, I'm sure the audience would have voted in favor of Lish receiving another letter from the busker. Well anyway, I had to be sure at that point. The second letter was scheduled to arrive. Sure enough, *bam bam bam*. There was Lish at my door with the twins and one of Angela's daughters. All the girls were wearing bathing suits and Lish had her black hair pulled back into a pony tail. She and Alba had blue face paint all over their faces. Another one of Alba's make-up experiments. Lish had a very strange expression on her face, under the blue, like she'd just been pinched in the bum by a stranger. She told the girls to find Dill and build a fort with him or something. Normally Lish remembered that Dill couldn't even walk, let alone construct forts, but like I said, she was looking weird.

"He's hanging in the hallway," I said, referring to Dill.

"Can we take him down?"

"Sure, just hang the Jolly Jumper over the doorknob so you don't bash into it every time."

"Okay Lucy, this is it." Lish was making coffee and bubbling over with talk. "He's written again. It's gotta mean something. I'm going to find him. He can't come here right now 'cause of some drug charge, he can't cross the border and he's broke 'cause the festival in Detroit got rained out. He's on his way to Denver, Colorado. Oh Lucy, I'm gonna go there. I don't care. I've got nothing to lose. I have to do *something*—if it doesn't work out at least we'll have gotten the hell out of Half-a-Laugh for a while anyway."

"What do you mean *we*? Are you taking the girls? You didn't tell them, did you?"

"That their dad's written, or that we're going to find him?"

"Either. Oh, god."

"No, no, no, nope. Not yet. But I think I will. They have a right to know."

"Yeah, but you've said what difference does it make, they don't even know him, and if you don't find him, it'll just be a major letdown for them."

"Either way it's a letdown. They're old enough to know they had a father. They think he's abandoned them, even though I told them he didn't even know they existed. It might not break their hearts, but still . . . If there's a chance of finding him, great, if not, no loss. Back to square one."

"Oh god, Lish, why don't—"

"What, I thought you'd be excited! This is great news! He's not that far away. Let me read you the letter."

The twins came into the room wanting a drink, and Lish poured them some apple juice and shooed them off into the other room. She was so excited she put the juice into the cupboard instead of into the fridge. Lish opened the letter and then lowered her voice a bit and tried not to smile.

"Hey Baby," she read, "The more I think about you the more I regret ever leaving you. I'll be in the middle of my show and a picture of you will come into my head and I'll forget my next bit. I've been doing the same shtick for years and I'll forget. I know we didn't have much time together but what we had was amazing. I love the way you laugh and the way your black hair fell all over the pillow when we made love. I love the little blue veins behind your knees and your long fingers. I want to see you more than anything else in this world. But I can't cross the border because six months ago I was charged with obsession (of you) ha ha no possession (of drugs) and now I can't get into Canada. The festival in Detroit was rained out so I didn't make any money. I'm going to hitchhike to Denver. I hear they've got a great street scene. And it's nice there in the fall. Course it's not the fall but soon it will be. If you care about me or even remember me you could send a letter to Denver, Poste Restante, I might get it. I might not. Anyway I've got to keep moving. I'll try to sneak across the border somewhere, somehow and get into Canada to see you. Otherwise I'll keep writing. All my love to you Lish, (It says here on your drivers license that your real name is Alicia. That's the most beautiful name I've ever heard. I sleep with your wallet.) Love, Gotcha."

Lish opened her mouth and laughed. "Okay, he's a lousy writer, but hey, he's got other qualities." All I could do was sit there and stare at my cup. I thought how odd it was to be sitting drinking coffee while my child played in the other room with the children of my friend, another mother, and I didn't know a damn thing about love. It didn't make sense. I noticed a chip on the cup. My mother would have thrown the cup into the garbage right there and then. Lish was right, it was a terrible letter. But still, Lish was buzzing. It had done the job. She was laughing. She was happy. She was a fool, but at least she was happy. Suddenly Lish began singing: "Wise men say only fools rush in but I can't help falling in love with you." She had rolled the letter into a microphone and she was singing into it. Her face was painted blue. What a kook. *Trez bizarre*, as Teresa would have said before she quit French Immersions.

We were all going. Lish, Alba, Hope, Maya, Letitia, Dill and me. Lish had made arrangements with Rodger to use his old van and we were all going to Denver to find the busker.

A few weeks before we left Dill had croup. For babies, it is a bad thing to have. All you can do is sit in the bathroom with the door closed and all the taps running hot water so there is steam everywhere. The steam loosens up the chest and allows the baby to breathe normally. At least that's what's supposed to happen. I read this in my Benjamin Spock book which I kept under my bed so people like Terrapin wouldn't see it. They didn't believe in doctors, especially male ones. Anyway, so that's what we did, Dill and I. I turned on the sink tap and the bathtub tap full blast and then I sat on the floor, leaning against the tub, with poor Dill on my lap. It was one of the worst nights of my life with Dill. I was afraid he would die. I phoned the hospital and told them how Dill was coughing. They told me to continue doing the steam thing. They said there was no reason to bring him in to the hospital because there was a three- to four-hour waiting period and by then the attack would be over. *Attack.* They told me my son was being *attacked* and I would have to wait four hours for them to help him! They told me to relax. As if. Why didn't I just invite a few friends over for movies and popcorn while I was at it?

Dill and I sat in the steam. He coughed and coughed. I took off his undershirt and he sat in my lap in his diaper. I tried to nurse him. He coughed and cried. I cried and hoped that the hot water would not run out. I sang songs. I listened closely to his cough. Was it getting a bit better? Little beads of sweat were popping out on Dill's head. I noticed how tiny Dill's chest was. I noticed how I hadn't been cleaning the bathroom floor very well. I didn't want to call Lish. Or Teresa. Or Mercy. Or Terrapin. Or Sing Dylan. Or any of them. I wanted to handle this. Then I wanted my mom. Then I looked at Dill and thought, oh my god, I'm *his* mom. And then I wanted my mom even more. Finally Dill fell asleep in my lap. The attack was over.

I was so tired I fell asleep right there on the bathroom floor. I had a dream that I was in Venice, Italy. All by myself. I was standing by some water and I had a camera around my neck. Suddenly two huge polar bears came out of the water and one took a a big bite out of the other one and then they disappeared. Then two huge whales did the same thing. And then two other animals I couldn't exactly identify. All this time I didn't take any pictures, even though I had a camera around my neck. I decided to leave Venice but as I turned to go my mom appeared beside me and said, "Don't worry, we're really not picture people." She took the camera from around my neck and it blew away and disappeared. Then she and I sat down. And that was the end of the dream.

We couldn't leave right away like Lish wanted because Hope and Maya refused to miss any school. We would have to wait until the end of June. This was a good thing anyway, because there were a lot of details to work out. When you're on welfare, you are not allowed to leave the province. Everyone does from time to time, but you have to make sure you're covered in case your dole worker decides to surprise you with a home visit or if one of your appointments falls into the period of time you plan to be away. Also, Rodger was going to do some work on the van, make sure it would get us to Denver and back. And we wanted to find a tent and sleeping bags somewhere, maybe a pawn shop, because we couldn't all sleep in the van and we certainly couldn't afford motels. We couldn't even afford the gas to get us there, but Lish said she had a plan.

So in the meantime, all we had to do was get through the rain and the bugs for two more weeks until school was out and we had come up with the extra cash to get us to Denver. Lish's parents had to come to Winnipeg on some business. Her mom phoned and said they'd be staying at the Four Seasons with the rest of the conventioneers, but they would try to make it over to Lish's place at least once over the weekend. Her mom told her it was important for her to be in Winnipeg as well because it was a kind of cosy spousal convention, where her absence would be noted and all sorts of rumours would fly and Lish's dad's job might come into question because of his questionable stability and marital standing.

Later we were sitting around at Lish's place, drinking coffee and eating Lemon Loaf, burning patchouli incense and talking. We agreed we would never act like Lish's mother: not trying to see our kids when they were only a few blocks away and we hadn't seen them in six months and some *man* forbade it, some man trying to get a promotion.

"Would you like a beer?" asked Lish. She wandered over to her fridge and took out two bottles. "Glass?" she called from the kitchen.

"No, thanks," I said.

She handed me the beer and sat down with her own. "What the hell," she said.

We were quiet for a while. Lish drank her beer in about three minutes and went to the fridge to get another one. She held one up and looked at me. I shook my head. She came back and sat down in her big brown chair and flipped her legs over one of the chair's arms. "You know," she said, "I'm a lot like him in some ways."

"Like who?" I asked.

"Like my father," she said. She had a sip of her beer.

"He's never come here to visit us. He's never called to say hello. Years ago, when I told him I was pregnant with Hope, he said, 'I expected more from you.'" Lish had another sip.

I grinned. "More kids?" I asked.

She smiled, and sighed. "We both want what we want, he and I," she said. "So fucking badly."

"And what would that be?" I asked.

She paused. "Another beer," said Lish. "Yourself?"

"Half," I said.

Suddenly Lish blurted out, "That's it. I'm going there. I'm taking the girls to see them. And Lucy, you and Dill are coming along! GIRLS, WE'RE GOING TO SEE GRANDMA AND GRANDPA AT THEIR HOTEL!!!" she shouted. And so we did. Lish told the girls to dress up, and because Lish did not believe in telling them how to dress, they put on bizarre outfits, too small, too big, clashing colours, discarded costume jewellery, and, of course, garish face paints in place of real make-up. Hope made a fake cigarette out of rolled-up paper and put it behind her ear. Lish put on a black sequined dress she had picked up at the Junior League, and her long square-toed shoes. She polished her spider and put it on the lowest part of her brim so it looked like a third eye. She doused herself with patchouli oil and rose water. She put on all her clanging bracelets and a ring on each finger. She tossed the rest of the Lemon Loaf in a Safeway bag to bring to her parents. I changed Dill's diaper, gave him a cracker to chew on, and we were out the door. The twins in the wagon with Dill sandwiched in between, the older girls dancing along behind it, Lish, bent over in her sequined dress and square-toed shoes, and me, taking turns lugging the wagon to the Four Seasons Hotel. It was only sprinkling outside, and besides, Lish said she didn't give a flying fuck if we got soaked. She had a plan.

The doorman of the Four Seasons was not sure what to do with the wagon when we got there. He held the door open for Lish and the girls and at the same time tried to help push the wagon over the door stoop. It was harder than he thought, and he let go of the door. The door swung back into Lish's face. The wagon perched in between the doors. Hope and Maya started pushing it from the back and the twins began to laugh. The doorman stood up and looked at Lish for guidance. She said, "Look, just everyone let go of the frigging wagon. I'll do it myself." She backed out and tried the revolving doors. This time the wagon wedged itself into one of the sections and wouldn't move. Lish told the girls to get out and squeeze through the space. The older girls stood outside helplessly. "Go through the door, Jesus," muttered Lish through the glass pointing to the non-revolving door. The doorman ran to that door and pushed. Hope and Maya were pushing too. "For Christ's sake. . ." Lish moved the doorman away from the door and Hope and Maya burst into the hotel and fell on top of each other.

"I hope you're not expecting a tip," said Lish to the blushing doorman. He laughed, and Lish rolled her eyes at him, straightened her hat and told her girls to follow her to the elevator. The man behind the front desk leaned over its marble surface. "Excuse me, ma'am?"

"What."

"What are you going to do with your wagon? And who are you looking for?"

"Mom, the wagon's still stuck. You can't leave it there. Geez." Maya looked disgusted and straightened Hope's cigarette.

"I am not going to do anything with the wagon. The doorman—" Lish stretched this word out and paused briefly after saying it—"will somehow remove it and put it in a suitable place until I come back to get it. I, we, are going to the convention in the ballroom on the sixth floor. Is there a problem with that?"

"Well, are you a member of the convention or . . ."

"Yes, I am." Lish put one of her hands into the other one and cocked her head. Dill had fallen asleep on the way to the hotel and I stood beside Lish holding him over my shoulder and shifting around from one foot to the other, trying to assume a confident stance like Lish's, but thinking I looked more like a refugee at an appeal hearing. Please sir, I felt like blurting out in broken English, grant my infant son and me asylum at the Four Seasons Hotel.

"Are you sure, you don't—"

"I don't have a sitter, you're right," said Lish. "This convention came up out of the blue and I didn't have enough time to get one. Fortunately, my girls are used to this type of thing. They come out for every Kids At the Office Day and are very well-behaved." Alba was grabbing her crotch, desperate to pee, and Letitia had pushed every floor button of the elevator. Hope and Maya were chasing each other around the potted trees in the lobby. Lish went on, "I really must go. I have an 11:30 presentation to make on Bank Security Measures." Lish grabbed Alba's hand away from her crotch and called to the others, "Girls, time to go." The front desk guy pursed his lips and started clacking away at his computer.

Lish spotted her parents in the ballroom immediately. John was holding forth on some hot banking news. He had a sharp dark suit on. He was talking very loudly. As a child Lish could never lose him because of his booming voice. The men he was talking to were inches shorter than he and they gazed up at him while he boomed. John glanced around the room, looking over and around their heads. Lish's mother smiled demurely at his side and picked a piece of lint off the back of his jacket.

I wandered over to the buffet table and lay the sleeping Dill on the floor underneath it. He was getting very heavy. I stood and looked over the trays of food and kept my eye on Dill while Lish went over to talk to her parents.

"GRANDMA GRANDPA GRANDMA GRANDPA!" The twins sprinted to their grandparents. The look on Lish's mom's face was one of pure surprise and delight. The look on John's face, one of pure horror.

"Girls, *oh how wonderful*, I'm so glad! I was going to call you to see if we—"

"How the hell did you get in here, Alicia?" John still had a a big smile on his face but the words were forced through the spaces between his teeth.

Lish stood there and smiled. She straightened her hat and readjusted her bracelets. Alba leapt at her grandfather and smeared yellow face paint all over his dark suit jacket. People were beginning to stare and raise their eyebrows.

"Hi Dad, hi Mom."

"Alicia, collect your uh . . . children . . . and come with me. Mary, did you invite them here?"

"Dad," said Lish, "there's something I need to ask you."

"Alicia, dear, I'm so glad you're here," said Lish's mom. "And the kids, oh you precious girls, come here and let me hold you. Oh John, isn't this wonderful?"

One of John's friends strolled by. He was holding two drinks in his hand and had loosened his tie. He smiled at Lish and said, "Well, well, who have we here?"

"Hello, I'm Lish, this is Alba and Hope and Letitia over there and Maya."

"How da ya doo. My name's Howard Bloethal, I'm very happy to beat you and your famlay. Whaddaya do uh . . . uh . . ."

"Lish. Nothing. I'm on social assistance."

"Well, isn't that great, you must be very happy and whad-beeyoodivul girls I gotta go now ggg goodbye."

John said, "Thank god he's too drunk to notice anything. My god, is that a spider Alicia?"

"It is," said Lish, "but Daddy, can I talk to you for a sec—"

"Look," he interrupted her, "come with me, all of you. We'll sort this out." He spoke in a loud whisper, "Why are you doing this to me, Alicia? It's not fair, showing up like this out of

the blue. Everything I do I do for you and your mother. I'm trying to do my work here. I don't deserve this kind of treatment."

Just then two more suits walked up and slapped John on his
back. One asked, "Who's the pretty lady, John?"

"My name is Lish. I'm John's daughter and these are his
granddaughters. That's my friend Lucy over there, and her son
Dill." She turned and waved and I forced a weak smile. I
glanced at John and he appeared to be tearing the skin off one
of his thumbs. He looked up at the ceiling and for one second I
felt I knew what he was going through. Help, his look said, and
I thought, fellow refugee.

Mary was hauling treats from her purse and passing them
out to the girls, hugging and kissing them. They were all talking
at once. Mary asked them if they'd like to visit the buffet and
have a snack. They wanted to show her their wagon stuck in the
door and perform a play for her. They wanted to know why was
Grandpa mad? He wasn't, Mary told them, he's just busy and
doesn't handle surprises well. Would they come over? Well . . .

Lish tried to move closer to her father, but one of the men
standing around decided to strike up a conversation with her.
He asked, "So your father tells me you're in business for yourself? Working out of your home?"

"Ha ha ha, yeah, you might say that." Lish looked at her
father.

"Mmmm, what's that smell?"

"Oh, my patchouli, or it could be this lemon loaf." Lish
swung the Safeway bag around. The men nodded, clued out.

The conversation between Lish and John's buddies was
picking up. John stood to one side, smiling, tearing at his
thumb.

"What does your husband do, Lish?"

"Oh, well, I don't have one, thankfully, I already have four
children ha ha ha."

She looked over at me for confirmation, but I snapped my
head away from her glance, toward the buffet table, and crossed
my fingers. Dill was making noises under the table and I could
smell his diaper.

"Oh, well, is their father helping you out uh . . . financially, or . . ."

"Not really. The father of the older two lives in his van or at his mother's and is a poet. The father of the twins doesn't know he is, and can't come to Canada because of a drug charge, although I'm planning to go to Colorado to find him and show him the girls, you know, have a little fun . . . he's a fire-eater . . ."

"That's it. Alicia, come with me now." John steered Lish towards the giant doors of the ballroom. Lish tossed the Safeway bag with the lemon loaf at John's friends and said, "Here, just for you . . ."

Outside in the hall, John practically slammed Lish into the wall. His face was a deep shade of red and looked like dried fruit. Before he could bring himself to speak, Lish said calmly.

"Give me a thousand bucks and I'll leave."

I could hear John yelling. "COMING IN HERE LIKE THIS WITH YOUR RAGTAG HERD OF KIDS DRESSED UP LIKE TARTS ASKING FOR MONEY WHO THE HELL DO YOU THINK YOU ARE—"

"I'm your daughter, John."

So that was it, John wrote Lish a cheque for a thousand bucks. Then he got his dark suit and his dried fruit face back into that ballroom, in a hurry to explain all to the boys. Mary walked Lish and the kids to the lobby and they had some of the free coffee and doughnuts and talked. Mary wanted to get a cab for Lish, but Mary never really had money of her own. Mary said she would try to make it out to Winnipeg soon to visit Lish and the kids, but she had a sad look on her face when she laughed. In any case, they were coming out for a niece's wedding in the fall and they'd see each other then. She did like Lish's outfit. "Leave it to Lish," she said, and she said the girls were gems. Lish told Mary that she intended to use the money to go to Colorado to find the twins' father, and Mary wished her well. She apologized for John and gave each of the girls another candy and a big wet kiss and a hug. She agreed with the girls that the wagon must certainly have been stuck but now it sat outside the hotel on the sidewalk tucked behind one of the fat pillars. The front desk clerk looked anxious to see it go.

On the way home I asked Lish if she was okay. She said, "What do you think, Lucy? Do you think I'm okay?"

I said, "I think you might not be." She looked at me. She was crying. I took her hand and we walked home in the rain.

So we had the cash, the van (just about fixed) and the destination. All we needed was to fix welfare, make sure we wouldn't get caught leaving the province, let alone the country, and wait until Hope and Maya got out of school.

Lish had decided not to tell the girls about the busker actually being their father unless we found him. Until then he'd just be a friend we were trying to locate. I felt like my life had just lurched involuntarily into fourth gear. Maybe chasing after the busker wasn't the best thing for Lish to be doing and for me to be encouraging. But I just wanted what was best for her and the kids. I wanted her to be happy. And at least we'd be getting away from Half-a-Life for awhile. That could only be a good thing, regardless of where we went or what we found. Or didn't find.

My dole appointment was coming up again. I needed to postpone it a bit, otherwise my next one would fall somewhere in the time when Lish and I had planned to be in Colorado. I decided to phone Podborczintski and lie. It was something I was getting pretty good at. I made the call at 9:10 in the morning and was on hold until 9:55. The whole time their muzak played Billy Joel's "Honesty." Not too subtle.

"Hello, Mr. Podborczintski?"

"Case number please."

That was charming. Welfare language meaning Hello. "Uh, 5040388920."

"One moment while I punch you in." On hold again with "Honesty." "Yes, Lucy Van Alstyne. How may I help you."

"Uh, yeah, I have an appointment with you for June 21st and I'm going to have to change it, like move it up, because I have a funeral to go to on that day."

"Whose funeral is it?" I guess he wanted a case number and a computer printout in front of him.

"Well, it's my mother's funeral."

"I see. Unfortunately, I'll need a death certificate to prove she's dead and a letter from the person officiating at the funeral to prove that her funeral is indeed on June 21st. What time is the funeral?"

"Oh, it's in the afternoon. Two o'clock."

"Well, your appointment is for 10:15 in the morning. Technically you'd be able to make it for your appointment and still get to the funeral for the afternoon. I realize you're distraught; however, my hands are tied with regards to policy."

If I had been Lish I would have reacted differently. I would have started to cry or been outraged. I would have demanded to speak to his superior, threatened to contact my MP, take it to the press, insisted on proof that this was indeed policy. I would have made a scene.

"Oh, well fine then, see you June 21st."

"Very well, June 21st it is, and uh . . . I'm sorry about your mother. I lost my mother to cancer only six months ago, so I know what you're going through."

Interesting. I should have asked to see old Mrs. Podborczintski's death certificate. Well, so much for that. I'd have to go for my appointment now and call from somewhere on the road with an elaborate story about why I couldn't make it for my next one. Lish would be with me. She could help with the details. I could picture it in my mind. Some phone booth in Wyoming, maybe, all five kids running around squawking, Lish trying not to laugh, saying, "Tell him that . . . Tell him oooh . . . ha ha ha."

When I was a kid I remember my mother telling my dad to act like a man and stand up for his rights. The car dealership behind us had wanted to buy our back lot and pave over it to make more room for new cars. They said if my dad didn't sell, they'd have the area zoned for commercial use and then we'd have to sell for even less than they were offering us now. My dad took to his bed for one week. He asked my mom to cancel his classes for him. Sometimes I'd peek through the door to his bedroom and he'd be lying there on his bed staring up at the ceiling. Sometimes he'd be sleeping. The room smelled stale. When he finally came to the breakfast table, he said, "I don't want a fight. They can have whatever they want." My mom exploded. "Why can't you fight for what's yours? Why are you always such a coward? What are you afraid of? So you lose, big deal, at least you'll have stood up for your rights. You are so weak. Okay, fine. Let them bulldoze down all your chokecherry trees and your Saskatoon trees and all your stupid flowers. See if I care."

Then my dad did something terrible. He put his head down close to his bowl of cheerios and cried. Terrible sucking, murmuring noises. My mom said, "Oh for Pete's sake," and left. My dad cried and shook and told me he was sorry.

Mercy had a job working for the Disaster Board. She had been transferred over there temporarily from her other government job because she was so good at organizing files and receipts and complaints, separating the genuine from the bogus. Lish and I watched her leave one morning, mosquito netting and bike helmets on both her and her daughter's heads, reflectors on the bike and on their rain jackets and on Zara's backpack and

Mercy's briefcase. We marvelled at her routine. The truth was, most of us in Half-a-Life were afraid of jobs, so our feelings for Mercy were a combination of jealousy and disgust. We'd all had jobs at one time or another. Most didn't last long. We had a problem with authority. Maybe we were lazy. A lot of people figured we were stupid. But even being on the dole was better than working. We didn't want to leave our kids at a daycare or with a sitter. Some of us wouldn't have been able to maintain the schedule, up at dawn, home at dusk, bed by 9:30, do it again the next day. I think a lot of us lacked confidence, too, in ourselves and in our ability to stick with a job and do it well. Having children was easy. There was no choice: we were stuck with them and this worked out for us, more or less. And besides, being on the dole and having children at the same time was a job. Who says we didn't earn our money?

But to get back to Mercy: at precisely 5:10 she and Zara would be back at Half-a-Life. She might visit with one of us briefly before making supper for Zara and herself. Zara would be in bed by seven o'clock sharp, otherwise she'd have a fit, according to Mercy. Zara had to get up at six every morning to make it to daycare on time for Mercy to make it to work on time, so it made sense. Mercy would then clean up from supper, re-arrange her tiny apartment, do laundry, maybe some paper-work. By 9:30 she was in bed. The next day they'd do it again.

During one of her brief visits, Mercy told us Bunnie Hutchison, the Minister in charge of Welfare, had applied for flood disaster relief money from the province. On her form she had said she didn't have insurance and needed money for dam-aged carpets, lifting tiles, shifting foundation, loss of clothing (including numerous fur coats left in a cedar closet in the base-ment), loss of television, VCR, CD player, stained cedar wood from her sauna, fridge (from mini-bar), ruined leather from the mini-bar, pool table, bathroom cabinet, washer, dryer, motors, tools (belonging to her husband), and a two thousand-dollar aquarium which housed eight exotic South American piranhas who died when the aquarium's climate control was altered by the cold rain water splashing up against it.

Mercy told us she had done a routine check of Bunnie Hutchison's city tax bill and found out that she did indeed have insurance that covered flood, sewage and any other type of natural disaster. How odd. Must have been an oversight on Bunnie's part, thought Mercy. When she showed the file to her supervisor, he took it and said, "Oh, that's fine, I'll handle this."

I realized later that Mercy was trying to tell me something about Bunnie Hutchison, but at that point I guessed that Mercy was merely talking about her day at work, and pointing out that even provincial government ministers make mistakes. That evening I lay down with Dill. I sang to him and he fell asleep with his arm around my neck. From my bedroom window I could see more rain clouds puffing up, getting ready to dump their load. I thought of the clothes I'd pack for Dill and me. I thought of the games and food we could bring for the kids and the tapes we'd bring to listen to. I didn't think about the real reason why we were going. For Lish this adventure had a purpose, an end. For me, it was just an adventure.

That evening I watched Joe deliberately smash his 1976 Dodge Dart into a pole in the Half-a-Life parking lot. The next day he'd report it as a hit-and-run accident and claim the insurance money for it. He and Pillar would be able to buy another week's worth of groceries and when they were flush they'd buy another beater for a hundred or two hundred dollars.

The next day was my appointment with Podborczintski. This time Lish had agreed to look after Dill, which was a big relief. It was almost exciting, like going out. Going out on my own, even to the dole. In the lobby I passed Terrapin hauling a small dead tree through the side door. She was building a shrine out of *papier-mâché* and chicken wire. She needed the space in the lobby because her apartment was too tiny. The shrine was supposed to be a tree with a kind of shelf around the bottom. It was her contribution to the Homebirth Network's march at the legislative grounds. The tree was the tree of life, and the shelf was there for gifts. Her kids were playing cat's cradle and arguing about something. Terrapin was frowning at them. The chicken wire wasn't doing what it was supposed to.

"No Dill?" she asked.

"No Dill," I replied.

When I got to the welfare office, I walked through the doors with ease, no stroller to maneouvre, and I marched up to the desk of the first officer like an old hand and said, "Case number 5040388920, 10:15 appointment with F. Podborczintski, sir." I clicked my shoe against the other one and brought my hand to my head in a salute.

"Cute." The woman behind the desk was not amused. "What time did you say your appointment was?"

Without having to worry about Dill squirming in my arms or crawling off on the wrong coloured line I was able to stand perfectly still and stare into this woman's eyes.

But I felt kind of stupid. I had made what I thought was a bold move, but I didn't know exactly what to do next. "10:15," I said.

The woman looked at her watch and said, "You're late."

I glanced at the big caged clock on the wall. "It's not even 10:20. I'll have to sit and wait for ages, anyway," I said. "I'm sorry I'm late," I added, suddenly feeling like an eight-year-old kid.

"I don't need attitude from people like you." The woman's head quivered while she spoke.

Attitude! Hadn't I just apologized? "Hey, we're here to worry about my needs, not yours, hey hey," I muttered, feeling like a moron, like a failed stand-up comedian. I was only trying to be funny, even friendly, but our senses of humour weren't gelling right then.

"The yellow line," she hissed. This time her head bobbed and her jaw clenched and two white spots appeared on her cheeks.

I followed the yellow line, past the bulletproof glass shielding the cashiers, into the holding area. I thought of the white-capped mountains of Colorado and sunshine and the open highway. Sitting in the holding area, I overheard two guys speaking in French. Then their names were called by a man in a suit. I overheard bits of their conversation. They were applying for emergency money.

". . . fuckin' wet here, had to sleep in the truck . . . broke down in Kenora . . . had to use our gas money for repairs . . ."

"Alright. Your names are Jean—"

"We're trying to get to Vancouver . . . work there . . . we're from New Brunswick."

The dole worker in the suit told them to come with him. Then he said, "Oh, I'll take one of you at a time."

Poor guys.

"Ah merde . . ." One of the guys said something to the other in French. The dole worker stopped him and said, "No consulting. This way, please."

If their stories were exactly the same they'd be made to do lumpy labour, maybe lugging dead cows around a slaughter-house or filling up potholes, maybe something to do with the flood, for a day or two, stay at the Sally Ann until they had enough gas money to get the hell out of Winnipeg.

The woman next to me had on mustard-coloured stretch pants and a tank top that read "Life's a Bitch and Then You Die." She jerked her head at the two guys and said, "Bullshitters."

I didn't say anything. Nobody wants to be associated with any of the other welfare bums in the building. This is one of the harder parts of the job of being on the dole. It requires complete denial. You must be still and patient.

Eventually Podborczintski called me into his little office. I noticed he had a new piece of art on his wall. It was a crayon drawing of a boat and a box and a tree and looked like it must have been done by his grandchild. He looked old enough to have grandchildren. I'm sure he could positively identify the father of each one, too.

We did our usual dole chat. No, I hadn't found out who Dill's father was. No, I hadn't made any money in any way since my last appointment. No, I hadn't received any gifts of money from my family. The only shocking thing about the meeting happened at the end. Podborczintski told me he was sorry about my mother dying. He told me he was trying his best to help unfortunate people like me. He had a daughter himself and would be devastated if ever she had to turn to social assistance to support her children. He said he wished he could be the father to all these poor children, to show them love, a future, a male role model that they so desperately need. I didn't know what to do, so I tried to change the subject.

"That's a nice picture you got. By the way."

"What? Oh, that. Yes, yes, isn't it beautiful? You see, that right there illustrates the potential these children have to turn the ugly reality of their lives into something beautiful. Lucy, I hope you recognize that your child, despite his random arrival in a world of poverty and absent fathers, knows that he is special, that he is loved, and capable of making change, of creating beauty from the mess around him."

"Oh, yes." I shifted around in my chair. "Are we done?" I asked him.

"Oh, yes, yes. Wait. I'll have to schedule a home visit. I'll be dropping in sometime in the next couple of weeks. Home visits are a necessary component of my job. They are put in place to allow for a more precise assessment of the client's needs and to ensure that nothing—well . . . I imagine you know the routine." Suddenly Podborczintski seemed awfully tired.

He smiled and stared off toward his window. If Podborczintski was planning a home visit I'd have to be home and not traipsing around in Colorado with five children and a crazy woman looking for a fire-eating street performer. It was a problem.

I cleared my throat and asked, "Can't we make a specific time for the appointment? I'm not always at home, I'm outside a lot. Because I have lung problems and the rain is very good for them. You see."

"I'm sorry, Lucy, but the nature of home visits is such that they allow for a random, unplanned visit. We need to know that there is no, how shall I say . . ."

I nodded quickly. Podborczintski was sparing me the details, and I was sparing him the embarrassment of reciting them.

He quickly added, "Also, we need a look at the floor plan of your apartment to verify that you have, indeed, two bedrooms and so on."

"Right. OK," I said.

You know that expression *gulping air*. That's what I did when I got out of the dole building. Really, I stood on the street and gulped air. God, life could get complicated.

Before I got back to Half-a-Life, it had started to rain. Sing Dylan was outside with a shovel, trying to dig what looked like a sloped ditch away from his basement window. This time Sarah wasn't helping him. I asked Sing Dylan where she was, and he told me she had gone to apply for a part-time job at the carnival that was coming to town. To prove to her social worker that she was productive and deserved to get her son back, she had to apply for a certain number of jobs per day. He pronounced it *carney val*, with a rolled *r*, so at first I didn't get it.

When I got upstairs to Lish's apartment I noticed it was really quiet, and Lish's apartment is rarely quiet, not even at night, especially not at night. I knocked on the door. Nothing. I checked and it was open. It was dark in the hallway, so I groped around for the light switch. The light came on and there they were: Lish, Hope, Maya (home from school for lunch) Alba, Letitia and Dill all dead, slaughtered, with streaks of red food colouring coming from their mouths and their eyeballs bulging grotesquely, unblinking. I found out later that Dill had fallen asleep on the floor, and his habit of sleeping with his eyes half-open had inspired the girls to mount this production. Lish had

106

been forced to go along with it for added effect. Her hair looked great splayed out over the kitchen linoleum. Funny, yeah, but murder has never sat well with me. So my initial gasp was really authentic and the girls were tickled pink.

Anyway, Lish got up and told me we were going to a party that night, come hell or high water. We were stepping out. Teresa had offered to babysit, so "youse guys can get pissed for a change," and had even offered me a dress to wear for the evening. The party was at the home of a friend of a friend of another friend of one of Lish's night-time paramours. Apparently it was some kind of film wrap-up thing and Graham Greene might even show up. Teresa told me that in exchange for babysitting I had to ask someone about the chances of her getting hired as a flagger on any upcoming shoot.

Teresa took Dill and the girls an hour before we were actually leaving because, she told us, the time spent getting ready, preparing, dressing, preening and talking about getting laid is the best part of any party, really. The actual party is usually a bore, and odds are you don't get laid.

It took me about five minutes to decide not to wear Teresa's red fake silk dress and to wear instead my super tight jeans and black t-shirt. Hopefully Teresa wouldn't see me leave. I'd have to crumple the dress up a bit and blow cigarette smoke on it and put some of my blonde hairs and maybe a smudge of lipstick on it. Watching Lish, on the other hand, prepare for this party, was another story. She did take an hour to get ready. First of all, she had to find her black lipstick and that took fifteen minutes. It took her about half an hour to comb through her hair, a concession she only makes when going to parties. Then she changed her mind about a dozen times about what she wanted to wear. First, it was her ripped up underwear look, pantyhose, nightgown, with leopard skin fake fur vest and knee-high red rubber rain boots. Then she thought that was too flip and people like Graham Greene would think she was insane. So she changed into a floor-length shimmery black skin-tight velvet dress with buttons down the front, and added black gloves up to her elbow and put on her square-toed black shoes. This was much more elegant and mysterious-looking, but she looked like an eel or a skindiver or something. Plus, the rolls around her middle stuck out. Finally she settled on a pair of black tights and a huge green loosely-knit sweater and her red rubber boots, because we'd probably have to walk back after the buses had stopped running. She slapped her spider hat on, of course, and splashed patchouli and rose water all over her neck. I have a feeling she put some on her crotch when she went to the can, but who knows. I would have if I had been her, but I wasn't her and I didn't think any guy would even notice me, let alone get close enough to my crotch to smell it. I had the impression this Graham Greene guy was more refined. She also managed to find all fifteen bracelets for her arms. Even though she could have been one bright green and red smelly, jangly mess with crows' feet and belly flab, she wasn't. She was beautiful. Then, she started to cry out of the blue, and I thought, Oh god, why is she crying now? But before I could say anything, Lish said, "Luce, don't worry, I just like the way I look right after I cry, and I usually feel more in control, funnier and more, you know, reckless. Crying releases some kind of bravado inside me. Plus my lips go puffy and my eyes sort of shine."

"Oh. Kay, cry your head off then. But we should go soon."

"Yeah, yeah, I have to cry for at least a good ten minutes for the right effect. And it has to be serious open-mouthed pathetic crying. So, okay, here goes."

While Lish cried I stared at myself in the mirror. I looked like a wide-eyed kid going to her first mixed-sex party. I was hanging around with some kooky older mother who had to cry before we could leave. I had left my child, *my child*, with a woman whose last name I didn't even know. Some hot shot actor guy was going to be at the party, but I knew he would not talk to me or notice me. Tight jeans looked bad on me. Loose fit would have been better. That's it. I looked like a reject from the 'seventies.

"Kay, Luce, I'm done. Are you ready?" Lish definitely looked puffier and her eyes shone. For a moment I imagined her and Graham Greene as my parents: giving me a big pile of crackers and then dashing upstairs for the nearest bedroom, the house pet rubbing against my leg and whining for my crackers. I'd kick him.

"Yeah. I'm ready."

I drank way too much at the party. Lish shone like a star, charming everyone, being smart and funny. She knew how to talk to men so that they talked back. The guys at this party were not like Joe or Sing Dylan or Rodger or any of the guys she brought back to her apartment. They wore sweaters that were pastel-coloured and drank beer from glasses. They felt good laughing and talking with a wacky single welfare mother. I didn't think any of them would ever marry women like us, or even date us, but a little drunken flirtation—maybe even sex— away from their real lives was okay. For them, stretch marks were like jock straps or Jack Daniels or facial hair, or ejaculation: a little benchmark on their way to becoming real men. "Oh yeah," they'd say, "I've had sex with a woman who's had kids. I've fucked a mother!" I wondered what they thought might happen; that their penis might get lost inside like a surgeon's rubber glove accidentally left behind in the patient's body?

Pillar told me that Joe woke up one morning and his penis had swollen up like a turnip—like an S-shaped turnip with bubbles. He freaked. He screamed at her, "What did you do to me? This is my *dick*!!!! This is my life, my future, this is *grotesque*!!! Pillar made the mistake of laughing all day about it. Even before they found out it was only a wasp bite, actually three of them, and not some terrible disease. Apparently he'd been drinking red wine all night before going to bed and getting stung and that's why he hadn't woken up. Before he got to

the doctor he had said, repeatedly, I am very *concerned* about
this, you know, *very* concerned about this. And that would set
Pillar off all over again. She told us she actually wet her pants
laughing, but she felt it was worth it.

Like I said, I drank way too much. I remember hearing Lish
telling some guy we were hitting the road in search of a man
she once knew, and who was the father of her twins. I remember him saying, "My goodness," and asking her to excuse him,
he needed another beer. I had the feeling we were becoming
cartoon characters in that place: Lish was trying to make her
life seem funny and reckless, charming and dangerous. Sexy.
Maybe it was, I don't know. Graham Greene didn't talk to us at
all. But a lawyer did. Well, he talked to me. I think Lish terrified him.

"But you look too young to have a kid," he said to me in
some kind of backhanded compliment.

"I am."

"Oh, ha ha, you are, good one. I'm sure you're capable of
raising a child, but . . ."

I had the feeling his only idea of a mother was his own and
the mother of his own children, a woman who was probably
right now administering Tempra or something, chasing out
monsters, maybe getting sloshed in front of the tube wondering
why her husband had to work so much and thinking of her lost
youth. I didn't know if he had a wife or kids, but I was sure he'd
had a mother. Mothers you can be sure of, fathers, well . . .
they're the kind of people whose heads always get chopped off
in pictures.

I found out that this man's name was Hartley Weinstein of
Weinstein, Weinstein and Vrsnick. I wish that he could have
come right out and said, "I want to fuck you," because that is
obviously what he did want. He didn't talk to the other people
there, his age, other professionals, film people, people he
knew from work, people who knew him, people who wouldn't
fuck him.

At first I felt sorry for his wife, I just knew he had to have one, and then I felt mean. I thought, well, she could be all those women who stare at me and Lish in the rain, with our Safeway bags and our secondhand clothes and our many children and our inferior strollers and our lack of men and cars. I stopped feeling sorry for her and decided to fuck her husband just for revenge. Then I felt sad with a really big feeling of wanting a boyfriend, some guy my age in jeans and runners, all wiry and muscular, with his arm around me, giving other guys the evil eye, carrying a picture of me, and Dill, I guess, in his wallet, and throwing me over his shoulder, throwing me onto a bed and making love to me in a bed. Making Love to me in a Bed and then sleeping with his muscular arm lying across my stomach, and his hair in my face.

This was my thought as I got into Hart's Ford Aerostar. He chucked the kid's car seat in the back, thinking I was too drunk to notice, I guess. Stupidly he held my hand as he drove and then all I could think about was my dad holding my hand on the way to The Waffle Shop. My dad had big brown hairy hands with chewed nails. Hart had narrow white bony hands that didn't seem much bigger than mine. His nails looked crisp and even. He had tassel shoes and the heel of one kind of slipped off his foot when he had it on the gas pedal. He mentioned something about the farmers getting enough rain this summer. The thing was this guy Weinstein wasn't really that much older than me. Really, he told me, he was only twenty-four, which made him only six years older than me. He told me that he didn't think he approved of welfare. I had no idea where we were going. He seemed interested in coming to my place. More slumming I guess. Too cheap to get a room. Wife at home. Why not. Fuck the Rich than Eat them.

By the time we got to Half-a-Life, I had gained a more positive perspective on the whole thing. In fact, I couldn't stop laughing. Hart looked nervous about me laughing. He tried to chuckle in the spirit of things, but he sounded nervous. He said, "You're crazy, aren't you?" in a voice mixed with disbelief and appreciation and a tinge of hostility. He sounded like an actor doing a first reading. I realized he wanted me to be crazy, nutty, making up for poverty with *joie de vivre* and skid row toughness. And tenderness, you know the type. Wise beyond my years. Street-smart, but still yearning for love in all the wrong places. Hollywood. We managed to sneak past Teresa's place. I couldn't exactly be crazy and tough and tender and generally fucked up and not caring, just enjoying the desperate edge of poverty, and not needing anyone—or so I tried to tell myself—with a ten-month-old baby on my hip. Besides, Dill was probably fast asleep on Teresa's living room floor anyway and why wake him up? This was going to be the first time I'd had sex in a bed. Then I started laughing all over again.

Hart took off his shoes at the door and promptly stepped on a hard block and then another. Then he stepped on another and said, "What the heck?" What I wanted to do right then was sit down at the kitchen table with Lish and have a good laugh. At that point Hart might have welcomed it as well. But Lish was still stranded at the party, she'd have to make her own way home, and somehow I knew she'd do it with a lot more class. Hart and I stood smiling at each other. Then he walked down the hall to the bathroom and I ran to my bedroom and chucked the diapers, clothes, toys and books off my bed and onto my floor.

I heard the toilet running. I yelled, "Jiggle the handle!" but I don't think he heard me. If it kept running it would eventually run all over the floor and Sing Dylan would have to fix it. I went into the hall to yell it again and I saw him in the light of the bathroom for a brief moment before he switched it off and headed my way in the half-darkness of the hallway. He wore a gleaming white t-shirt and black socks pulled up mid-calf. He had removed his glasses and put water in his hair to slick it back. My heart sank. He'd looked better at the party. Then again, I probably had too. He grinned and rubbed his hands together and said, "Ready or not." Then for a brief second I envied his wife sitting at home on the couch alone, or lying down with the baby. She'd be relieved he was getting his rocks off with me, and not with her, and the joke was on me! I smiled sweetly at Hart, overcome with sadness really, and led him by his little hand to my messy bedroom. Then I lay there staring at the ceiling and thinking about Dill.

And my toilet which was still running. Hart rubbed his black sock against my bare foot and then ran his big toe up my shin to about my knee. Unfortunately he spoke. "You hot little tomato you." I smiled sweetly again. I closed my eyes and thought about my non-existent nineteen-year-old boyfriend with the muscular arms and the jeans and the picture in his wallet poking out of a hole in the back pocket of his jeans. Hart started rubbing my belly like I was a kid with a stomachache (which come to think of it I was, getting there, anyway) and then moved his hand down to my pubic hair, hesitated for one brief dramatic moment and plunged one of his skinny white fingers into my vagina. Sigh. That area taken care of for the time being, he proceeded to move up to my breasts. Like switching on a car. Ignition, wipers, radio, okay we're ready to go!

I could see him with a long pointer pointing to a pie on the blackboard. Attend to bottom half of woman, then, moving the marker, from there proceed to top half, maintaining pressure on bottom, until all lights on dash are on. Contact! Proceed to drive. He started to kiss his way up from my bellybutton to my right breast, stopping briefly to lick the hard flat area in between my breasts. I wondered if Dill had had trouble going to sleep over at Teresa's. Hart pulled my hand and steered it in the general direction of his dick and then demonstrated how he wanted me to move my hand. Standard. See chart. Back to the breast. His tongue wrapped itself around my nipple and one of his hands moved up to squeeze the wide base of my breast.

"HOLY SHIT!!!!! WHAT THE HEEEELLL!!!" Suddenly Hart was hollering.

By the dim light of the street lamp shining into my bedroom window I saw Hart's face, lifted up off my breast, white, dripping, covered in milk. Dill's milk. He looked like a kitten stopping for a breath while drinking from a big bowl of cream. Warm milk dribbled out of the corner of his mouth. A little geyser shot out from my nipple for a few seconds and then petered out to a few drops. They sat poised, shimmering and white, pure, on the very tip of my pink nipple, with no place to go. Hart's hot tomato had sprung a leak.

"For Christ's sake," Hart spluttered. He got up and stumbled to the bathroom. I rolled over and buried my face in my pillow and laughed and laughed and shook, trying to muffle my laughter. From the bathroom Hart yelled, "Jesus, thanks a lot, I can't believe you're laughing!"

"A merry heart doeth good like a medicine!" I yelled back and then laughed really hard. After a minute or two I got up and got dressed. I noticed the sun coming up. The sun! I could hear Hart struggling with the toilet handle. I asked, "Doncha have to get back home, Hart?" I assumed our night of passion was over and our lives would resume their opposite courses. Hart came out of the bathroom, fully dressed and looking pale and frightened without his glasses and without the blurriness that he once had, when the booze had had a firmer grip. He looked about fourteen. He forced a smile and looked at me as if I was his captor and he needed to pee.

He asked, "What was that? Was it milk?"

"Yeah. What did you think?" I couldn't believe it. He was still under the impression that I had spontaneously shot out some mysterious white fluid from my breasts.

"Do you have a baby!!!"

"Yeah. I have a baby. I breast-feed him. I told you I had a baby, at the party."

"Oh, my god."

"It's a pretty normal thing to do, Hart."

"Really? I mean still?"

"Yeah."

"Oh geez. You must think I'm an idiot."

"Look, Hart, don't you have to get back?"

"No. My mom's in Florida."

"Excuse me?"

"She won't know when I get in."

"You live with your mother?"

"Yeah."

"Oh," I said. "What about the baby seat in the mini-van?"

"What? Oh right. Oh geez, it's my brother's mini-van."
Hart looked like he was going to cry. Every single person who
entered my life in any way seemed to be on the verge of tears.
That can make a person feel insecure.

"Look," he said, "would you like to see me?"

"I can see you, Hart. You're standing right in front of me."

"No. Like, another time. Or whatever."

Then I realized that Hart might be interested in seeing me
again, in dating, in becoming my boyfriend, in becoming Dill's
step-father, maybe adopting him, after marriage of course,
building a home for us in Linden Woods, having more kids
together, a cottage at Victoria Beach, and matching shorts, side
by side burial plots, oh my god. Not that I didn't want some of
that. I just didn't know if I wanted it with Hart.

"No," I said. "Well, maybe . . ."

"Oh."

I could hear the building coming to life. Out of my kitchen
window I saw Mercy leaving for work on her bike with Zara in
the seat behind her. Off to deal with the flood disasters. Sing
Dylan was at the wall with his hose and soap, scrubbing at the
letters. I realized I had to get Dill. Teresa would probably be
pissed off at me for leaving him with her all night.

Hart headed for the door.

"Would you like some coffee or something?" I asked.

"Nah, I should get going. I've got to work in the morning."

"I didn't mean to be so abrupt, you know, I just was under
the impression that this was a basic one-night stand and so I
wasn't really thinking about . . . you know."

"Yeah. It doesn't matter." Hart looked around, considering
my offer, and then, deciding I wasn't a total bitch, added,
"What the heck, okay, I'll have a cup of coffee, if you're having
some."

"I am."

"Okay."

It turned out that Hart had never wanted to be a lawyer. He had
wanted to be a jazz saxophonist. I told him he could be both
and he said, naah, he didn't think so. I said look at Woody
Allen, or you know Bill Clinton, they still find time to play
their horns. Hart grinned. He told me he had had a girlfriend
who had gone insane or something, and his mother was starting
a new relationship with some American. His dad was living in
Toronto. His brother sold junk bonds and was trying to get a
divorce from his wife. The mini-van belonged to his brother.
But Hart said he wouldn't miss it. He preferred his Miata.

By now Teresa had called and said Dill was playing happily
and I could go down and pick him up whenever I felt like it
(she told me she had seen the mini-van so she understood) but
before noon because she had to go to a job interview, something
Mercy had told her about, something like flood inspector for
people's flooded basements.

Apparently they were hiring anybody. I guess a flooded
basement would be one good way Teresa could extinguish herself. Ha Ha. Hart asked me if I was still involved with Dill's
father. I said no. I showed him pictures of Dill and he said Dill
was cute. He said he looked like me. I liked Hart right then. He
said he was sorry if he had upset me. I told him I was sorry if I
had upset him, and I said, "If there is ever anything I can do for
you . . ."

"Thanks. You too."

Though what that might have been I wasn't sure. I was
pouring us more coffee when there was a knock at the door. I
thought it must be Teresa with Dill or Lish to talk about last
night or maybe Sing Dylan wanting to fix the toilet. I peered
through the little peephole. It wasn't any of those people. It was
Podborczintski. He had a vinyl briefcase in one hand and a
windbreaker zippered right up to his chin. He had brown pants
on that had wrapped themselves weirdly around one leg. He

was stroking the top of his head in swift jerky motions, trying to get some hair to stay there. "Oh," I called out to him through the door. "Hang on!" I ran to the kitchen. "Shit, Hart, you have to get out of here. Real fast."

"Okay. Why?"

"Cause my welfare guy is here and you're not supposed to be. Hurry. Hurry."

Hart got his shoes on. I threw his cup in the sink. God, Dill should have been here. Hart shouldn't have. What would Podborczintski think? How was I going to get rid of Hart? I said to him, "You're going to have to go down the balcony."

"What? You're crazy." This time he sounded sincere.

"No. No. Come on. Hurry." I grabbed his arm and pulled him towards the kitchen. "Hang on Mr. Podborczintski, I'm just getting out of the tub," I yelled. I yanked the sheet off my bed, ran to the balcony and tied one end of it to the balcony railing.

"Forget that, it doesn't work," said Hart. "Jesus Christ." He started laughing. For a split second I was full of admiration, but I said urgently, "Okay then, what are you going to do? Hide? Podborczintski is gonna check the floor plan to make sure I'm getting the right amount of rent money."

"No, I'll pretend I'm your, uh, meter man."

"I don't have a meter in my apartment."

"Okay, okay, I'll be your minister. You need counselling."

"Then why am I in the bathtub?"

"Fuck."

"Fuck."

"Okay, I'm going to jump."

"You'll kill yourself."

"As if."

I slapped Hart on the back and smiled. "Atta boy," I said. He was becoming more and more like my fantasy of the perfect boyfriend.

He ran to the balcony. We stood there looking at each other for a moment. I kissed him and he blushed. Then he threw his shoes over the side. Sing Dylan looked up from his job washing

117

the graffiti and stared. Hart crawled over the side and lowered
himself down the railing. He was hanging on, dangling there.
He grinned up at me.

"You're crazy," I said.

"Yeah," he said. "Bye."

Then he let go and fell onto the grass below. Thud. He lay
there for a second. I threw his glasses down to him and he
missed catching them, but they didn't break. He got up and
put on his shoes and ran to the mini-van. I ran to the door. I
opened it wide with a big smile on my face and Podborczintski
squinted at the sun that now shone in his face. Teresa, holding
Dill and followed by her son, was coming down the hall peering at Podborczintski, unsure. I called out, "Hi!!!! You're back!
Great!"

Podborczintski looked at me with a puzzled expression and
then saw that I wasn't talking to him, but to Teresa and Dill, but
before he could say anything, I went on, "Thanks for looking
after Dill, Teresa, how was he, how were you, Dill, oh c'mon
over here, let me give you a great big hug and kiss, there you go,
thanks, Teresa, hi Scotty, okay well . . . ."

I was doing a lot of talking because I didn't know what to
say.

When I stopped to catch my breath, Podborczintski said,
"Sorry to get you out of the bath."

"What? Oh yeah, no problem, I was . . . ready to get
out . . . yup, it was time alright. So . . . c'mon in. Teresa, thanks
again, see ya later."

Teresa stood there staring. I guess she was wondering if this
was the guy I had brought home for the night. Podborczintski?
How could she? I put Dill down and Podborczintski made little clucking noises to him. We were still all bunched around
the doorway. Dill crawled over to Podborczintski and began to
pull himself up one of his brown trouser legs. After a few seconds Podborczintski picked him up, holding him away from
his body, and said, "Hello there, little fella." Dill smiled.
Podborczintski said, "*Well* well well, he certainly doesn't object
to strangers picking him up, does he?"

"He gets that from his mother," said Teresa making a face at me from behind Podborczintski. "Well, gotta go," she added. "I've got my interview. Lucy, you should consider going for an interview for this job, they're hiring anybody, they've got sixteen thousand flooded basements they still haven't—"

"Teresa, this is Mr. Podborczintski, my case worker from *Social Assistance!*"

Teresa's face froze, and she stammered, "Oh . . . oh." She made another face meaning *oops, major gaffe,* behind his back and said she was pleased to meet him, she had to go. I wondered if she thought I had brought Podborczintski home for the night. Obviously I couldn't do a lot of explaining right then.

Podborczintski did the inspection and got out of my apartment in a hurry. If he noticed the bathroom was as dry as a bone and not steamed up from a bath, he didn't say anything. He seemed satisfied the dole was giving me the right amount of rent money. As he was leaving, he asked me again, of course, whether or not I had found out who Dill's father was. Again, I said, "Nope, sorry." I wondered when he would stop asking me that question. I saw that Hart had left his card on my pillow. John Dillinger would not have left a business card on my pillow. How could I have told Hart, the attorney, that I'm attracted to outlaws, dead notorious ones at that?

Lish and I had things to do. We had to get ready for the trip. I'll tell you right now I had misgivings. We only had about ten days before we were supposed to leave. Rodger said the van was working alright, except for the sliding door. Around sharp curves, one of us would have to hang onto it, he said, so it wouldn't come right off. But the van wasn't the real problem: this whole trip would be pointless, futile. I knew it. Lish didn't know it, but I knew it. She was so excited and the twins were excited, though they still didn't know it was their father we were out to find, and even the older girls were looking forward to hitting the road. They hadn't been out of the city since the last time Rodger's van was working, and that was five years ago, when

Lish was volunteering for the Busking festival and the kids were off with Rodger and his mom, at somebody's cabin in Alberta.

At least Podborczintski had checked out my apartment. I didn't have to worry about his coming when I was gone. I had one dole appointment before we left and that cash would come in handy. Tanya told us we could use one of her beer coolers in our van for food, so we wouldn't have to eat in restaurants. Much. Even if we didn't find the busker, we'd be getting a bit of a break from Half-a-Life. With all the rain, and the prospect of school ending for the summer, the mothers in the block, as well as the on-again-off-again fathers, were getting tense. Serenity Place too, apparently, was getting rowdy. I had noticed the cops over there three times in the past week. They always had one woman cop, so you know it's a domestic dispute. That was kind of satisfying, really, and the more stressful things got over there, the more organized Sarah became.

She had landed the job with the carnival, which only lasted a couple of weeks, but still, she was getting out of Half-a-Life every day. And, in the evening, she was still helping Sing Dylan scrub the graffiti, (someone had recently written KILL THE RICH THEN FUCK THEM and this was too much for Sing Dylan, so he had thrown an orange tarp over it when they weren't hosing it down). And he and Sarah were also busy digging the trench away from Sing Dylan's basement apartment, toward the front doors of Serenity Place. They were serious about revenge. Sarah wanted her son back, and she wanted to show the women, especially Sindy, that she could fight back. Already, when it rained, you could see the trickle heading over there. But it hadn't arrived yet and we'd need a really big storm for it to make it all the way. And a deeper trench. So Sing Dylan and Sarah had a purpose, a goal. Okay, it was a mischievous one but hey, they deserved it. The women in Serenity Place would stand around watching Sarah and Sing Dylan dig and laugh at them, and sometimes call out to them, insults and things. Once one of them even said, "You're not gonna get your kid back if you're sleeping around with a Paki." They hadn't seemed to figure out what the trench was all about. Sing Dylan and Sarah just kept digging, and digging, in the rain, in the mosquitoes, in the sun, sometimes at night. The women in Serenity Place would soon be flooded out and revenge would be Sarah's and Sing Dylan's. At the end of the day I imagined Sing Dylan saying to Sarah, "Thank you. Thank you kindly."

When Emmanuel came to visit, Sarah stopped digging and put on her peach t-shirt dress and they sat together on their balcony playing checkers and sucking on Freezies. Sometimes Sing Dylan would look up from his digging and give the thumbs up sign to Emmanuel, which always cracked up me and Lish. Another thing, Emmanuel was coming for longer and longer visits: when it wasn't raining, he was out in the parking lot roller blading and riding his bike, and when he and his mom said goodbye, they smiled instead of cried. Sing Dylan shook his hand.

Lish was acting funny, too, in a good way. She was giddy and full of beans, pushing for the high yellow note, as Vincent Van Gogh would have said, as Lish herself told me: the high yellow note being that kind of intense but temporary manic creative force. If Vincent Van Gogh had given birth, he'd probably have called birthing the high yellow note.

I knew Lish was excited about leaving, which didn't exactly make my mood any better. But it was fun to see her so happy. Everything she did, she did with a little flourish. Like, when she picked up toys and clothes and things, she'd pick them up, throw them in the air so they spun and then snatch them before they fell to the floor. When she put milk in her coffee, she'd stir it and then ding the spoon a couple of times against the side of her cup and then slice the air with the spoon, like a symphony conductor. And then there was the little patch of sunlight on her kitchen wall. It didn't last very long in the morning, about twenty minutes or so. And with the rain and everything, there was only ever enough sunshine for it to materialize about once every two or three weeks, so it wasn't a regular thing. It was a square of white light on the wall beside the fridge. It came through the kitchen window. Lish would stop to spread her fingers in it briefly, making goofy shadow monsters, birds and rabbits. Then she'd dart off to whatever errands she was performing that day. I had seen her doing it a couple of times when she thought I wasn't looking. She didn't talk about it with me, and when Terrapin told Lish that she and her kids played shadow puppets instead of seeing movies, Lish told her to get a life.

So Lish was happy. She was buying food for the trip and learning about Colorado in the encyclopedia at the library. She was gathering little games and craft things the kids could do in the back of the van and checking out maps and routes and interesting places along the way, like the Badlands.

"You know, nothing, well just about nothing, lives in the Badlands," she said. "They're called the Badlands because cowboys knew they could die there on their treks across America. Isn't that cool? I mean, *nothing* lives. Everything's dry and hot and flaky."

I could see the appeal. The rain hadn't stopped in ages. Mercy was going nuts down at the flood disaster board, and more and more people were losing all their possessions. Farmers were committing suicide and some disease from rotting cattle was spreading to the farm animals that were still alive. The Infectious Disease people said there was a slim chance the disease could be spread to humans, and only if they had a lot of contact with animal fecal material. (Just walking down the street it's hard to say who those folks would be.) One good thing, the mosquitoes had died out a bit. But about the flood: some guy had invented a sandbag-filling machine. It could fill them in one tenth of the time it took to fill them by shovel. Apparently he was going to just hand the machine over to the government to fight the flood and then try to market it to the States and other places. But the government, I think it was Bunnie Hutchison, refused his offer. She said it was better to put the single men on welfare to work shovelling than to try to use something with no track record of success. What made her think single men on the dole had a track record of success?

But speaking of Bunnie Hutchison, apparently Mercy did

have some dirt on her. It was true, she had filed for flood relief money, claiming she had no insurance when she actually did. Now a group of welfare mothers was going to try to frame her. Mercy was their key, their secret weapon. This was the plan—blackmail. The mothers would tell Bunnie Hutchison that Mercy would suppress the file, but she would have to do something for the mothers in return: she would have to save the child tax credit. At Half-a-Life, there was a petition being passed around to sign. Even at Serenity Place, they were signing up. When all the petitions had been filled out they'd be presented to Bunnie Hutchison. Mercy would have to remain anonymous in case the plan backfired and she got into trouble and lost her job. The petitions were to be put in Bunnie Hutchison's mailbox along with a note saying, "We, all of us, knew what Bunnie Hutchison was up to at the Disaster Board. Comply with our wishes, give us back our extra one thousand dollars a year, and nobody'll be the wiser." This was the plan. Naturally, Mercy was nervous. She was always nervous, but now she was really nervous. She didn't want to lose her job. She had already been under observation because of Joe.

Joe and Pillar were going through a bad time. Joe had been unfaithful. He'd got drunk after one of their big fights and picked up a girl of no more than sixteen, in a bar. They'd had sex in Joe's car and Joe ended up with a case of genital warts which, naturally, he'd passed on to Pillar. Pillar freaked out and told Joe they were history. She had her warts burned off, had an AIDS test and told the kids that their father was mentally ill. He had to leave. But, as so often before, he talked his way back into her heart and her home. He appealed to the kids, he showered her with affection and bought her flowers and said it would never ever happen again. He blamed his actions on booze and depression, on feeling unloved and unappreciated. He turned it around. If Pillar had been more attentive, Joe wouldn't have been forced to sleep with the girl. Poor Joe. Pillar said there were certain things he'd have to do if he wanted to come back. One was get a job and support them. Lish and I thought he should have to get the name *Pillar* tattooed on his penis. As his penis grew, so would the letters of her name *Pillar* get stretched out, maybe in red or black, on his swollen member, forever reminding him where it belonged. Pillar told Joe that she was tired of living with a fuck-up. She told him the only way he could be a fuck-up in his personal life was if he was brilliant in a career. Then you can get away with it because you're special. Look at Chaplin, or Picasso. But Joe wasn't an artist and Pillar was nobody's muse.

For a while Joe did lumpy labour. Every morning he went downtown to the job centre and sat around waiting to be told where to go. One day he had to sweep roads, one day he had to pick up garbage, one day he had to move pig parts from one warehouse to another. One day he had to clean the sludge from the porto-toilets on a construction site. One day he was sent to work in a glass factory. He had steel-toed boots, but no work gloves, and when he came home after twelve hours in the glass factory, his hands were all cut up. Pillar poured hydrogen per-oxide into his open cuts and Joe's screams could be heard throughout Half-a-Life. Pillar felt bad. She told Joe the next day he could wear a pair of the kids' hockey mitts. He shouted, "OH I CAN, CAN I? WELL THANK YOU VERY MUCH!!! THIS IS FUCK-ING GREAT. I'M THIRTY-EIGHT YEARS OLD AND I HAVE A WIFE AND THREE KIDS AND I HAVE A CAREER PICKING UP GLASS OFF THE FUCKING FLOOR WEARING CHILDREN'S MITTENS!!" Then for two weeks he didn't go to the job centre. He lay on the couch and drank gin and slept. Pillar told us he wore the same sweatpants every day on that couch.

Mercy heard about Joe and Pillar, as we all eventually did, and she said she would try to get him a job at the Disaster Board. Like I said, they were hiring anybody and everybody. When Pillar told Joe that Mercy might be able to get him a job with the disaster board, he yelled, "MY WHOLE FUCKING LIFE IS A DISASTER. I'M FUCKING WAY OVERQUALIFIED FOR THAT JOB I'LL TELL YOU. WHY THE FUCK WOULD I BE INTERESTED IN OTHER PEOPLE'S DISASTERS I CAN BARELY FUCKING KEEP UP WITH MY OWN. WHY DON'T *YOU* BECOME A FLOOD INSPEC-TOR IF YOU'RE SO EXCITED ABOUT IT?" And then he started laughing in a deranged way. Pillar told him she would, but she couldn't count on him to look after the kids when he could barely look after himself. She told him inspecting flooded basements was a lot less work than looking after three kids, and if he had half a brain, he'd get out of those grimy sweatpants, and take the job. Pretty soon, the dole would force him to do more lumpy labour, or he'd have to move out so Pillar could get the dole herself as a single mother. And where would Joe go?

So Mercy got him the job as a flood inspector. He had to go into people's basements with a clipboard and all sorts of forms. He had to get down all the information about every room. Like what the walls were made of, whether or not there was carpet or insulation, and how old everything was. He had to draw out the floor plan with windows and doors and everything colour-coded on graph paper with the square feet and the place where the water entered. He also had to make lists of everything damaged, how old it was, what it had cost, how much time had been spent cleaning up and on and on. It was complicated for Joe and he was one of the slowest inspectors. Mercy's bosses were asking her, "What's with this guy?"

Well, it turned out he was casing every house for his own purposes. He was taking note of which windows were unlocked, which doors had dead-bolts, and, more importantly, which ones didn't. Where the VCRs were kept, and whether or not there were home alarms installed. The first house he broke into, the owners caught him red-handed and said, "Hey, you look familiar." They figured it out and reported him to the cops *and* the Disaster Board. He was fired, naturally, fined, and put in jail. And Pillar was really alone with the kids, and Mercy was doing her best to make up for her error in judgement. So, she was in no position to get caught blackmailing Bunnie Hutchison, Minister of Families and Welfare, in a crazy scheme concocted by angry mothers on the dole.

With Joe on his way to jail for a couple of months, Pillar could focus on what she considered his good qualities. Instead of getting him out of her life, she seemed to resolve to make their relationship work upon his release. Lish and I were over there having coffee. The kids were colouring all over the back sides of disaster board inspector sheets. Pillar had a lot of them around for scrap paper. Dill was playing with Joe's guitar, dropping bits of toast inside it and then trying to get them out.

Lish asked Pillar, "What do you like about Joe?"

"Well, he's very loyal, you know . . ."

"Loyal? Yeah? But Pillar . . ."

"Yeah. And he's independent. He doesn't run with the pack."

"Anything else?"

"Yeah." Pillar hesitated and put her hair behind her ear. "He's affectionate, you know, frisky."

"My god, Pillar, what is he? A dog?"

"Lish, I'll tell you something. He's a man. And I'm damn happy to have one. You would be, too. I know it. When Joe and I wake up in the morning I'm so happy, really. Like, I tremble with happiness. My chest tightens, my eyes burn with tears of happiness. Sometimes. Like I can't believe I've got Joe. This world is so fucked up and cold and mean it's amazing Joe and I could ever even get close enough to each other to have kids. He's got a problem with employment, sure, but . . ."

"Not to mention other women," added Lish.

"That was not really his fault."

"Oh god, Pillar. Honestly, you know what he wants? He's got this perfect picture of domestic bliss: you wearing a red dress or something and no underwear and washing dishes, supper in the oven—and boning you from behind while the kids watch YTV in the other room. That's his idea of happiness."

"Well Lish, you don't even know him. At least he didn't knock me up and then disappear. At least I'm not chasing him around the countryside. At least I have more than a spoon to hold onto at night."

"Yeah, well, Pillar, he's not exactly going anywhere, is he? Even if he wasn't going to jail, he wouldn't leave here. He's got it so good. You just keep forgiving him, blaming yourself for his mistakes, cooking his dinner, smiling at his stupid guitar songs and fooling yourself into thinking you've got something really fine. The guy's a loser, Pillar."

"Yeah, well, he's my loser."

I was confused. Maybe Pillar had a point. When you're a mother on the dole you don't get a lot of opportunities to meet men. And it's damn lonely at times. Maybe Joe was better than nothing after all. Then again, is it stupid to want something better when you are on the dole? So maybe Lish was right. Why not roam around the countryside looking for the real thing? What have we got to lose? Pillar could probably do better than Joe, but could Lish ever find the busker? And make him stay put? And would she want him after she got him? And if you keep having kids with different guys? What does that mean? Try every nationality, say. Sitting at the kitchen table could be like a UN meeting. All God's children, black and yellow, brown and white. Well, I know for a fact that Dill's father must have had some kind of red hair gene in his body. He certainly doesn't get that from my side. Red hair is recessive, right, so I would have to find the grandparents or the parents of every guy I had an encounter with and see if they had red hair. There could be baldness or dye jobs thrown in there, so really the chances of finding a redhead are remote. And besides, they probably wouldn't want anything to do with me. Or Dill. I would have to concoct some sort of story about who his father was. Immaculate conception wouldn't work. So what happens if Dill decides to go off and find him? Some fictional man? And comes back all bitter telling me I'm nuts for leading him on that way and then he becomes a serial killer of women who look like me.

Why didn't I just tell him the truth? What was my frigging problem? 'Course I've created fictional men before. My dad, for instance. In a story in school. I wrote a poem about him, but it wasn't really him, about him sailing and me drowning and how he sailed right past me at two hundred miles an hour and plucked me from the freezing water of Falcon Lake. Then we both climbed the rigging and brought her home. I realize now that you can't be up in the rigging when you're sailing a boat, but the image of me and him up there silhouetted against the setting sun, all tanned and tough, was a good one. What actually happened was that my uncle took my dad out in his

catamaran and my dad fell off the edge and ripped his swim-
ming trunks and had to sit in the hold with a towel around his
bottom until they got back to the dock. My mom and my aunt
were sitting on lawn chairs and when they saw him they burst
out laughing and my dad said, "I'm so happy to be the butt of
your joke," and my mom said, "Oooh good one. A merry heart
doeth good like a medicine, Geoffrey." She appreciated any
joke. She loved to laugh. She was always laughing at the goofy
things I did. She was a great audience. She'd had a good life, a
funny life. The day my dad dies is going to be a lot sadder than
the day my mom died. I know that for sure.

I had never really known my dad, and now I wasn't giving
Dill the chance to know his dad. Maybe I should write down
everything I know about every guy I was with and then let Dill
choose who . . . but what difference does it make? At the very
least, I knew I was his mother.

Things were wrapping up at Hope and Maya's school. As soon
as they had picked up their final report cards we could hit the
road. Lish had actually volunteered at the school a couple of
times. She hadn't wanted to, but the girls had convinced her
that it would be fun. And, they said, if she was so critical of
school, she should really know what it was she was being critical
of. The first day she volunteered she took the twins with her.
She thought she could put them off the idea of school by showing them what it was about. But everything had changed since
Lish had been in school. The teacher and the kids thought Lish
was cool. They wanted to know about the spider on her hat.
Desks weren't lined up in rows. Instead they had tables, and the
kids moved from one to another, depending on their activity.
The kids chose their own themes and read their own stories to
the class. They conducted their own scientific experiments.
They moved freely around the classroom, using playing cards
and string and books and their own shoes for math exercises.
They had mice, and plants, and painted scenes on the windows.
Some listened quietly to music in the hallway if they were

feeling uptight and moody. Others were encouraged to sign up for one-on-one conferences with the teacher to talk about stuff. They baked bread and charted the progress of the moon. They were up-to-date on the flood disaster. Parents were encouraged to volunteer and offer suggestions. The kids had their own personal files on the class computer. Nobody was sent to the principal's office. Nobody was made to feel stupid. The teacher ate lunch with them. They put on plays and poetry (their own) readings and dances for whoever was interested. The twins ended up loving it and crying when they had to leave. They made Lish promise they would be able to go to nursery school in the fall. I was there when they were begging her to sign them up for the fall.

"God," said Lish, "I think I'll have to have another baby."

"Why, Lish?" I asked. "Just think, all your girls could be in school. The twins at least for half days and you could have some time to do your own thing, go out, get a job, go to university, oh I guess not, but you know, learn how to make shoes, paint, read, lie in the park. It would be great."

"I guess. I don't know. Besides, when all your kids are in school, the dole figures it's time for you to get a job. Now that you have no excuse to be at home."

"So. Maybe you'd like that. You could decorate other people's houses or help them plant gardens or read books to blind people. You could have your own personal catering business with all your garlic dishes. You could set up a secondhand shop. You could sew costumes for the theatres. You could freelance and work out of your home and have your own hours, and you know how to do tons of stuff."

"I think it would be easier to have another kid."

"Are you kidding? With who?" I threw my arms up in the air. "At least have one with somebody who doesn't live in a van or disappears. Then at least have a kid with someone who has some cash, someone who would stick around and help you out, invest in RRSPs or cook a meal once in a while."

"I don't want anyone to help me out."

"Why not?"

"I don't know. Because you have to compromise then. At least with no man around I don't have any expectations. If I don't have any expectations, I'll never be disappointed. And, I'm too disagreeable."

"You are not disagreeable."

"Yes I am."

"No you're not."

"Yes I am. Dammit."

We both started to laugh. In two days we'd be leaving Half-a-Life, not for long, but for awhile. And that was a good thing, too. I thought it would be nice for Lish to get another letter from the busker. Just to encourage her, strengthen her resolve. And so she did. This time it was a postcard with a picture of a sunset.

Dear Alicia,

Did you get my other letter? I'm doing pretty good here in Colorado. The inside of my mouth is burnt to hell but hey, at least I'm not wearing a suit and tie. I've had my picture in a few local papers and had a late night spot on TV. I'm becoming something of an institution around here I think. That is, if you can call a fire-eating clown an institution. A bunch of us are sleeping in a tent in Denver. We always get moved along by the cops, so the park changes just about every night. One of my buddies was shot when he was doing a show downtown. He's from Australia and so he doesn't have any medical insurance. We're taking care of him ourselves. We're cowboys man! At night I cover myself with a blanket made out of your hair, metaphorically speaking. Of course. Well, gotta go. Someday I know I'll make it to Canada again. Has it stopped raining up there?

Love, Gotcha

Yup. Lish was psyched. "God," she said, "he's a terrible writer." And then she kissed the postcard. I was unimpressed with that but Lish didn't notice. We were Colorado-bound. Everything was happening according to plan. If you can believe it.

Our main problem was going to be Dill. He was a good kid, happy most of the time, but he was only ten months old and it's not easy to be stuck in a car seat all day when you're ten months old. We'd be making a lot of stops. And of course there were all the girls to entertain him, and as long as we weren't making a lot of sudden stops and starts he could be taken out of his car seat and allowed to sit and play in the back with the girls.

Lish had her money from her dad. I had some extra cash I had saved. And Sing Dylan had given us some money he said he had saved for a rainy day.

Good one, Sing. Naturally, it was raining when we left. It was a good thing, too, because without the rain we wouldn't have noticed that the left windshield wiper didn't work, and we weren't going far without it. We stopped at the first garage and had to spend fifteen dollars on a new wiper. Lish was fuming. She couldn't believe Rodger was so dense that he hadn't noticed the wiper was broken. Where had he been living? The Sahara? So that was our first major expense. I told Lish that it was better than getting caught in a downpour somewhere in the middle of nowhere and finding out, but she said she'd rather have made it outside city limits before something went wrong. She had a point. At least the sliding door was still on.

I want to tell you right now I was feeling okay about the way things were going. There was something I needed to know though. That was how optimistic was Lish feeling about finding the busker and what exactly he meant to her. Part of me knew that he was more like a sweet memory, a dream, but not a flesh and blood thing really, a person. 'Course the twins were proof of his existence, but Lish never knew the busker in a big way, never actually, you know, loved him, really. I mean, how could you after a week? Wouldn't it be better if she never found him?

131

It would be, wouldn't it? That way he could just remain a sweet memory. And living in Half-a-Life, it helps to have these memories.

As for how optimistic she felt about finding him, well, that was another story. She seemed to waver between being absolutely positive to thinking she was a total fool for even trying to find this guy, let alone giving a damn about him. After all, he had stolen from her, ditched her, been busted for drugs, lived in a tent, and as far as she knew wrote terrible letters. Sometimes she talked about how great it would be to spend just one passionate night with him, just to feel young and crazy and alive again. Sometimes she talked about marching up to him after a show with the twins and grabbing the hat he threw down for money and saying, "We'll take that, thank you very much. By the way, these are your children, you low-life prick!" And then marching off. She never talked about bringing him back to Half-a-Life. You have to be strong to live in Half-a-Life, and frankly I don't think Gotcha would have lasted a week. It's a nutty life when you try to combine romance and taking care of little kids. Now this is what we had in the van. And actually, it was quite amazing that we had the van at all.

Up until the evening before we left, Rodger was going to change his mind about letting us use it because welfare had scooped him up for some kind of job demolishing the old meat packing plant and he was going to have to use it to get to work. Fortunately, Safety Canada or some such thing stepped in and said it was utterly criminal to send inexperienced men on welfare in to work with explosives and dangerous chemicals and heavy machinery. Only skilled workers could do that. What the hell, Bunnie Hutchison was going to try to get around it. She probably wouldn't have shed a tear to see a few single welfare recipients go up in smoke or die slowly from asbestos poisoning. Rodger said welfare was getting too dangerous and he decided to just be done with it and live once and for all off his mother and write short stories in her basement until something better came along. So we got the van after all, complete with a bumper sticker that read, "I Brake for Hallucinations," a back bumper that we had to hang onto the van with wire and pry off when we needed to put oil in the engine (which was in the back behind the bumper), and an ignition that could be started with a screwdriver. This is what we filled it with:

- one tiny ripped pup tent (some of us would sleep in the van)
- one Coleman stove
- one cooler full of fruit and vegetables and crackers and juice and some beer from Tanya and alfalfa sprout and cucumber sandwiches on rice cakes from Terrapin (who seemed to be getting skinnier and skinnier)
- one ghetto blaster and assorted tapes
- candles for emergencies and ambience
- paper
- markers
- Barbies
- toys
- books
- diapers
- sunscreen
- Dill's ultra-deluxe two-hundred-and-fifty-dollar stolen stroller. (It had become a bit beat up after the women in Half-a-Life started borrowing it for bringing home the groceries.)
- bag of clothes for each of Lish's kids, one bag for Lish, and one bag for Dill and me
- maps
- spare tire
- tire jack
- jumper cables
- motor oil
- pillows and blankets
- two inflatable air mattresses
- two women
- five children

Teresa had promised to get our mail and cover for us if any dole patrols showed up, but that probably wouldn't happen. She told us, "Youse all have a great trip and don't turn around halfway and come back neither. And get me some cheap American smokes." She would also make sure our toilets didn't overflow and the rain didn't come through our windows. (Even when they were closed, rain would gather on the window ledge and sometimes seep under the caulking and run down the wall.) Nobody in Half-a-Life had their beds against the walls, and kids were constantly falling out of bed. In public housing it sounds like an explosion. Mercy, who is so tense all the time, bangs on the door of whoever she thinks fell out of bed so she can tell us not to move the kid too quickly, not before checking all the bones. Apparently she heard of a kid who had fallen out of bed the wrong way, broke her neck, and was paralyzed from the waist down forevermore.

It's funny that Mercy is working for the Disaster Board because we think her life is a bit of a disaster—that is, the way it's set up so disaster can never happen, so pinched and safe and boarded up from every danger. And yet she's the one who tells us we're fooling ourselves thinking we're secure. You'd think, with that philosophy, she'd be the one to let loose, flirt with danger, live on the edge, take risks. Her motto is: "Disaster can strike anytime, anywhere." According to her, Dill could choke on a piece of Lego, Hope and Maya might go to school one day and never return. These things we women of Half-a-Life knew. But I think Mercy was still hung up on that disappearing Mercedes, the car she was named after because it was the last memory her mother had of her father. Mercy was just trying to keep things from going away or getting lost. Her photographs were all wrapped up in plastic and binding. All her toys and books put away in the same place each time; her bike helmets and mosquito netting, too. Her fluorescent clothing, her never-changing routine, her obsessiveness with the safety of her daughter, her nervousness. It occurred to me that she and I were the same, sort of. Both our mothers were dead and our fathers were just, well, they were just out there. And so was Dill's and so was the twins'. And so was Lish's. All these missing fathers, not even dead and buried. That would be easy. No, they were just out there somewhere, like space junk orbiting planets populated with wives and girlfriends and sons and daughters.

Speaking of fathers, the day we left was a Friday. Deadbeat Dad's day. Sherree's ex was back for Jasmine. Sherree, who was a born again Christian, and Jasmine lived in the basement with eight or nine cats. Tanya's kids were going off in separate directions and the librarian was there to pick up Teresa's and Marjorie's boys, both his. Also a couple of others I had seen but didn't really know. The mothers who were saying goodbye to their kids had their lists of things to do and things not to do, for the fathers: brush their teeth, don't lose their clothes, and so on. I don't know whether it was harder to keep them for the weekend or to say goodbye.

Even Sarah came out. It wasn't her weekend to see Emmanuel, she was just out for the social occasion of Deadbeat Dad's day. That morning everybody was huddling under umbrellas and black garbage bags. Sarah got wet like always: she didn't seem to mind the rain. Sherree's ex had barely said hello to Jasmine before he looked pissed off and fed up with her. I remember Lish telling me that when Maya or Hope—I can't remember which one—was born she had gone over to Sherree's place to show them the baby, and Sherree's ex had said, "Don't point that thing at me." Now he hurled Jasmine's little plastic knapsack into the back part, it wasn't really a seat, of his Camaro and said in a very irritated tone of voice, "I said hurry up, get in the damn car already."

Terrapin was actually allowing her daughters to go out with their father, a macrobiotic software programmer who had had a nervous breakdown but was recovering, thanks to the Lord and a daily journal of affirmations or some such thing. Terrapin said she could feel his pain, and although at first she was angry when he had his breakdown, she was now sympathetic. She was just so thankful he wasn't put on any mind-altering medication. She was sure it was diet-related, though I didn't know how that could be, because the man looked like he hardly ate anything at all.

Another couple was exchanging insults over the heads of their two kids, and the two kids were hitting each other.

Apparently he was accusing her of putting his phone number in the *Buy and Sell*, advertising all sorts of things really cheap: like VCRs for ten bucks and a 1992 Volvo for one hundred dollars and furniture for free and stuff like that, so he'd get tons of phone calls and be driven up the wall. She said it was the only thing left for her to do to get even with him, and all the other women, even Sarah, were laughing; she said she'd already had three arrests for assaulting him—one more and she'd lose custody rights, maybe even visitation rights. This was stupid, because she actually seemed like a pretty good mother, she just had it in for her ex. Lish told me that even this woman's own mother was on her ex's side. Both thought she was crazy because she had been misdiagnosed as a schizophrenic. They never thought to get mad at the doctor. Anyway, so now all she could do to him were non-violent things like the *Buy and Sell* prank. I think she also wrote country songs about him and performed them at amateur Saturdays at the Blues Jam.

Geez, I tell you, we'd never have had kids if we'd known it would turn out like this. And besides, Lish said that women are always hornier when they're ovulating because it's nature's cruel trick to get them pregnant. During that time the body takes over the brain and they get themselves in trouble. It's not the brain talking, it's the egg. Well, Lish never thought having the baby was a problem. She just wasn't sure she could handle having the man. It made me think maybe I was better off not knowing Dill's father. I couldn't see myself shouting instructions from the front door of Half-a-Life every Friday evening and waiting, lonely and worried as hell, every Sunday evening for Dill's return, waiting to see if his hair had been cut, or worrying about him growing fond of some other woman. Some of the women in Half-a-Life worried about their exes leaving the country with the kid or kids. Especially after the movie of the week had been on because it was usually about some nut who kidnaps his kid or tries to swap him with a different one or something else entirely freaky. I doubted Camaro Guy was up for that, let alone any of the other Deadbeat Dads. But if some kid wasn't home at six on Sunday, oh boy, the cops were called, and there were police escorts home for the kids, trailing the father's car all the way to Half-a-Life, cursing and crying and recriminations and shouts of *see you in court* and name-calling and sad, mixed-up kids. Like I said, it's amazing how love can turn so rotten.

I noticed Jasmine had a little tear in her black tights that tore a little more as she crawled up onto the front seat of the red Camaro. I could smell the unmistakable odour of fried hamburger. Even if some of the mothers were losing their kids for the weekend, they weren't saying goodbye to cheap meat and noodle dishes. Somewhere in between the time the women said goodbye to their kids and went upstairs to their quiet apartments, they'd have to find something good, maybe the look of the sky or the smile on their kid's face as they drove away or a whiff of something that reminded them of a long time ago or a coupon for a two-for-one deal at Safeway or an invitation to the Scrabble tournament with tequila in the block that night. Something good, otherwise I would imagine the quiet of an empty apartment could kill you.

Anyway, Lish had spent about an hour deciding what to wear for our first day on the road. She was wearing a pair of Hope's pink plastic sunglasses and frosted lipstick to match. Her hair was plastered back, held in place by her hat. Her spider had been polished for the occasion. Her black t-shirt was cut off so low in the front that with every little bump in the road her breasts jumped up and down and teetered for a while afterwards. She was drinking Roots ginger-ale and belching on purpose in between gulps. Around her neck, she had her good luck charm in a little leather pouch. The charm was actually Maya's dried up umbilical cord with some rosemary and a couple of bay leaves thrown in. She had stuck the postcard of the sunset from Gotcha onto the ceiling of the van above her head. The kids, in the back of the van, were quiet. Their black eyes shone and I noticed they were holding hands. Nobody said anything. We all stared off to the side or ahead of us down the highway.

This was the first time Dill had left the city, our city. Centre of the universe. And right now an official disaster area. His head had fallen onto his chest. His rice cake had fallen to the floor of the van. He was asleep.

By suppertime we were well and truly on the road. If things worked according to plan we would make it to Fargo, North Dakota by the kids' bedtime. The van could only go about 55 miles an hour without starting to shudder, and with the load of stuff and all the kids and everything we really didn't want to push it. Mercy had told us that a vehicle could be controlled when a tire blows at 55 miles an hour but not faster than that. She said that good tires were the most important safety feature of any vehicle. She said after 40,000 kilometres of wear and tear most tires are liable to blow. But at a hundred bucks a pop who can afford new tires? Not us, that's for sure. Or Rodger. Or anybody else I know except my dad, and he didn't need new tires, because since my mom's accident he rarely ever drove. Anyway, we'd go slow. It would be a bit of a drag.

Like my mom, I was fond of driving fast. I remember a family trip we took to Quebec, and my mom almost went insane because my dad was driving so slow. When we got to Montreal, she said that was it. She told my dad to take a nap in the back seat and she'd drive. She said, "Geoffrey, if we're going to get anywhere in Montreal we have to drive like Montrealers do." By the time we arrived at our hotel my dad was pale and stiff in the back seat. My mom was flushed with excitement and enormously proud of herself. Actually, the last time I talked to my dad just before Dill was born, he said he wasn't driving anymore 'cause of night vision or lack of it or something. He said he only needed to go to the university and the grocery store, and why bother insuring a car and risking an accident to boot? He had invited me and Dill to his house to visit him, but I figured if he was too stubborn or terrified to keep a car of his own and use it to visit us, then damned if I was going to bus it to his place with Dill and bags and stroller and stuff. Just because my mom, his wife, died in a car—well, she died in the ditch, but she wouldn't have got there if it hadn't been for the car about to be stolen—didn't mean that he could just refuse to drive a car. Hadn't my mother had any effect on him at all? I mean, while she was counselling women to get up and leave their husbands, live, start fresh, take a chance, move, move, move, drive away now, he, her husband, was just dying inside. Had it ever occurred to her to give him the same advice? Or had it ever occurred to him to take that advice? Probably. But something that occurs to us doesn't mean it's going to happen, does it? Look at Lish and me.

Here we were, going to Colorado to find some guy because it occurred to Lish that we could. I mean, people travel, they go places, they try to find people. Why not us? But that didn't mean we'd find him. That didn't mean we wouldn't go back home to Half-a-Life and the rain and Serenity Place and sad Sarah and Sing Dylan and Podborczintski and all the other people and start doing the same things all over again. All it meant was that we had decided to do something adventurous and then we had done it. If it didn't work out the way we had hoped it to, fine. Who cares how it all ends? We had taken the steps toward something. Anything. Some people wouldn't understand how important that is for a woman on the dole. It's like that song, "The Tennessee Waltz." My mom used to play it on the piano. It starts off beautifully: "I was dancing with my darling to the Tennessee Waltz, when an old friend I happened to spy. I introduced him to my darling, and while they were dancing, my friend stole my sweetheart from me. I remember the night and the Tennessee Waltz. Now I know just how much I have lost. Well I lost my little darlin' . . ." But then we get the cold hard cruel facts of the song and it's just way too sad. If we could just block out the second part of the song from our minds and sing the first part. But we can't. The first part of the song is so beautiful because the second part is so sad. We can't have one without the other. It doesn't turn out like we thought. But still it's a beautiful song.

I was lost in a reverie about this when I heard Lish's voice: "Lucy!"

Dill had slipped down in his car seat and looked like he was choking to death. His head was where his waist should have been, squeezed between the back of the chair and the bar in front, and his legs were dangling close to the floor of the van. Lish slammed on the brakes and pulled over to the side of the road and I scrambled over to Dill to rescue him. I managed to get him out of the seat with all the girls hovering around saying, "Is he alright, is Dilly alright," and Lish sitting behind the wheel muttering, *oh my god oh my god oh my god.* Dill was absolutely fine. In fact, he loved the attention and started giggling as the girls stroked his head and arms and back and stomach, and Lish and I stared at each other and at him and back at each other. I knew Lish was going to have another fit like the one about the curbs and the strollers she had had in the curry restaurant.

"You see," she began, "you see, Lucy? Just because we're poor we have inferior fucking car seats, borrowed secondhand pieces of shit that sooner strangle a kid than protect him. We're driving in a piece of shit with bald tires held together with rope and wire, and why? Because we're poor! We can't even travel to a stupid place in the States without risking our lives. No wonder people like us are always dying before everyone else. We have to live with all these stupid risks, even in our apartments. Bad wiring, leaking Freon from our inferior fridges, mice in our walls, roach spray making our hair fall out, wet mouldy rotten drywall and insulation that makes our kids cough all night, windows with broken screens so kids can fall out of them, burnt out lights in the hallway, elevators that don't work, neighbours that are psychopaths, obscene graffiti on the walls, cops circling round all the time but never when you need them—"

"Lish, the car seat thing could have happened to a rich kid, too. He's fine, don't worry. I probably did the strap thing wrong. It's not because we're poor, we're stupid." I laughed.

"Yeah, but we're poor because we're stupid. And being poor makes us more stupid."

"No, it doesn't. It makes other people think we're stupid. You know there are so many pissed-off people who are considered much more successful than me, but I think I'm happy. I feel happy. I don't know why. I have Dill. I'm young. We're on the road. Stuff's happening. I wish it was enough to be happy. It should be, you know. That should be the mark of success, you know, just a general feeling of happiness. I mean considering everything, I think I'm fucking amazing for being happy. *Happy, happy, happy,* isn't it a funny word? You know some guy could come along and say *you still happy? Gosh darn,* he'd say and shake his head and say, *Well, okay, here's your cheque for five million dollars, keep up the good work.*"

"Jesus, how much caffeine have you had today, Lucy?"

"Oh, about ten cups, but it's not that. Just moving, you know, this moving ahead thing makes me feel awake and—"

"Happy, yeah yeah yeah. But you worry a lot."

"Yeah, that's true, but maybe worrying makes me happy. It motivates me. I think worrying must relax me. I'm very optimistic about my future."

"You are?"

"Yeah, I am. And so are you, or we wouldn't even be in this stupid van travelling down the highway. You wouldn't get up every morning and put on music and cook your garlic dishes and have real fun with your kids who actually like you, and go to the library and wear your goofy pink dress and play in that little sunlight on your wall. What do you want anyway?"

"I do not play in the little sunlight on my wall."

"Yes, you do. When you think no one's looking, you stop and make these little shapes and stuff and you—"

"Lucy. I do not play in the little sunlight on my wall, as you put it. I perform complex shadow puppet theatre."

"Ah." We were both laughing. In fact we were really laughing hard. And driving slow. And people passing us were staring at us, as if two women laughing hard in a beater van with five kids in the back of it was the strangest thing in the world.

"Oh Lucy, why can't we get paid for the things we're good at?"

"Well, in a way we do. You know, by the dole. We're like government employees, you know, freelance ones. Those people who just passed us wouldn't have had anything to stare at if they weren't paying taxes to keep people like us alive."

"Hmmmmmm. It's a good thing I didn't introduce you to my dad at that convention. He'd hate you."

"Really?" I said.

"Guaranteed," said Lish.

I was shocked. It had never occurred to me that somebody might hate me for being on the dole. I hadn't meant to be on the dole. I wasn't planning to be on it for a long time, not forever, anyway. I didn't want anybody to hate me. What would happen if I started hating everybody before they could hate me? I'd have an awful life! I'd be a terrible mother! I'd become an alcoholic! Fuck him, I thought, why would he hate me? He didn't even know me!

We had been on the road for fifty minutes and not one out of the five—well, out of four, really; Dill had a diaper on— children had asked to stop to pee. There had not been one argument, not one shriek, not one bad word, not one painful accident (besides the car seat incident, but that was only painful for everyone watching it happen to Dill and not for Dill himself), not one spilled box of apple juice, not one object thrown from the window, and not one automotive breakdown. *Uneventful*, a gossip columnist would have written of our trip at that point. We passed flooded fields, abandoned homes and barns, machinery, and even whole deserted towns. The highway was clear of water, other than the shallow puddles this morning's rain had formed. The ditches, though, were full of dark, dirty water. Every now and then we saw a piece of some kid's abandoned raft. In Morris we saw a big billboard that read, "Give money to the chamber of commerce. Help pay for the flood victims' hotel bills." Lish had read that they were all covered by the government, so she snorted when she read the billboard. We wondered if Mercy's blackmail plan would work with Bunnie Hutchison. We saw a billboard that read, "Jesus is the way, the truth and the light."

We saw another one reading, "An unborn baby's heart starts beating at four weeks."

Hope read every billboard out loud to herself and said, "Hey mom, Lucy, didja know that a baby's heart starts beating when it's four weeks old?"

Lish hollered to the back, "An unborn baby's heart, Hope."

"What?" Hope yelled to the front. "Stubborn? A stubborn baby's heart starts beating?—"

"*Unborn, Un-born*," Lish yelled back.

"How can you have a baby that's *unborn?*" asked Hope. "You have to be born to be a baby."

"Hope," said Lish. "A baby that's still in the womb is unborn. It's alive in there, it's just not out yet."

"Well," said Hope, "you have to be out to be alive, don't you?"

"No," said Lish. "The babies inside eat and pee and all that stuff living people do."

"Oooh, yuck," said Hope. "How big would the heart be? About the size of a lentil? MOM? I'M ASKING YOU A QUESTION!"

Lish put in a k.d. lang tape and turned the volume up. We chugged along through Morris and St. Jean and some other places. We were headed for Emerson and the border.

Rodger had assured us that he had removed all traces of marijuana and anything else from the van. Unfortunately, there was nothing we could do about the "I Brake For Hallucinations" bumper sticker. Lish had taken off her sunglasses and hung them on the neckline of her shirt. Dill had dozed off again and the girls were drawing. It was our time of the day. Dusk. My favourite time. This time and very early morning. These were the times people like us made sense. Before and after the hullaballoo of the work day, before and after the real time, when interest rates and house taxes and rental equipment and bad debts and loan payments and funeral homes and car washes and TV repair shops and malls and soup kitchens and utility companies and garages and car dealers and daycares and daytimers and mandates and agendas and health clinics were all busy and we were hustled off to the wings. In the early morning and at dusk we emerged, purposeful, engaged, necessary. People stopped and smiled at us. We smiled at ourselves. During the day, the busy busy work day, we were temporarily forgotten. We mothers and children. Like the smell of Simonize floor wax and the distinct orange of Mercurochrome, we were reminders of another time.

"Okay, Lucy," said Lish. "When we get to the border, let me do the talking, not that we have anything to hide, I just don't want them to get suspicious."

"Suspicious? Why would they get suspicious of me? Of totally normal me? Look at you. They'll take one look at you and think you're some kind of escaped mental patient or something. Me. You gotta be kidding."

"No, no, Luce, you see I'm so obvious, they won't even bother to bother me. They'll worry about you. You know, being so normal and together-looking."

"Yeah, well, they'll worry more about me if I don't say anything. Why don't I fire up a chain saw and wave it out the window when we go past? Why don't I just pretend to be dead in the back of the van? Geez, I can't help it if I'm normal-looking."

"No, no, they have a strict policy on bodies going across the border. You can't even go over with the chicken pox. Rodger and I tried when Hope and Maya were two and three and they took one look at their spots and made us turn around and go home."

"Well, you should have been at home anyway, if they were sick."

"So, Lucy, when they ask us where we're going, we have to know, and when they ask us how long we're staying, we have to know that, too, and how much money we have on us, and we have to prove that the kids are ours. Or maybe that's coming back. Is it going or coming? Now I can't remem—"

"Lish! Look at that sign. Over there. Look. Where I'm pointing."

"So? You want to buy honey? I don't think we can bring honey across the border. You don't feed honey to Dill, do you?

Kids under a year aren't supposed to eat honey for some reason. Mercy told me that, naturally. Although Teresa used to smear it all over her kid's soother to quiet him down and he lived, so who knows?"

"No. No. Oh my god. You know what, Lish? That's the place, right under that sign in the ditch. Where my mom died. I know it. Right under that honey sign. I can't believe it's still there. You'd think they'd have taken it down."

"Geez, I guess. But, well, why? They're still selling honey. Probably."

"Yeah, I know, but who would feel like buying honey from a guy who has his billboard right over the place where somebody died? Like, was killed."

"I don't know. But Lucy, I don't mean to sound callous or anything, but nobody but you and your dad really would know that somebody, I mean your mom, died there. You think he should move it over a bit or just take it down completely— Lucy?"

"What." I had started to cry. I wasn't going to cry anymore about it but now I had started to cry. Now I was crying just like everybody else seemed to be. This was turning out to be one wet summer.

"Do you want to stop for a minute by the sign or . . . ?" Lish was peering into the rearview mirror.

"No, no. Well. Okay. Yeah, okay. Do we have time?"

"Lucy. Of course we have time. Time is what we have."

"Fine."

"Okay. KIDS WE'RE STOPPING. SIT ON YOUR BUMS AND IF YOU HAVE TO PEE, GET READY TO DO IT NOW. Or maybe not Lucy? Would it be okay if like they peed here if they have to? Or we could wait, we're almost at the border."

Lish stopped the van and she and I got out. I stared at the honey sign.

"Lucy?" said Lish.

"No, no. Of course they can pee here. Geez. She's not buried here. Look at that sign. It's peeling. My dad said when my mom died they had just put up this new honey sign, 'cause

the guy, the honey guy, came out to check his new sign when
the cops were here and my dad and everything right after, and a
lady cop who was with my dad asked me later if he was okay
because he kept asking the guy *Do you sell a lot of honey? Do you
sell a lot of honey?* and you know my mom lay there. And now
the sign is peeling and all worn out looking. It's so weird, like
because for me my mom died, you know, like yesterday. She
dies almost every day in my mind, you know, it's fresh. But look
at that sign. God, you must think I'm a total basket case. I'm
sorry about this."

"You don't have to aplogize Lu—"

"Lish!"

"What?"

"The kids are trying to get out of the van. You better go and
let them out before they bugger up the sliding door."

Lish muttered something and moved along the shoulder of
the highway back towards the van. I stared at the ditch and the
sign. I couldn't go into the ditch because it was full of water.
The honey sign, which was stuck into a farmer's field on the
other side of the ditch, had water about two or three feet up its
post. Why on earth would someone want to steal that stupid
car? I could picture my mom lying there wearing my dad's big
windbreaker and her wool skirt and sneakers, lying there on her
back as she always did when she slept, holding that big briefcase
of files across her chest. Or had it been flung beside her or way
off into the field? All I know is that the guy who killed her flung
it out of the car after her, or at her. The records of those
women's lives. My mom was desperate to keep them, to preserve
them and protect them.

The guy had actually thrown them out of the car at her.
Why? Did he think it was the right thing to do? Was it some
crazy notion of his of respecting her last wishes? He hadn't been
thinking of the right thing to do when he slammed his gun over
my mom's head and threw her in the ditch to die. Why did he
give her the files? The files of all those women trying to escape
their lives, trying to find something better, trying to find happiness. 'Course they wouldn't have all the details, like whether or

not they played in squares of sunlight on their walls, if they
wore spiders on their hats, if they ate hamburger every other
day, if they had ever made love in a yellow canola field tenderly
or passionately or awkwardly. If they preferred dresses or pants,
if they shaved their legs or didn't, or if they preferred red peppers to green. Stuff was happening. Even in Half-a-Life. Little
things, but it all added up to something big. To our lives. It was
happening all along. These were our lives. This was it. My mom
was hanging on to the lives, the recorded lives, of these women.
We might escape, but what if we didn't? What if we lived in
Half-a-Life all our lives, poor, lonely, proud, happy? If we did,
we did. These were our lives. If we couldn't escape them, we'd
have to live them.

When my mom died I wanted to know every detail of her
life. When did she have her first perm? Had she suffered from
post-partum depression? Did she have a lot of friends when she
was a little kid? Why did she want to be a therapist? Didn't she
sometimes just hate her clients? Was she in love with my dad?
Had she ever had an affair? With a woman? Did she enjoy sex?
Did she have any recurring nightmares? How did she get that
scar on the back of her leg? Who could tell me? Why hadn't I
found out all these things when I'd had the chance? And suddenly it occurred to me that Dill and Lish's kids and all the kids
of Half-a-Life might want to know the details of our lives, too,
right down to the last squalid detail.

Sometimes you can keep someone almost alive, still alive,
by remembering the details, by always remembering. I could
hear the girls laughing at each other as they squatted by the side
of the road, peeing. Lish was giving them instructions. Dill was
still sleeping. Good ol' Dill. He had no idea who my mom was,
who his dad was, who the twins' dad was, where we were going,
when we'd be back. All he knew was that he was with me right
now and right here. I thought of my dad, scared stiff in the car
while my mom sped around enjoying herself, unafraid.
Sometimes the memory of the living hurts worse than the
memory of the dead.

It came to me suddenly that while I was spending so much

time remembering my dead mother, I was forgetting to remember my father, who was alive. My mother may have been what I needed, but my father was what I had.

"Lish," I called over to where the others were. "I've got to make a phone call."

"What?" Cars were swooshing past us, their occupants staring at us curiously. A VW van drove past us slowly and two guys in it gave us a peace sign and honked their horn. Lish and I rolled our eyes at each other.

"At the border. I have to make a call."

"Who're you calling?"

"My dad."

"Really?"

"Yup."

"Okey doke."

We were still kind of hollering at each other because of the wind and the cars and everything. The girls were just finishing up. Letitia was crying a bit because she'd peed on her dress, her favourite dress. Alba, in her bossiest voice, was telling her, "Well, you should have spread your legs farther apart and lifted your dress high, right mom? Right mom? RIGHT MOM? MOM, MOM, LETITIA SHOULD HAVE SPREAD HER—"

"YES ALBA! She should have. Drop it already. She's already forgotten about it. Good grief. Lucy, Lucy, I'm sorry this has all gotten so . . . GET IN THE VAN," she yelled, "YOU'LL FALL IN THE DITCH LEAVE THAT GARBAGE ALONE. Geez Hope, Maya, haul Alba and Letitia into the van," Lish said.

"Ugh, she's covered in pee, I'm not touching her," said Hope.

"ALBA HELP YOUR SISTER RIGHT NOW FOR GOD'S SAKE HER DRESS IS ALREADY DRY."

"I always have to do everything, why can't Maya. . ."

"Oh no, Dill's awake now, Luce," said Lish. "He looks pissed off. Maybe you should nurse him here. It's okay, Dilly, your mama's coming. Can you guys entertain Dill for a sec? Luce, I'm sorry this has all got so, you know, emotional." She quieted down a bit as we got closer to each other. Lish dragged out the word *emotional* to make it sound ironic and comical. She knew it was one of those words that didn't mean a hell of a lot and sounds cold when you just say it. "Are you okay?" she asked.

"Yeah, yeah, I'm just fine. But now I'm leaking all over the place. My right breast feels like it's going to explode. I better nurse him."

"Well, so far in one short stop we've got you crying and leaking milk, we've got the girls peeing on themselves, we've got some more rain coming right now, we've got fresh honey, we've got Dill screaming, we've got the girls bickering, I could use another cold root beer, or better a shot of tequila, and hey hey hey we've been on the road for all of ninety minutes. Isn't travel relaxing? I told you we needed a holiday."

"Okay. Well let's just drive to the border and then we'll give the kids a chance to run around for a bit and I'll nurse Dill and call my dad and you can just sit . . . and like that."

"Think he'll be home?"

"My dad?"

"Yeah."

"Definitely."

"Lucy?"

"What."

"I'm, you know, sorry about your mom. ALBA," she said over her shoulder, "STOP TALKING ABOUT THE DRESS."

"I know. Thanks."

We both took big cartoon breaths with our mouths clamped shut, and looked at each other for a second or two. Then I said urgently, "Lish, watch what you're doing or we'll hit the ditch. I can't swim."

"Right."

In the fifteen minutes it took us to reach the border Letitia had removed her dress and panties and shoes and sat stoically, completely naked, in the back of the van. Alba was waving Letitia's panties out of the window, threatening to show them to passersby. Letitia refused even to look at her, let alone take the bait and lunge for her panties. Hope and Maya were arguing about how many planets there are, nine or ten or thirteen or twenty-three, and Dill was back in his car seat chewing on an uncapped Crayola marker. A glorious fuchsia dye stained his lips, his teeth, his tongue, his cheeks, his hands, and his saliva, mixed with breast milk, was drooling out of the side of his mouth in fuchsia.

The guy at the border pointed at Dill behind us and said, "I think the baby has a problem." As Lish had insisted, she did the talking. I think the border guys were a little confused, not sure exactly what to do with us, but it gave me time to wander off to a pay phone. Lish started filling out some forms and I took Dill with me to the phone. The girls romped around in the patch of grass behind the Customs building.

I dialed and listened to a few rings. The answering machine came on. My dad's voice sounded far away and serious, very professional: "I'm sorry I am unable to answer the phone at this time. Please leave a message with your name and number and I will call you as soon as I am able. Thank you."

"Uh. Dad. Dad? It's Luce. I'm calling you from the—"

"Lucy?" My dad had picked up the phone.

"Hey Dad. Screening your calls?"

"I'm just trying to avoid Mrs. Sawatsky. Do you remember her, from down the street?"

"Yeah. So what, do you owe her money or something?"

"No. No. It's not that. She's quite determined to have me for dinner some night and I'm not sure."

"What? You mean like a date? Geez."

"Well. No. No. Regardless, I have no intention. . ."

I couldn't believe it. My dad on a date? This was ridiculous. The peeling paint on the honey sign, my dad on a date. How long had it been, anyway?

"How are you doing, Lucy?" asked my dad, "And Dillinger? How's the apartment working out for you?"

"Oh. Great. How are you?"

"Very good. Very good. Uh."

"Dad?"

"Yes?"

"Why don't you say hi to Dill?"

I put Dill's mouth to the receiver. Fuchsia marker ink got all over it. "Say something Dill. Say hi to Grandpa. Say hi, Dill."

"Mom," said Dill. I heard my dad saying some things like *Hello Dillinger, how are you?* It always cracked me up to hear my dad say Dillinger.

I took the receiver. "Did you hear that, dad? He said *mom*. I guess it was the first word that came to mind. He's pointing at the receiver now. I think he remembers your voice."

"Oh. Well. It's been quite some time since . . . uh . . ."

His voice would be all that Dill would remember of my dad because he had never seen my dad. We had talked a couple of times on the phone, though, to arrange for me to get stuff from the house and things like that. I know it seems weird that a grandpa did not see his grandchild, but I don't think it was that he didn't want to, just that he didn't know how to. I think it made him sad. My mom, me, Dill, everything in his life hadn't turned out the way he had thought it would. I think he thought I wanted him to leave me alone. Which I did—but then again I really didn't. But how was he to know. "So Dad," I said, "I'm at the border with a friend of mine and her kids. We're going on a little holiday."

"Oh yes? Very good. Do you have a reliable vehicle?"

"Yeah. Very."

"Good. Good."

"Dad. You know we drove past the honey sign."

"Oh yes."

"So. Dad."

"Yes, Lucy?"

"Why don't we get together some time?"

"That's a good idea. Very good. I'd enjoy that very much. When will you be back?"

"Oh. A few days. I'll give you my number and you can call or I'll call you back when I'm home."

"Very good. Just one moment while I get my ballpoint pen. There we go."

I gave him my address and phone number, and then said,"Well okay. I guess I better get back to the van."

"So uh . . . the honey sign. It's still there, is it?"

"Yup. It's still there."

"Well. I imagine there's a lot of water in the country?"

"Oh yeah, tons. Everywhere."

"Very good then. I uh . . . I appreciate your calling me, Lucy."

"Okay. Sure. So I'll see you soon?"

"You bet. Very good."

"Bye."

"Goodbye. Uh . . . Lucy?"

"Yeah?"

"Drive carefully. No speeding, hey hey."

I laughed. "Okay, Dad. See ya."

This was one of the longest conversations we'd ever had. I wondered if my dad was trying to slow his life down to somehow make up for the fast and furious pace my mom lived life at. She sped through her life while he tried his hardest to cling to the rigging. Just to stay afloat. My mom didn't care about sinking 'cause she was always moving, like a waterskier skimming along the top of the water. If you slow down, you sink, seemed to be her motto; if you sink, you drown. Maybe it was best if my dad and I talked to each other over the phone, on our way somewhere. Phones and imminent departure force a person to speak. Hey, he even cracked a joke—about the speeding. My mom used to measure everything in terms of driving time. I'd ask, "How long is the average labour, mom?" "Six hours," she'd reply, "the time it takes to drive to Regina." But my mom drove too fast everywhere and my dad would say, "No, no, it takes at least seven hours to drive to Regina. And that's with only one coffee stop." "Oh, that's ridiculous," my mom would say, "you can easily do it in six." Anyway, my labour with Dill wasn't six or seven hours or the time it takes to drive to Regina. It was exactly three-and-a-half hours.

Even my mom couldn't have driven to Regina in that amount of time. Everyone said *Oooh, that's short for the first baby*. And I was thinking *Yeah, about the time it takes to drive to Grand Forks*. I mean, you can't just sit in the back seat of a moving car all the way to Grand Forks from Winnipeg and imagine you're in acute pain and your insides are lurching around wildly the whole time. That would seem unbearable. When you're in labour all sorts of odd and mundane things happen and the time goes by. A road trip to Regina or Grand Forks is far less exciting than being in labour. That is, if you've ever been in labour.

I had to pry the phone out of Dill's hand and he started to cry. I wandered into the waiting area so I could sit down and change his diaper and nurse him. When I got there the girls were walking around and around on top of the plastic orange chairs singing to themselves and Lish was arguing, mildly, with the Customs guy. It seemed he was suspicious of us. Why did we want to go to Colorado? To see a friend. Where does this friend live? In Denver. All these children are yours? Yes. And hers. How much money do you have? When do you plan to return? Do you have any communicable diseases, open sores, fruit, pets, firearms, telephones, or otherwise deadly weapons? Finally he asked, "What do you do in Winnipeg?"

"I raise my children."

"I mean for a job? Your line of work?"

"Like I said—"

"Yeah, yeah, every mother's a working mother, but what is your source of income? Do you understand that question?"

"Yes, at night I perform delicate bowel surgery on uninsured American geriatrics. That is my reason for wanting to enter the United States." She raised her voice. "I'm on SOCIAL ASSISTANCE. ISN'T THAT BLOODY OBVIOUS?"

"You're going to have to calm down, ma'am, if you want this application processed."

I tried not to stare at both of them. The girls didn't seem bothered by this exchange. But I was worried that we wouldn't be allowed into the States if they knew we were on the dole. We weren't supposed to leave the province, let alone the country. Did they know that?

The big guy behind the counter and a couple of smaller older ones who seemed more relaxed all huddled back behind a desk. Then they started talking about us and looking at us and finally went into a little room. They closed the curtains on the window separating us from them.

Lish was mad. "What the hell is this? Albania? I wouldn't even want to get to their stupid country if it weren't for Gotcha. I can't do a damn thing without some government asshole stepping in to okay it, to fucking monitor my entire life. Why don't they just fucking put me into a zoo and watch me on those little video cameras?"

"Shhhh. Lish. We have nothing to hide. They're just bored. The big young guy probably has a lot to prove. They have to go through the motions. Just sit here and relax. You want a jawbreaker?"

"No."

"I do."

"I do."

"I do."

"Me too."

"Oh, for Christ's sake."

I bought four jawbreakers for the girls and told them to keep them hidden from Dill because I was afraid he'd choke on one. All the girls sat in silence then, their jaws moving like crazy around the big bulges in their cheeks. Slowly black jawbreaker juice trickled out of the corners of their mouths. Dill was pulling himself up to all the girls, one by one and saying something like *Wha Da Wha Da* and pointing to their mouths and to me and Lish *Wha Da Wha Da*. The girls, caught up in the excitement of the conspiracy against Dill, remained silent and opened their eyes wide and shrugged their shoulders, black juice trickling down their chins and their bulging cheeks. Finally, the Customs guy called us over, very seriously, as though he were going to tell us we had inoperable tumours all over our bodies.

Lish said, "Oh. Coffee break's over, eh?" to the guy, who
didn't smile or even look at her.

All he did was barely move his head quickly down and back
up and say, "Enjoy your stay."

"Gee thanks,"said Lish. "Can you guarantee—"

"Lish!" I said, "we should get going." I didn't want her to
start crusading again. If she started lecturing this guy we'd never
get across the border.

"Right," she said. "Let's go." I couldn't believe it. She was
agreeing with me! And then she looked at the guy and said,
"Thank you," and she smiled at him!

We picked up all our stuff and herded the kids toward the
van.

"Proud of me?" she asked. I nodded. "I just get so fucking
pissed off sometimes . . ."

"Apparently," I said. "Let's go."

"You know," she said, "I feel like that puppet in Mr.
Dressup, what's her name? Casey?"

"I think it's a he," I said.

"Whatever—have you ever noticed how bitchy she is?"

"He," I said. "Yeah, he's got a short fuse. I would too if all I
had for company week after week was an old man and a dog."

"And if you were a puppet," added Lish.

"Right," I said. I nodded.

"And Lucy! You're Finnegan! You're the dog! You keep nodding and not saying much." Lish loved this idea, she was laughing. She put her head next to mind. "What's that Finnegan?"
she said in a high voice. "You want to get going?"

"Woof," I said.

Letitia was staring at us. "Finnegan doesn't make any noise
at all, Lucy," she said in a serious tone. Lish just laughed.

The United States of America. Both Lish and I had, of course,
crossed this border many times when we were younger and were
travelling with our parents: weekends at the Holiday Inn in
Grand Forks or Fargo or sometimes even as far as Minneapolis.

Wearing our new Levis over the border so Mom didn't have to declare them. Not to mention the new sneakers, underwear and t-shirts. But since we had become adults ourselves, and poor ones at that, our trips anywhere had been almost non-existent, unless you count the laundry room downstairs. That little lift we once felt entering another country wasn't there this time. Everything looked the same, except that the roads were better than in Canada. Had my dad and I been talking about my mom? Not really, I guess. And yet he had made the crack about speeding and I had mentioned the honey sign. Only the two of us could have known what we were talking about. Maybe that was progress. Maybe we just didn't realize it was. Do we see ourselves growing old or do we wake up one day and startle ourselves looking into the mirror? It happens in steps. So I told myself that our conversation was progress.

Soon Dill would be walking and my dad would think he'd always walked, knowing he hadn't really, but somehow not believing it because he never saw it. Maybe we can't imagine what we've never seen. If Lish doesn't see Gotcha again, ever, she will retain her memory of him: the memory of passion, if not love. If Podborczintski asks me who Dill's father is, I still will not be able to give him an answer. At least I know who mine is, and I could say I was talking to him just the other day.

Lish had changed black t-shirts from one that read "Talk Minus Action Equals Zero" to one that had the Pepsi-Cola logo on it, but instead of the swirling letters spelling Pepsi-Cola they spelled Peepee Caca. She'd designed it herself. Since we had arrived in the United States she had taken on a more serious look. And I noticed the fields were drier over the border. It was getting hotter. The kids were playing some game having to do with catching up to the disappearing patches of water on the highway. Naturally they kept disappearing just when we were getting close. The game consisted of getting all excited by going oh o h OH OH GONE! over and over. I remembered a sign I had put on the back window of our car when I was travelling with my parents. It read "Help I'm being Kidnapped!" Nobody seemed to care. They all went swooshing past, grinning. Even when I gestured madly for them to cut the car off and rescue me they laughed. Some just looked annoyed. Others didn't look at all. I grabbed my neck and shook my head, sticking out my tongue and rolling my eyes. I pointed a finger that looked like a gun to the side of my head. I did everything to get noticed. Nothing. Nobody stopped. My parents didn't even turn around. The radio kept playing the hog and crop report. The cars kept whizzing past and the patches of water kept disappearing. I guess I looked like I belonged in the back of that car with that woman and that man. I suppose some people just sense if someone belongs or not.

All the girls, except Hope, who was too sophisticated to be naked in the back of a van, had removed their clothes. Dill was chewing on a shoe. The van wasn't making any weird noises yet and we were almost in Grand Forks. Geez, Podborczintski would be mad if he found out we had left town. I smiled. The dole. Daddy to us all. Would we ever stop running away and needing it at the same time? Anyway, right now we were looking for one of those low-slung fleabag motels with a lot of burnt-out neon and an angry teenage son or daughter left behind the office counter who you can be sure never heard of hotel management courses. We were, after all, on a fixed budget. I had reminded Lish that we had all the camping gear in the back of the van, and she had looked at me and arched her eyebrows and said, "Who're you kidding? We're not Terrapin and Gypsy. If I'm gonna meet the love of my life after five years I'm not gonna have that refugee look you get after camping with kids. It's overrated, trust me. Maybe one kid and the Marlborough Man to start the fire and put up the tent. Then maybe. You know, wine spritzers and no bugs and hand-knit sweaters and perfect roasted marshmallows and bird sounds coming off the lake. A little skinny dipping after the *one* well-behaved child has happily gone to sleep in the tent. Then maybe. In the meantime, look for a motel out your side. We've got more practical survival skills, Luce."

After we had put the kids to bed and they were sleeping and Lish and I were lying awake in the dark, I noticed she was very quiet. Our limbs made the only noises as they rubbed, from time to time, against the stiff motel sheets. Then Lish sighed and spoke. "Maybe this is stupid."

"What? What's stupid?"

"This. Just taking off in search of some guy I met five years ago and happened to get pregnant by. I think it is. Stupid. What the fuck am I gonna say to him anyway?"

"How should I know? Like I'm an expert in communications."

"But it could be good. I guess."

"What?"

"This."

"Yeah. I guess. For sure."

Only me and Teresa back at Half-a-Life knew that there couldn't be anything, good or bad, between Lish and the busker. Because it hadn't been anything to begin with: I know I should have learned my lesson a long time ago when me and my cousin wrote those fake love letters to her brother and permanently screwed up his life. Who did I think I was, anyway? Lish's life wasn't a Brazilian soap opera, and it wasn't up to me to decide what happened next. For all I knew Gotcha was married with three kids and living right in Grand Forks working at Wal-Mart.

This whole crazy thing was really because of my selfishness and a big fear that without Lish's happiness my own would crumble. And if that happened, what would happen to Dill? That's about what it amounted to. I figured if she got some postcards from the busker saying how much he really cared and thought about her and then he just up and died somehow, dramatically, trying to reach her . . . I thought that would be a better way to remember him. And for the twins too. Better a dead father than an absent one. I thought. Look at my mom. I seem only to be able to remember the funny, good things about her. I miss her, but her death is less painful than my father's life. He only makes me feel sad. And I wonder why we could never get it together just to get along, just to feel relaxed with each other and laugh suddenly at the same stupid thing. What happened in between the time he held my hand all the way to The Waffle Shop and called me his bombshell blonde and my adulthood? Better dead than absent, I say. Or I think I say. Now I just don't know. I realized after calling my dad at the border that things could always, maybe, change. Better a late father than an absent father.

But it was too late to turn back. Was it wrong to make up a person when they're gone? We do it when they're dead, so why not when they're missing? Not dead, neatly buried in the ground, but missing. Teresa was my accomplice. To a certain degree, she depended on Lish, too. This was the plan: when we got to the Badlands we'd call to ask about the mail and Teresa would tell Lish that another postcard had arrived. One from a friend of Gotcha's, saying he'd been killed in a drive-by shooting coming out of a movie theatre in downtown Denver. Just like John Dillinger.

I used to think my mom had staged her death. She must have been burnt out from the stress of counselling people and had plotted her death (hell, if I could fake a death, why not her?) and had taken off to South America. Speeding through banana plantations in a Land Rover, doing crossword puzzles in Spanish, laughing at the world and her great escape as she whizzed along patting the top of the Land Rover with her hand. You know how all mothers are slightly nervous about getting their baby mixed up in the hospital. Well, how do I know it was really my mother in that coffin? Well. I do. I know it was her, because if she was still alive she'd know about Dill and the three of us would have lunch more often. I was a fool, a major league fool. My dad at least figured it out that mom was gone for good and maybe he was a lonely recluse because of it. But he knew the truth. And let it be.

"Lish?"

"Yeah?"

"Good night."

"Yeah, okay, good night. The kids were pretty good, weren't they?"

"Yeah Lish, they were. They were very good."

"Sweet dreams, Lucy."

"You too."

Frankly, I was tired of dreaming. And I was feeling wide awake. More awake than I had felt in months. I needed to convince myself of only one more thing. That what I was doing was right. That my life was funny, and Dill was a lucky boy, father or no father. I would go through with this whole Gotcha business and hope that later on sometime I could tell Lish the truth and we could laugh. If I never told her the truth, I hoped that we could laugh, too. At the age of eighteen I told myself I would be happy. And if I could do that, I could finally embrace the sadness and the truth of my mother's death and remember her for who she was.

That night it rained. When it rains so much it feels like cotton in your ears, like big woollen socks brushing up against the nerve endings in your brain, rubbing and rubbing. A constant background noise. That night it rained like every other night so far that spring. Our fleabag motel was only about twenty feet from the highway and every car and truck that whizzed past on the wet road sounded like fabric ripping. Not only that, but Lish was snoring like some kind of wild animal. Her kids were used to it and Dill was so tired he slept through it. But geez, it was loud. I called her name loud and then louder. "Lish you're snoring." "Thank-you," she'd say extremely cheerfully. Then she'd stop for a few minutes. Then she'd start up again even louder. With the ripping fabric sound of the cars on the wet road right outside our window and her snoring, it was like being in the middle of some ferocious jungle kill. I told myself to remember to mention it to her. She definitely had some kind of nasal problem. But soon I was screaming, "LISH YOU ARE SNORING!!!"

Nothing.

"LISH ROLL OVER YOU ARE SNORING LIKE A WILD PIG AND I CAN'T SLEEP!!!"

Grunt. Snort. "Again? Look at that. Gotta turn on to my side. Gotta *turn* onto my side. Thank-you . . . zzzzz." More grunting.

Lish's snoring didn't bother her kids, but my yelling did, and Alba woke up and said, "Mommy? Lucy's mad at you. She's screaming."

"No, Alba, I am not mad at your mother. I'm trying to get her to stop snoring because I can't sleep."

"Ha Ha Ha. My mom doesn't snore. Ha Ha Ha."

"Yeah, Alba, she snores like a wildebeest. You're just used to it."

Then Letitia woke up. "Used to what? What's Alba used to?"

"Nothing."

"What's Alba used to? Tell me what Alba's used to?"

Hope said, "Shut up."

Maya said, "You shut up."

Then Dill woke up and started to cry and I had to get up to nurse him and I stepped on Hope and she started to cry and said she wanted to go home.

"So go," said Maya. "Hitchhike."

"Shut up," said Hope.

"How many seconds do you think I can hold my breath for, Lucy?"

"I don't know. I don't care. Go to sleep."

"I could hold my breath and pass out."

"Kay."

"I'm telling my mom you said that."

"Good. Tell her to roll over, too."

"Why?"

"Look. Everybody just shut the fuck up and go to sleep."

"That's twenty-five cents in the swear jar."

"Hope, we don't even have one of those any more. Not since the twins. After they were born Mom said we could all just start swearing a lot as long as we didn't hit anybody " said Maya.

"Oh right," said Hope.

"Well, that's no fair that you had a swear jar and we didn't, is it Letish," said Alba.

"Kay, so just get one. You don't even know what a swear word is. Sucks," said Hope.

"Fucks," said Alba. "Ha Ha. Did you hear what I said, Letitia? I said—"

"SHUT UP!"

Then Lish said, "Okay, thank you. Gotta turn onto my side. Gotta *turn* onto my side."

In the morning we were getting along a lot better. Somehow we had managed to fall back asleep and wake up in time to get free coffee and doughnuts before they were taken away for the day. Our battery was dead in the van because we had forgotten to switch the lights off and the teenager who had been working behind the front desk the night before now had a chance to do something real. He looked happy when we told him we needed a boost. His neck was covered in huge hickeys that he must have got after we took the room. He pulled his car up to our van and blasted music out of speakers in his trunk. He had those silver sticky letters on the back of his car and they spelled "Dream Weaver." His back tires were jacked up and the interior of his car was black. He had a garter belt hanging from his rearview mirror. He said to us, "I'll jump youse no problem. Hey, cool bumper sticker, hallucinations, yup, I've had a few of those too. Hello trouble. But what the hell, you gotta live from time to time. Whadya got under the hood? Holy shit this thing's ancient. Yeah I wanted to get 'Red Phantom' put on my car it's more you know of a guy thing? But my girlfriend said Dream Weaver was hot and actually she paid for it so . . . it's kind of gay but fuck can this baby move when she has to I'm telling you. Ohhhhh yeah."

It occurred to me that he was probably only a couple of years younger than me. Or maybe even my age. He didn't seem to wonder why two women with five kids were travelling around in an old van. I wondered what his girlfriend was like. She obviously liked to give hickeys and drive around in hot cars. He was probably crazy about her. I wanted to be her. I wanted to touch his arms. I really wanted to touch his arms. I wanted to forget about Dill just for a while and feel those hard brown arms. I wanted to ride in the Dream Weaver with him and see those dirty hands of his holding onto the wheel. Driving fast. I wanted my life to go back about ten years so I could do it over and figure things out before I went ahead living it. And everybody else's life, too. I wanted him to be Dill's father. I wanted my mother. I wanted my father. I just wanted.

When he bent over to hook up the cables from his car to our van, his jeans slid down slightly and the girls could see the crack in his smooth, hairless ass. They talked about that for at least an hour while Lish and I had some peace in the front. Or as much peace as you can feel when you think you're searching for a man you don't know if you hate or love, and as much peace as you can feel when you're headlong into the biggest lie you've ever told and wonder if you've done the right thing or ruined somebody's life forever.

We were headed for the Badlands, for Murdo and Wall Drug and blank and blank and. I kept meaning to bring up Lish's snoring problem, but I thought really it was just a problem for me and I didn't normally sleep with her, so why bother. Really we didn't talk much at all during that stretch to the Badlands. It had stopped raining. The fields were turning into grassy sandy plains. The earth was getting dryer and the air was getting warmer and as we approached the entrance to the Badlands I could see that not much lived around there. Nothing we could see, anyway. It was sort of a relief to see all that eroded rock and sand and hot air. There was less life than Lish and I and all the kids were used to, living in Half-a-Life public housing during one of the rainiest, most mosquito-infested summers in the history of Winnipeg, city of extremes, city of thunder, centre of the universe. And the absence of all that life, all that noisy relentless non-stop life, was quite a relief. In the Badlands you kind of see the miracle of your own living body in the midst of all this crumbly clay. It's standing out for a change, as a unique living thing instead of more of the same. Then there's the movement of your limbs and the way your eyes dart over a landscape and the urge to pee and the dryness in your mouth and the ability to recall a childhood memory just by feeling the texture of the dry sand as it slips through your fingers.

It was in Cactus Flats that everything was supposed to happen. According to the plan Teresa and I had made, Lish and I would call Teresa to find out what was happening and she'd tell me that Lish had received a postcard from one of Gotcha's friends, saying that Gotcha was dead, killed outside a movie theatre, shot randomly by some drug dealer or buyer or whatever. An American thing. She'd say that in the postcard the guy, Gotcha's friend, had written that Gotcha had never forgotten Lish and up to the day he died remembered her the most fondly of all the women he'd known on the road. As the most fun. And he'd never forget all that wild black hair. *And* that he always regretted stealing her wallet. It would say that his parents had already retrieved the body and buried it in their local cemetery in—the guy couldn't remember where Gotcha was from—but he'd never forget him. And, oh yeah, he loved kids and had always wanted one (or two) of his own. It would say that Gotcha had said that he was happy that Lish had that big silver spoon, at least, as a reminder of their love.

I had written the postcard before we left so Lish would be able to get her hands on it just as soon as we got back. It was written badly, like all the others, but I thought it important that I was consistent.

It was strange: tricking Lish this way, I was filled with a sense of well-being and an overwhelming sense of dread at the same time. Every five miles or so my mood would shift from one to the other, but I tried to ride it up the middle and focus on my project and convince myself it was for the best. I looked at the twins and tried to tell myself that Gotcha would never ever have shown up anyway, not after five years of no communication at all, and so for their father to be dead was best. Hell, even if he did show up some time, it would be a great story for the twins to tell their friends. Our dad died and came back to life so he could see *us*. Oh god, the next five-mile section of dread was coming up. What was I doing?

When I was eight, my parents bought a cabin at Falcon Lake, and every Sunday we went to church and Sunday School at an outdoor tent set up a few miles down the road. I had short hair and red jeans and a Jimmy Walker shirt that said "dyn-o-mite" on it and everyone thought I was a boy. I wanted to be a boy. So I said, "Yeah, my name's uh . . . Jimmy," and I got to go in the boys' Sunday School for weeks and play with the boys until one Sunday the minister guy came up to my mom and dad and me in the car and said, "So how's Jimmy liking Sunday School?" And they said, "Who?" And the minister smiled and smiled, looking back at me and them, and I buried my face in my mom's lap and cried all the way home, while my mom and dad tried not to laugh. After that I refused to go back to the outdoor church and so we all quit.

I think it was a big relief for everyone. Except for a while there I was hung up on the Rapture story that I had heard in Sunday School. If I came home from school and nobody was home, my dad gone, even my mom and her clients nowhere to be seen, no murmuring coming from her office, I'd think the Rapture had happened and I'd been left behind to fend for myself on earth while everybody else had managed to get taken to heaven. For those split seconds I'd be afraid and pissed off, too. I thought Geez, even my mom's clients who were so messed up managed to get to heaven and I, an innocent child, was left behind. Go figure. What had I done? What had I done? For a while there I couldn't go to sleep until I had gotten down on my knees and thanked God for everything in my life and asked to be forgiven for just about everything I had said and thought that day. I had scraps of paper with terrible things I had thought and said during the day so I wouldn't forget come forgiveness time. For some reason I never worried about dying during the day at school or something without being forgiven. It was only at home at night in my bed that I feared the morning would never come.

I also made myself read two pages of tiny print in the King James version of the Bible which is almost entirely incomprehensible. If I didn't do that I'd fear for my life and worry about eternal damnation. It got to be a problem, a real problem, though, because I'd lie in bed almost asleep and think an evil thought just because I knew I wasn't supposed to and then *poof* I'd be on my knees again praying for forgiveness. I had to be kneeling to be forgiven, this I knew. Eventually I told myself to fall asleep kneeling against my bed in a repentant pose so I wouldn't miss being forgiven for every single bad thing I thought before I fell asleep. During the day I was dragging myself around, totally exhausted and hurting from a terrible crick in my neck. My mom started to worry and took me to three doctors before she finally caught me kneeling at my bed, head in my hands, fast asleep at three in the morning. She had come in to close my window. She told me evil thoughts are normal and beneficial: they are God's way of preventing us from actually carrying out evil deeds. And when we have good thoughts, you know, kind and gentle ones, we'll be so pleasantly surprised that we'll want to have more. She told me there are two things I should not do. They were *lie* and *throw stones*.

She told me more things that night, but I didn't hear them, because I was sound asleep, beside her in my little twin bed. What I heard was *Don't lie, Don't throw stones.* That was good. I could do that. I could breathe easy. Since then I've lied a bit, okay a lot, and even thrown stones. But it's definitely a good base to work from. I'm still alive, anyway, and I'm not so tired. And if the Rapture's happened, nobody I know got picked to go up to heaven.

If Lish found out I had rigged this whole thing, I wouldn't be able to leave Half-a-Life as easily as I had that outdoor church. Public housing isn't exactly popping up all over the city. And I don't think anybody would be laughing. And I certainly wouldn't be able to cry in my mom's lap. But things might just work out. The next five-mile stretch of well-being was coming up and Lish was singing and the kids were quiet, listening. The van was still running, the children were happy and it was *not* raining.

Cactus Flats. Where history was made, thanks to me and my big mouth and my need to shape other people's lives. Was I like my mother? Would I die holding onto the secrets of other women's lives? I was acting more like a dictator than a mirror. If my mother reflected women's lives, I twisted them around like nutty putty. "I think we should call Teresa and see how things are going," I said to Lish that day in Cactus Flats. "You know, the *mail*." Could I be more obvious. Denver was only a day's drive away and I had to make sure we didn't get there. "Fine," she said. Just like that. We bought a carton of Camel cigarettes for Teresa and bourbon for Lish and then we found a pay phone. I do not remember any details about the town of Cactus Flats, other than that it was very quiet. In the phone booth Lish kept flipping her hair back so she could dial: every time it hit the side wall of the booth. She was wearing a black t-shirt with the sleeves and neckline cut off and it read, "She Who Must Be Obeyed." I was nervous, really nervous about the call. I was worried about how Lish would react. What would I tell her? Why hadn't I rehearsed that? And how would the kids, especially the twins, feel? Lish spoke to Teresa. I only heard what Lish said.

What?

No.

No.

No way.
No.
No fucking way.
No. Fucking. Way.
Yeah, read it to me.
Jesus.
No.
Did you say silver spoon?
How do you like them apples.
How the fuck do you like them apples.
Yeah.
Yes.
What? Yeah, it's still running.
Kay.
Bye.

I don't know why Teresa had to ask if the van was still running. It was rather inappropriate timing. I guess she just didn't feel the drama of the moment. At least she didn't ask if we'd got her cheap American smokes yet. Or maybe she had. How would I know? While Lish was talking I had the feeling I was drifting away, lifting off and floating up into the sky, away from Lish and Dill and the girls and out of this crazy lie I had concocted. Then the Badlands came to life and I came back to earth and the dusty quiet town of Cactus Flats, South Dakota, woke up briefly as Lish hollered at the top of her lungs, "GODDAMN FUCKING FUCKING FUCKING ASSHOLE!!!" The girls stared and I stared. Nobody mentioned the swear jar and Dill, in that marvellous way babies have, began to chuckle.

"I'm sorry. I'm sorry." That was about all I kept saying to Lish on the drive back to Winnipeg. She kept saying, "It's not your fault. It's not your fault." She had these crying jags and I told her she looked great afterwards. She laughed. When she cried I drove so we wouldn't go off the road. She told the girls point blank that the friend they were looking for had been killed in a terrible stupid accident and we were going home. Alba said we could still have a holiday and Hope glared at her and Alba stuck out her tongue. In the washroom of a gas station, Lish told me she would have to figure out how to tell the twins their mysterious father was now dead. It was anti-climactic. This was the big finish I was hoping for. Better a dead father than an absent one and all that. No more waiting, hoping, wondering. On with life! The twins could create the new Gotcha in their minds, in their hearts, in their stories at school, and in their conversations in the playground, and he would never let them down. *Never*. And they would believe he had died trying to find *them*.

But I didn't feel jubilant. After all, the twins had never really worried about their father. Lish had explained to them who he was, and that they'd likely never see him. They were content with that. They had been told the truth. And maybe when they were older they'd borrow somebody's van and hit the road looking for him themselves. Or maybe they wouldn't and he would become something they'd think about a couple of times a year, maybe the month of their conception, which would have been July, or whenever they saw a dark-haired handsome man performing magic on an outdoor stage. Who can tell? Why did I think that just because I could re-create my mother after her stupid death, they could or would want to re-create their dad's after his? After his fake one, that is.

And Lish. Obviously she had managed to survive all those years before I moved into Half-a-Life. I found her crying one day, assumed it was over lost love, and then concocted some stupid plan to return that love to her to make her happy, to keep her happy, so I could be happy. To think I could be a mother and so fucked up at the same time. If I wanted to fix somebody's life so badly, why didn't I start with my own?

Anyway, I kept apologizing to Lish, saying it was my fault, it was my fault, I shouldn't have encouraged her to take this trip. It was doomed from the beginning, *etc. etc.* I came as close as I could to telling her I had rigged the whole thing—until she finally told me to shut up and stop blaming myself. She said women always blame themselves when it rains at a picnic. She drove with one hairy leg heaved up onto the seat and her elbow resting on the window sill holding up her head. She had on the same t-shirt as on the day before. As we headed north toward Winnipeg a miracle began, slowly, to unfold: the sun came out. The prairie sun was finally doing what it was famous for. It was shining, hot and shining. "Well," said Lish, "There is a God. That big red swollen orb up there has finally found its groove and it's about darn tootin' time I'd say, wouldn't you, girls? Dill?"

Groove? I thought to myself. Groove?

We decided to bypass the fleabag motel in Grand Forks and camp instead. I was glad about that. The boy with the hickeys and the brown arms confused me. And I think any more confusion at that point would have made me certifiably insane. And anyway, Lish could afford to look awful from a night of camping. And we could tell Terrapin that yes, we had camped, because she was sure to ask. Lish tried to start a fire using the bourbon as lighter fluid, but it didn't work. She said, "Fuck it, who needs a fire," and started chugging the bourbon straight from the bottle. After a lot of swearing and sweating and second thoughts we got the tent up and then all seven of us went skinny dipping in the lake until a park ranger or warden came to tell us it was unlawful to swim naked in the lake. Lish rose from the water slowly and walked over to this guy on the beach, starkers. Her wet black hair hung around her body like a pelt. The girls shrieked with delight.

"Did you say 'unlawful'?" she said.

"Yeah," he said, smiling. "It means you're not supposed to do it."

"To swim naked?" she said.

"Yeah," he said again. The ranger and Lish were smiling at each other and he began to rub his hands on his thighs and clear his throat. Then he played with a little button on his two-way radio. He didn't look much older than me. I was trying desperately to keep my breasts under the water and still hold Dill without drowning him. I must have looked like some kind of deformed stroke victim. Lish, however, stood on that beach like Joan of Arc, big, naked, looking the ranger in the eye, grinning, shaking drops of water out of her hair, squinting at the setting sun like a self-contained fugitive. I wanted this scene to end promptly. Lish wanted it to go on forever.

They stood smiling at each other. Lish moved her hair around a bit and a few drops of water fell on the ranger's pant leg. She made a big deal of wiping him off and he laughed and looked up at the sky as if to say *Thank you God for this naked woman standing in front of me and rubbing my thigh.* He took out two cigarettes and offered one to Lish. She shook her head and shifted her weight to one leg. The ranger was having a problem lighting his cigarette and Lish moved around slightly to block the wind from blowing out his match. They were talking and laughing. He was a cute ranger. It occurred to me to look at his pants to see if he was getting an erection, but I couldn't really tell. I quickly looked away.

I tried to engage Dill and the girls in some kind of feeble splashing game but Dill started fussing about the water in his eyes and the girls began chucking wet sand at each other. I looked at the happy couple on the beach and wondered whether Lish would drag this guy off to the bushes any second and screw him while she was at it, but they seemed satisfied enough standing around and talking to each other.

What the hell was I supposed to do? There was no way I was getting out of the water naked, and I was starting to feel like a real idiot, hunched over like a clam and moving around trying to stay warm in the water and keep Dill from crying. I couldn't exactly nurse him underwater—he'd drown if he took a breath. I guess I should have known it wasn't my breasts anybody was interested in, except Dill, and it wouldn't make any difference if I exposed myself or not. It could have been Normandy Beach on D-day and Lish and the ranger wouldn't have noticed.

Lish walked over a few feet and pulled her bottle of bourbon out from a log, and handed it to him. He had a drink and

Miriam Toews

passed it back to Lish. Well fine, I thought, if that's the only fluid they pass back and forth. I swatted a horsefly off Dill's head.

Finally Lish turned around and looked at us and waved. I held up my hand for a second like a traffic cop, thinking *okay if you've had your fun with buddy boy you might want to get back to looking after your kids*, who were kind of drifting off down the beach by now.

The ranger started pointing in one direction and then moving his finger around his palm and then pointing again. He was giving her directions to some place. His, I imagined. I sighed. No way, I thought. I am not looking after your kids while you go off to some look-out tower with a total stranger.

Lish nodded politely while he spoke and looked off in the direction in which he had pointed. Then he smiled and said, "So?" with an animated shrug. Lish laughed. She said, "You never know." He dropped his head in a comic gesture of defeat and then looked up at the sky again, supposedly for guidance. He was really a very cute ranger. Then they shook hands and while they were doing that he briefly placed his other hand on Lish's bare hip. She smiled.

Then he just walked away into the bush. And Lish did the old brushing off her hands gesture that meant *well, that's over*, and walked back into the lake with so much energy that she left a little wake behind her.

"You just never stop making waves, do you, Lish."

"Oh, pa-lease, leave the comedy to me."

"You're not gonna go off with that guy later, are you?" I asked.

"Nah," she said. She cupped some water in her hands and splashed it on her face. "He's a nice guy, though," she said. "He's funny."

"He's pretty cute," I said.

"Yeah," said Lish, and we both stared off at the place in the bushes where he'd disappeared.

It's amazing how refreshing a little bit of water can be. Mixed with bourbon.

I guessed that it would take Lish some time for the truth about the busker to set in, to take hold and make her react. She was acting kind of weird, but she always did, so that wasn't a big deal. She kept looking at me oddly, sort of smiling, like she wanted to ask me a stupid question but was kind of shy about it. If she had given up the hope of ever seeing Gotcha again she had replaced it with a kind of silliness. Well, maybe that's a form of grief, I thought. She talked about their week together five years ago, and how she actually had never really known him and had gone for months at a time without ever thinking about him and how the twins had never known him either and never would and it's too bad he died for sure, but she didn't quite know how to feel. I understood. All the guys I'd had sex with, some even for a week or more, were vague fuzzy lost people I couldn't really remember. That one of them could be Dill's father was absurd. That the reason for his existence, which was such a big event in my life, was some man I couldn't remember, some shadowy figure I couldn't place, seemed crazy.

It was a strange sensation. Even knowing so much about Dill didn't automatically make me know his father. Sometimes you wonder. Like Nike running shoes. I saw a show about the people who make them: sour-looking Asian women getting a few bucks a day making shoes that sold for a hundred bucks a pair. Sometimes you just wonder where these things come from. But usually you don't. Usually I just enjoyed Dill without wondering how exactly he got here.

Anyway, Lish felt good that the busker had been trying to reach her, that it would have been a chance for the kids to meet him. But would he have come back again and again or just fizzled out and left the kids feeling that awful feeling of loss instead of just curiosity, which is a lot easier? He didn't even know that he had kids and probably she would think he was alone and horny when he wrote the postcards and realized Winnipeg wasn't too far from Denver—and hadn't he had a good time with some woman from Winnipeg once upon a time? Maybe it could happen again. Sometimes that's what Lish figured he was thinking. And sometimes, it seemed she believed he wanted only her, in a tender, spiritual kind of way. At least that's what she said. As for me, I didn't know which was worse.

When we stopped at the border, the guy asked us had we purchased any firearms, telephones or pets. Lish said, "Yes, and a large quantity of drugs and lesbian porn we are hoping to sell in schoolyards." Fortunately Dill had woken up when the van stopped moving and was hollering as loud as he could and the guy didn't understand Lish and said, "Yes it is, isn't it."

Getting back into Canada was a breeze. They had to let us in even if they didn't want to. When we passed my mom's ditch and the honey sign, Lish asked, "Do you want to stop?" and I said, after a couple of seconds of wavering and Lish's foot hovering between the brake and the gas pedals and an enquiring expression on her face, "No."

Lish told us a story about her mother and father. It was the girls' favourite. The twins liked to hear it over and over. Both Lish's parents had been raised on farms. Farming was the main event. Her mother's family bought John Deere equipment and that was fine. But when their daughter, Lish's mom, began dating her neighbour, Lish's dad, the shit hit the fan, because Lish's father's family used Massey Ferguson equipment. In that area there was an ongoing feud between John Deere users and Massey Ferguson users. Something about the French buying one brand and the Ukrainians buying another, originally. Both camps swore up and down that theirs was the best, and because farming was their life, it was a big deal. So, for a John Deere girl and a Massey Ferguson boy to be dating, that was asking for trouble. It was like the Montagues and the Capulets. In the only café in the neighbouring town the John Deere clan sat on one side and the Massey Ferguson sat on the other. Sometimes the more good-natured farmers would try a little bit of friendly debate with someone from the other side, but they'd get glared down so fast even the waitress forgot to refill their coffee cups for the rest of the day. (The waitress's family was a Massey Ferguson family, but she said as long as there was no fighting, she'd serve the John Deeres in the restaurant same as everyone else.) Everyone waited eagerly for someone from the other side to get their arm cut off or a piston blown because of a faulty part, but when it happened to one of their own it was very hush hush. Repairs were done in the night, so no one from the other side would notice there was a problem.

New farmers were courted and wooed by both sides and it was always tough for them to make the choice. Usually it depended on whom the kids played with: even when they're fighting over farm machinery, parents want their kids to be happy. So potential farm equipment buyers bought John Deere if their kids were best friends with a John Deere family, and Massey Ferguson if it was the other way around. Farm families are very loyal to their friends. So anyway, Lish's mom and Lish's dad couldn't help falling in love even though they knew it was a dangerous thing to do. Neither one of them gave a damn about farming, let alone farm equipment. When Lish's mother's father found out about the courtship, he said, "I forbid you to see that boy," and her mother turned around to face the stove. The whole feud was really a male thing. The farm women just sighed mostly. And Lish's mom said, "But I love him. I love him more than I've ever loved any old John Deere plow. Yeah, if I get pregnant I'm going to name my baby *Massey Ferguson!*" She yelled it out at the top of her lungs. Well, this was too much for Lish's dad. He stood up and said, "If I ever, ever, *ever* hear you speak those two words again I will banish you from this house and you will *never* be allowed to return, so help me god." Lish's mom's mother said, "Oh, honey, sit down."

Lish's mom said, "*Fine*. This whole place stinks like pigs anyway and there's nothing to do. If your John Deere crap is more important than your own daughter, why don't you just go out there and . . . and . . . and screw it. Goodbye. Mom, I'll call you later. Goodbye."

"Goodbye dear. Are you sure you don't want supper before you go?"

"Yes. I'm sure." She slammed the door behind her. Lish's mom was off to find her Massey Ferguson man and start a new life off the farm. On her way down the long driveway to the gravel road she passed a John Deere hauler parked on the side, and she removed her panties and flung them onto the hauler. Then she flipped up her skirt and mooned the whole lot of them, her mother, her father, the pigs, the barn, the flies, the sadness, the boredom, the stink, the John Deere equipment.

"And," said Lish, finishing the story, "I think that was my mom's first and last act of rebellion. Isn't it amazing how men fall head over heels in love with wild women and then turn them into doormats?"

I asked, "Why didn't she name her first baby Massey Ferguson?"

"Oh well, by then she wasn't so angry. Too bad really. She hasn't been angry since. Just sighs at the stove."

We were approaching the city limits. We passed a sign that read "Congratulations Winnipeg and Welcome Visitors! Bite rate down from 48 bites per minute to two!!! We've survived!!!" And there was a bad painting of a family of mosquitoes holding suitcases waiting at an old-fashioned outdoor train platform.

"Oh well, that should draw the tourists," said Lish.

As we were rounding the corner of Broadway and Main, the sliding door on the van fell off. Luckily the kids didn't fall out, but a bunch of clothes and diapers and garbage and toys that were leaning up against it did and ended up lying all over the street. We were almost home, so Lish stopped and heaved the door into the van. "MOVE OVER, KIDS," she yelled. "I'M PUTTING THE DOOR IN HERE." I picked up all our stuff from the street. Some people honked. Others peeled around us and gave us the finger. Some just looked at us. "OKAY, DON'T FALL OUT OF THE VAN, JUST STAY WHERE YOU ARE. LET'S JUST GET THIS PIECE OF CRAP HOME. I'LL DRIVE SLOW. HI EVERYBODY, WE'RE BACK. FRIENDLY MANITOBA. DIDJA MISS US????" Lish yelled at everyone around and waved and smiled. "Fucking impatient sons of bitches," she muttered under her breath.

"Mom," said Maya. "You're supposed to say I'll drive slow-*lee*. Mrs. Loopnik says so."

"Yeah, mom," said Hope.

"*Yeah,* mom," said Alba.

"*Yeah, mom,*" said Letitia.

"If I had PMS I could slaughter you all and not do a day of time."

"You always have PMS, Mom," said Hope.

"Yeah, ha ha, *permanent menstrool system,*" said Maya.

"Ha ha, good one."

"Ha ha, yourselves, what do you mean *always*, I'm always *pregnant*. You can't have both. Mrs. Loopy ever tell you that? And you girls call yourselves educated. Hey, hey, look people, it's Sing Dylan. He's still scrubbing that old fence! Some things never change, boy oh boy."

Sing Dylan turned around and waved. And Lish honked the horn MEEP MEEP MEEP MEEEEEEEEEEEEEP as we drove up to the front doors of good old Half-a-Life.

Stuff had definitely happened at Half-a-Life over the very short time we had been away. Mostly it was that the sun had come out, and that had changed everything. Kids were running around the parking lot, and riding tricycles, bikes, roller blades, skateboards. Old rusty barbecues had been chained to light fixtures and other parking signs in the parking lot, and bags of charcoal were sitting underneath them. Some of the older kids were chucking them at each other. Obscene sidewalk chalk drawings were everywhere, kids falling down and howling, mothers standing around and smoking and talking. Other mothers were leaning against their balconies, shouting instructions and being ignored. Terrapin was squatting in a leftover puddle looking at waterbugs with her daughters, pointing at something with a grave expression on her face. Sing Dylan had almost removed all of the FUCK THE RICH THAN EAT THEM graffiti on the North Wall. He should have been happy, but he seemed kind of sad, worried. Then we saw Teresa.

She had cut off her hair and left a couple of long strands in the back. She was wearing a yellow tank top and cut-offs. She was running for our van barefoot over the little pebbles on the parking lot and so she kind of hobbled and grimaced and swore the whole way over. The way she was hunched over and wearing a tank top and rushing so eagerly and everything reminded me of the old lady tourists you see in Vegas. Terrapin called out to her to come and see the beautiful bug and Teresa said, "Get a fucking life Hairpin *ouch ouch*." I thought she was very desperate to get her cheap smokes and again I wished that she would play along with this death thing a bit better. But when she finally made it to the van, she didn't mention the cigarettes or Gotcha's death or the postcard or the trip or ask how're the kids or what's the van door doing in the van. She ran to Lish's window and heaved her giant yellow breasts onto the door frame and panted for a few seconds and then said in one breath like a big yellow balloon losing all its air, "Hurry up, you gotta hurry, Mercy's in *labour*! She refuses to go to the hospital. She said the last time she was in the hospital to have Zara they almost killed her. She refuses to lie down and give birth until her stupid apartment is sterile, so a bunch of us are busy trying to get it ready for her to have the baby and it's early so her midwife, we didn't even know she was fucking pregnant, isn't around and she says she can just do it by herself but not until the place is totally clean and so *hurry*!!!"

"What did you say! Mercy! In labour? Are you serious? This is a joke, right?" Lish was already parking the van in front of Half-a-Life.

I thought to myself, wait, not another set-up. Poor Lish. I thought I was the only one lying to her. Maybe Teresa had really got into all that secrecy and plotting and didn't want it to end. But how would she see the end of this one? She's not some kind of Steven Spielberg even if she wants to be a flagger on film sets. You can't just fake a new baby. At least not in Half-a-Life, where everyone has more than enough experience with real ones. This was getting ridiculous. Mercy hadn't even looked pregnant. But then again she was always wearing those big long-sleeved men's shirts. And Mercy? Pregnant? When had she ever had the opportunity to get pregnant? She was always so organized, every second of her day planned and what was this about sterile? Her place was *always* sterile. But Teresa, who was huffing and puffing, trying to jog alongside the van as we pulled in, wasn't finished. "And Luce, your dad's here too and whatsisname, that guy you had at your place when Podborczintski showed up. They're both in Mercy's apartment trying to help. I think they're doing the bathroom."

"*What?* My dad? Hart? Teresa, are you sure, what are they doing *here*? Geez, Teresa, are you positive you know what you're talking about? Geeeez, Teresa."

I gave her a really nasty look like she had gone too far and could we all please just be normal and truthful again. I couldn't remember the last time I had given anybody such a nasty look. And I began to feel bad 'cause it was Teresa, after all, who had been my trusty accomplice in the Gotcha affair. I felt I was to blame, giving her a taste of subterfuge, and now she couldn't get enough. But she didn't seem to notice. She just started hauling all the girls and Dill out of the van and rushing us all up the stairs to Mercy's apartment.

"My dad? Hart? Why are they here, Teresa?" I yelled at her in the stairwell.

"I don't know. Your dad's basement got flooded. The toilet backed up or something and there's shit all over and he had nowhere else to go. He thought he could use your place while you was gone and Hart was here to see Sing Dylan."

"Sing Dylan? Why Sing Dylan?"

"'Cause. Something about him defending him in court. Sing Dylan finally managed to reroute all the water over to Serenity Place. And now they're flooding like crazy over there, at least they were a couple of days ago before the rain stopped, and they threatened to take Sing Dylan to court and 'cause he's an illegal immigrant and everything he'd be sent home pronto and so I found whatsisname's calling card at your place when I was checking it for leaks and called him and he said he'd defend Sing Dylan for free 'cause he really needed experience anyway ha ha in all areas, eh Luce?? But now he's busy with your dad helping Mercy, and Sing Dylan is back at the wall. He tried to help for a while but he got too nervous so he went back to his wall. He was just doing that rerouting for Sarah. For her honour, you know. It was revenge. But as far as I'm concerned it wasn't nearly enough. I mean what's a kid compared to a flooded basement? Anyway, I think that's like a cultural thing for him. Or whatever. Because of what the bitches in Serenity Place said about her and Emmanuel and him being taken away and everything. *Hurry up!*"

Okay. All that stuff about Sing Dylan flooding Serenity Place made sense, sort of. But my dad at Half-a-Life? Assisting in a homebirth? He hadn't even seen Dill, let alone changed his diaper or kissed his cheek. I don't know if he had ever held a baby or not. I guess he had held me, but he certainly hadn't seen me being born back then, and he never really exhibited any interest in babies or children. I don't recall him ever even saying the word *pregnant*. The odd time he had to refer to some pregnant woman, he said "expecting." And now he was ready to get his hands covered in afterbirth?

All eight of us flew into Mercy's apartment. The girls were terribly excited about Mercy's new baby, or the prospect of Mercy's new baby. Dill was looking alert, too, Teresa was all business, Lish was mildly amused and puzzled by it all, and I, stupidly, began to cry. If this much could happen, find a beginning and an end, and lead to more and more events transpiring, over a short period of three days, then how much had happened over the three years since my mother had died? And how would I be able to remember her when so much was happening? I was afraid to blink for a second or shift my thoughts to Mercy's baby or Dill or my dad or Sing Dylan for fear I'd lose her. So much was happening. And not only that, but things were happening without me making them happen. What wasn't happening was my mom wasn't catching a flight home to Winnipeg from somewhere in South America and John Dillinger wasn't alive and well living under some pseudonym in Des Moines or anywhere else. Gotcha, dead or alive, was never going to show up and neither was Dill's father, the way Podborczintski kept hoping he would. I hoped Lish's crying trick would make me look great, too, 'cause now there was no turning back. If Siskel and Ebert had been reviewing this scene they would have said my crying looked fake and exaggerated, because I was heaving and my face was all distorted and really I was a mess. But when you see people, you know, bawling their heads off, looking scary and awful, believe me it's real. They feel bad, it's not an act. I couldn't bear to lose her all over again, the woman I had created in my mind. Speeding down the highway with her elbow resting on the door and her hand tapping on the roof of the car. At that moment, all I wanted was to have my mother back.

The thing is, at that moment, there were about twelve people all rushing around Mercy's apartment trying to make it sterile and my breakdown went entirely unnoticed. Which was good because it probably wouldn't have been too good for the baby's karma and energy and all that to have some unstable kid crying for her dead mom in the same room at the moment it was being born. I was standing frozen in the kitchen of Mercy's apartment dealing with the rest of my life while everyone else had poured in looking to play a role in the story of Mercy's baby's birth.

I decided to wash my face, that old cure for everything that ails you. Wash your face. All you gotta do is just wash your face. Splash splash. At the end of the hall I could see Mercy kneeling on her hands and knees groaning, "Is it ready, is it ready? Just fucking tell me, is the fucking thing ready or *what* ooohhhhh-haaaahhhhhhhhh ooh okay okay okay okay hang on baby." She started yelling, "OOOOOOOOOHH WOULD SOMEBODY PLEASE TELL ME IS THE FUCKING THING CLEAN OR IS THAT ASKING TO MU-AAAAAAAAAAHHHHHHHH!"

I had Dill on my hip and I quickly headed for the bathroom. I could see Angela and Lish and Teresa already rubbing Mercy's back and smoothing her hair and murmuring encouraging things, and like I said, the last thing Mercy needed right then was me, the grim reaper. I opened the bathroom door and then I remembered what Teresa had told us on the stairs. My dad and Hart were cleaning the bathroom. Sure enough, there they were. We all looked at one another, and then I laughed and I laughed. Then I sat down on the toilet and I laughed some more. My dad and Hart were kneeling at the tub and scrubbing it with some kind of organic cleanser. The sink already gleamed and I could see my reflection in the tiles on the bathroom floor. My dad and Hart had sanitary napkins taped onto their knees—to cushion them or to keep them dry or to keep the common bacteria on their pants from getting onto the floor, who knows? They only stopped for a second to turn around and look at me.

"Hi, Lucy," said my dad. "We'll have to talk later. I've been put to work."

"Hi, Lucy," said Hart, with a less serious expression on his face. "I came here to get some legal experience, but now . . ."

And he and I burst out laughing. My dad turned around and almost smiled and touched Dill's arm. He kept his hand on Dill's arm, looking at it, and then, finally, he spoke. "From what I understand your friend has chosen to deliver the child in the bathtub," he said.

This made Hart and me crack up all over again. I couldn't believe my dad was cleaning a tub for some single woman in public housing who wanted to have her baby in the bath. And wearing sanitary napkins on his knees!

"If your fucking family reunion is over I wouldn't mind having my fucking baby already if nobody fucking minds OOOOOOHHHHHHHHHHHH I don't care if it's covered in dirt fill the tub and let's do it OOOHAAAAAAHAHHHAOOOH!!!"

My dad and Hart snapped to attention. If they were upset with Mercy's language, they certainly didn't let on. My dad filled the tub, expertly, I might add, feeling the water, swooshing it around to make it the same warm temperature everywhere. Hart got a bunch of towels ready and took on the same stern expression my dad had. They were totally focussed. These were men, finally, with a mission. I got the hell out of that bathroom just in time. Mercy lumbered in, telling everyone around her to just fuck off, and plunged into the tub. She yelled, "I JUST NEED ONE OF YOU TO CHECK THE CORD AND CATCH THE BABY. THIS BABY'S GONNA BE BORN ANY SECOND AND I MEAN ANY SECOND!!!" Immediately, Hart ran out of the room, leaving my dad the job. Teresa and Lish offered to do it instead but Mercy told them, "Keep all your kids away from the bathroom," and "Lucy's dad can hold me up if I need it." I barely heard my dad murmur something like, "But I . . . but I have never in my life done anything like this—" and Mercy answer him with, "Listen, it's pretty fucking straight-forward. I'm having a baby here, alright? Just do what I tell yaaaaAAAAHHHH—" I caught a glimpse of my dad's face just before Mercy yelled at him to shut the fucking door and he looked, well, he looked terrified. Kind of like the way he looked when he found out my mom was dead. I tried not to worry about him in there. I figured if we could all survive being born, then he could survive watching someone being born. I mean, I had never heard of, you know, the midwife or the obstetrician dying in childbirth. And the way Mercy had been clomping around swearing and screaming, I wasn't worried about *her* dying. So. Nobody was dying. That was good.

Lish and Angela and Hart and Teresa and Dill and me sat in the kitchen quietly, drinking coffee, making sure we didn't leave a mess, sometimes getting up and walking over to the balcony to watch the girls, who had become bored with the whole thing by this time and were playing in the parking lot in the sunshine. We were in shock. Mercy having a baby was the last thing we thought would happen at Half-a-Life. And why hadn't she told us? We could have helped out. Then again, it would be a great feeling of accomplishment to have kept a secret for that long, nine months, or actually, eight, in a place like Half-a-Life. Finally Teresa said it: "So does anybody know who the father is?" and all of us just kind of gawked at each other and shook our heads and, naturally, wondered.

It was kind of a sacred time, the actual birth and everything, so none of us, even Lish, made any cracks about who it might be, though we were thinking about it, and later on, maybe in a day or two, we'd be trying to find out and coming up with our own ridiculous scenarios. Birth is a special thing, but in Half-a-Life we all start our nosing around very shortly afterwards. Not only us, but the dole, too. In the lives of the kids of Half-a-Life there were only a few days of freedom, of possibility, of what-ifs, before the dole swept in and took snapshots, fingerprinted, and filed all available data on the origins and future of this child, case number whatever it was. And all the questioning started.

While the other women talked about their own birth stories and revelled in the special conspiratorial mood of the occasion and Hart played with Dill, I sat on Mercy's kitchen chair trying to sort things out. My mother's death, Mercy's baby, Gotcha's fake death, Dill's unknown father, my own father, who right now was helping to deliver the baby of a perfect stranger. He had never even seen Dill until tonight, his own grandson, and now suddenly he was Geoffrey Van Alstyne, midwife of the poor. I got up and walked over to the bathroom door. I listened to my dad saying over and over, slowly, in a soft voice filled with confidence, "Very good, very good, very good." I sat down on the floor in the hallway and listened to him coax the new life out of Mercy, a woman he had never met until then. At the end of the hall I saw Lish move towards the fridge and stop for a second, on the way, to make a shadow puppet with her hand in the square of sunlight on Mercy's wall. I could see Hart, awkwardly pretending to chew Dill's toes off, and I saw Dill's big wet mouth open, chuckling. If my mother had been in this apartment, she would have reflected happiness. If my mother was a mirror, like she said, I would have seen myself smile. And if my mother had been there she would have seen my life, and she and my dad would have spoken the words together, "Very good, very good, very good."

Mercy had a girl. The father turned out to be the same father her other daughter had. We were all a little taken aback by that: in Half-a-Life it's sort of assumed that siblings have different fathers. Mercy could control just about everything around her and keep everything in order, in nice, straight, clean lines. Except for her feelings about this guy. The Father. Most of the time she could keep him out of her mind and out of her apartment, but not always. And so, she had another baby. There are worse things that could happen. Since working for the Disaster Board, Mercy had a new life philosophy: to name what you fear, to look it in the eye and embrace it. And so she named her new daughter Mayhem.

You might think that my dad and me caught up on the years we had lost or talked about my mom or declared our love for one another. Wrong. After Mayhem's birth, he and I and Dill went back to my apartment. He sat at my little kitchen table and drank a diet Coke with ice and gave Dill a present. It was a microscope. He hoped Dill could use it when he was older. We talked about the rain, his wrecked basement, not much else. But there we were.

That night Teresa had a tequila Scrabble party. It was only going to be a Scrabble party, but then after adding up all the positive things that had happened, she decided it had better be a tequila party, too. Even Sing Dylan was celebrating, though not with tequila. Hart had managed to convince the women in Serenity Place not to sue Sing Dylan for flooding their basements. He told them that it would take months to get money for that but they could get money right away from the Disaster Board if they said their basements flooded naturally like everyone else's. Welfare mothers all understood the appeal of quick cash, and we rarely let convictions stand in our way of getting it. So Sing Dylan wasn't going to have to go back to wherever the hell he came from after all. Which was good. He had even managed, finally, to wash off every last trace of the graffiti on the North wall.

What was bad was the new graffiti. The morning after Mayhem was born, Lish and I looked out of her kitchen window and saw Sing Dylan back at his wall with his pail and his hose. Nobody could miss those big fresh yellow letters: EAT THE POOR THERE MORE TENDER. Lish really liked the sound of that, despite the spelling. Again. She said it was like a welcome sign to Half-a-Life.

Another thing we were celebrating was the success of Mercy's blackmail campaign. Bunnie Hutchison met with Mercy in person, secretly, and guaranteed that the child tax credit would be brought back, if she didn't breathe a word about Bunnie's bogus flood claim. An extra thousand bucks? When you're pulling in nine, hey, what's a little blackmail.

Unfortunately, Bunnie Hutchison has decided to set up what she called a Snitch Line to catch welfare cheaters. People are supposed to call some number if they know someone guilty of welfare fraud. So now Half-a-Life and Serenity Place, we're all battening down our hatches and gathering our ammo, 'cause there's sure to be a war. Again. Don't even ask me how Lish reacted to news of the Snitch Line. The Snitch Line, the Fingerprints, the Surprise Home Visits, geez, you'd think we were dishonest. Which brings me to Lish and the Gotcha problem.

I was troubled by Lish's unchanging mood. The whole point of that stupid exercise had been to resolve things for her, to stop the wondering and the waiting, to cement his love for her, to create a dead father for the twins to love instead of a missing one. About one day after I'd done it, I realized I had done the wrong thing. But still, Lish didn't know the truth and, in my mind, she should have been acting differently. Based on what she thought she knew. Instead she was pretty much the same. She burned her incense, played her music, read her books, cooked her garlic dishes, hung out with her kids, helped Mercy with her baby, made cracks about everything, railed against the system. Nothing had changed!

As for my dad, well, he asked me if it would be alright with me if he stayed for three days while he had his basement cleaned out, installed a back-up valve and a sump pump, and replaced his weeping tile. With the ground as saturated as it was, there'd likely be more flooding next spring when it thawed. My dad decided to forget about having a finished basement and just live on the main floor. Dill and I didn't really see a lot of him during those three days. The first night I let him sleep in my bed, and Dill and I slept on Lish's air mattresses. The second night he said he would sleep on the air mattresses and when I said *no no*, he said, "I honestly would prefer to." In the morning we drank coffee together and watched Dill perform feats of derring-do, as my dad put it. I hadn't, up until then, really had anybody else to enjoy Dill with. And it was a wonderful feeling. I mean I had Lish and the other women in Half-a-Life, but my dad was far more thrilled with the little things Dill did. He saw them as incredible achievements. I think he was even proud.

Whenever there was a ruckus in the parking lot or a loud thud he'd scurry over to the window to check his car, and at night he'd ask me twice if the coffee was off and the chain was on the door. He was mostly at his house watching the men work, but he'd always come back at suppertime and take us out to a restaurant. Dill was still mostly breast-feeding and eating rice cereal with the odd piece of actual food thrown into his diet, but my dad figured hamburgers and french fries were the way to go. It wasn't because he was cheap or anything; I think it was because for him I was still kind of frozen in time at the age of fourteen: the year before my mother died and before I went off the deep end. When his life made more sense to him. I didn't want to tell him that Lish had properly introduced me to things like curry and rotis. I didn't want him to think he should change his mind from thinking what he had always thought. That's the kind of relationship we had. At least it wasn't pasta he was taking us out for. I'd had enough noodles to last me a lifetime.

At the restaurants we went to Dill would fuss a bit and my dad would say to me, "Why don't you nurse him, Lucy?" So I would, and my dad would cross his legs, sit kind of hunched over, and chew on a toothpick and stare out the window, not saying anything. He always nodded at anybody who walked by us, kind of like a cop on his beat, as if he should have said, "It's okay, this lady's feeding her baby, nothing to see, keep moving, that's it." When I was finished, my dad would say to Dill, "Bet that hit the spot, eh?" or "There, that's the ticket. Yup," or "Dillinger's favourite restaurant, eh?"

His last night at my place, like I mentioned, we were having the tequila Scrabble party at Teresa's. Everybody was there.
Kids were running in and out. Nobody complained, because
everybody's kids were doing it. Sing Dylan couldn't tell us in
his polite way to keep the noise down, because he was at the
party too, and it was partly in his honour to boot. Tanya
brought in a vat of homebrew, and Teresa and Angela and Lish
were already half cut. Nobody was playing Scrabble. Teresa
made the smokers go out on the balcony because of little
Mayhem, and there were some kids there, too, dropping stuff
onto the parking lot. I noticed that Sing Dylan hadn't managed
to get any of the EAT THE POOR THERE MORE TENDER graffiti
off the wall, or maybe he'd decided to leave it there. Terrapin
had trapped my dad in a corner and they were discussing the
merits of home births versus hospital births. Well, Terrapin was
discussing, and my dad was nodding, looking nervously
around the room for an exit.

Eventually we all headed outside for the parking lot—all
except Mercy and Mayhem. They stayed on the balcony like the
royal family and waved periodically, at least Mercy did. She
couldn't walk yet, not too easily, anyway. Teresa brought her
ghetto blaster, covered in a plastic bag in case it should rain, and
we all sat around in the grass behind our building, talking and
listening to music. My dad was trying to talk to Sing Dylan
about ducts. I heard Sing Dylan saying *ducks? ducks?* and looking around shaking his head and shrugging his shoulders. I
noticed that Lish was drunk. Really drunk. She was telling
Gypsy that she was not a mean drunk. Sometimes she was
mean, she said, and sometimes she was drunk, but she was not
a mean drunk.

She said she was a gentle drunk. That she should get drunk
more often and she'd probably get a Nobel Peace Prize. She was
rambling on like this and moving her hair around from one side
of her head to the other. She looked over at me and waved and
then she smiled and then she whispered something into Gypsy's
ear. Gypsy smiled and looked at me and waved too. Then they
left, hand in hand, laughing and whispering, and went inside

the building. I sat on the grass wondering whether or not I should have another shot of tequila, watching Dill pull grass out of the dirt and put it carefully on his head. Every time he leaned over to pull more out, the grass on his head fell off, and every time he looked surprised. I was about to go over to where my dad and Sing Dylan were when I heard a scream and then Lish came careening around the corner, black hair flying around her head like a dust storm.

"It's him, it's him!!! Oh my god I can't believe it!! It's *him*!"

"Who? Who? What are you talking about?" I had run over to her and she was kneeling on the ground like she was in labour. Everyone had started to crowd around her and some had run to the other side of the building to see who it was.

"It's . . . it's . . . it's . . . oh my god, Lucy, this is a miracle."

"What's a fucking miracle Lish—just say it already!"

"Oh Luce, Luce, It's . . . it's . . ." She belched.

"It's whoooo??" I yelled.

"It's . . . it's . . . GOTCHA! He's come BACK! He's HERE! HE'S HERE!!!" And then Lish swooned like a silent movie actress and fell to the ground, dropping her beer bottle, her hair splayed around her, her white hairy legs sticking out of her gauzy skirt.

It was my turn to fall to the ground. My head was reeling like a cheap midway ride, and I felt like I was going to throw up. Out of the corner of one eye I saw my dad, holding Dill, walking over to me. This wasn't supposed to be happening. Gotcha was not supposed to turn up at Half-a-Life. Lish would never believe that he was dead and then came back to life, and besides, she'd tell Gotcha, and he'd say, "What? What? Denver? Drug deal? Drive-by shooting? Postcards? What?" And the gig would be up and Lish would be on to me and be furious and hate me and I'd lose my best friend and I'd have to move out of Half-a-Life, probably to Serenity Place, and spend the rest of my life an outcast, a liar, a loser, a good-for-nothing pathetic broken-down bitter welfare mother with no friends. But wait! If Gotcha was here and Lish was so thrilled, where was he? Why weren't they running up to Lish's apartment, to her kitchen floor, to the twins, to the older girls, to their new life together?

Lish opened one eye and then the other. She stood up and put her hands on my shoulders. Her breath reeked of tequila and beer and her hair was full of grass. She pulled me close to her and hugged me hard for all she was worth. Then she stood back, her hands still on my shoulders, and said, "Luce!"

"What!"

"GOTCHA!!!"

And she fell back onto the ground, laughing and looking up at me with what could only be described as love in her eyes. And then, *poof*, she closed her eyes and fell asleep. She had always loved a good performance.

"But Lish," I asked her over coffee and Tylenol the next day, "how did you know?"

"Teresa, your accomplice who can't keep a secret for a second, told Sarah, thinking Sarah wouldn't talk because she never does. Anyway, Sarah *did* talk. She told me before the party last night that the whole thing was just a big joke. She said she wouldn't want anyone else getting hurt from a lie the way she did. And besides, when you wrote about the silver spoon? Gotcha didn't even know about it. I took it after he had left. So even then I was on to you."

"It wasn't a joke, Lish, I was doing it to stop you from wondering. And waiting. I thought it would, you know, make things better for you and the twins if—"

"If he was dead instead of just out there?"

"Yeah."

"Lucy."

"Yeah?"

"Why don't you try to find Dill's father? It would be weird, but you could try to contact them all and get blood if they'd cooperate. You never know, it might work. Call their parents and see if you could see baby pictures of these guys, if there are any. They might hang up on you, but they might not. Why don't you do what you can? You might get lucky, you never know. Figure out when you conceived Dill and try to remember who you were with at that time, that sort of thing. You could do these things, you know."

"And if I never find out?"

"Then you never find out."

That afternoon my dad said goodbye to all of us at Half-a-Life. He had gone up to Mercy's apartment and had given Mercy a book about rocks, to give to Mayhem when she was older. Later Mercy showed us what my dad had written inside: "Dear Mayhem, We probably won't ever really know each other. But you will always be a special child to me. I'm sure your mother will be able to explain everything. Mothers are good at that sort of thing. Yours truly, Geoffrey Van Alstyne." Then it said, "P.S. Good! Luck!"

Downstairs Sing Dylan shook his hand and Teresa gave him a big wet kiss and a pack of cheap American smokes. "In case you wanna start," she said. He said, "Thank you, Teresa. Thank you kindly." He and Dill and I walked to his car. Joe and Pillar were leaning against it. Joe had his arm around Pillar's waist and they were talking to each other. For the moment, they were happy again. As we approached my dad's car they smiled and wandered over to a different car to lean against while they talked.

"Dad. How come you and Mom never had any more kids?"

"Well. I guess . . . it just didn't happen." Which I took to mean that sometimes it just did. He took my hand. It was dry and very big. I looked at Dill's own big hands, and finally saw the similarities. For a second my dad and I were racing to The Waffle Shop. Nobody else existed.

"Lucy?"

"Yeah?"

"Life is not a joke."

"No."

I walked back to the front doors of Half-a-Life. I looked up and saw Lish on her balcony. She had on a t-shirt that read "I'm With Her," and it had a hand on it with a pointing finger. She stood in a square of sunlight and brushed her black hair. Half-a-Life. Half-a-Laugh. Winnipeg, Manitoba, city with the most hours of sunshine, the centre of the universe. I was home. It's true that life is not a joke. But I knew my life was funny. And Dillinger Geoffrey Van Alstyne was a lucky boy.